Praise for ELMORE LEONARD PRONTO

"Delightful and absorbing. . . . *Pronto* is an expert, rolling read, funny and quirky. . . . While Leonard excels at low-life suspense, he's also a master fiction writer whose gift for dialogue and cunningly meandering plots any novelist would envy."

—*...Chronicle*

"Guar... ...of-the-art L... ...knowing t... ...for the absurd."

—*Miami Herald*

"Nobody but nobody on the current scene can match his ability to serve up violence so light-handedly, with so supremely deadpan a flourish."

—*Detroit News*

"From sly title through breath-stopping climax to funny wrap-up, readers will relish Leonard's latest roller-coaster ride. . . . The only problem with the book is that it ends." —*Publishers Weekly*

"The ... ...*Times*

"Ame... ...gives his readers everything they would expect: a sense of place and milieu, lively characters, drop-dead dirty talk, situations you can't describe in a family newspaper . . . and poetic justice flecked by the unfairness of life. The pleasure of *Pronto* lies in the unexpected."

—*Boston Globe*

PRONTO

Also by Elmore Leonard

Fiction

Djibouti

Comfort to the Enemy
and Other Carl
Webster Stories

Road Dogs

Up in Honey's Room

The Hot Kid

The Complete Western
Stories of Elmore Leonard

Mr. Paradise

Fire in the Hole (previously
titled When the Women
Come Out to Dance)

Tishomingo Blues

Pagan Babies

Be Cool

The Tonto Woman & Other
Western Stories

Cuba Libre

Out of Sight

Riding the Rap

Rum Punch

Maximum Bob

Get Shorty

Killshot

Freaky Deaky

Touch

Bandits

Glitz

LaBrava

Stick

Cat Chaser

Split Images

City Primeval

Gold Coast

Gunsights

The Switch

The Hunted

Unknown Man No. 89

Swag

Fifty-Two Pickup

Mr. Majestyk

Forty Lashes Less One

Valdez Is Coming

The Moonshine War

The Big Bounce

Hombre

Last Stand at Saber River

Escape from Five Shadows

The Law at Randado

The Bounty Hunters

Nonfiction

Elmore Leonard's 10 Rules of Writing

ELMORE LEONARD

PRONTO

WILLIAM MORROW
An Imprint of HarperCollins*Publishers*

For Joan, always

Ezra Pound: *The Cantos of Ezra Pound*. Copyright © 1934, 1948 Ezra Pound. Reprinted by permission of New Directions Publishing Corporation.

FIRST HARPERTORCH PAPERBACK PUBLISHED 2002.
FIRST HARPER PAPERBACK SPECIAL PRINTING PUBLISHED 2010.
FIRST WILLIAM MORROW PAPERBACK EDITION PUBLISHED 2012.

Library of Congress Cataloging-in-Publication Data is available upon request.

ISBN 978-0-06-212033-5

16 17   RRD   10

O N E

One evening, it was toward the end of October, Harry Arno said to the woman he'd been seeing on and off the past few years, "I've made a decision. I'm going to tell you something I've never told anyone before in my life."

Joyce said, "You mean something you did when you were in the war?"

It stopped him. "How'd you know that?"

"When you were in Italy and you shot the deserter?"

Harry didn't say anything, staring at her.

"You already told me about it."

"Come on. When?"

"We were having drinks at the Cardozo, outside, not long after we started seeing each other again. You said it the same way you did just now, like you're going to tell me a secret. That's why I knew. Only I don't think you said anything about making a decision."

Now he was confused.

"I wasn't drinking then, was I?"

"You quit before that." Joyce paused and said, "Wait a minute. You know what? That was the second time you told me about shooting the guy. At Pisa, right? You showed me the picture of you holding up the Leaning Tower."

"It wasn't at Pisa," Harry said. "Not where I shot the guy."

"No, but around there."

"You're sure I told you about it twice?"

"The first time, it was when I was working at the club and we went out a few times. You were still drinking then."

"That was what, six or seven years ago."

"I hate to say it, Harry, but it's more like ten. I know I was almost thirty when I quit dancing."

Harry said, "Jesus Christ," figuring that would be about right, if Joyce was around forty now. Getting up there. He remembered her white skin in the spotlight, dark hair and pure white skin, the only topless dancer he ever knew who wore glasses while she performed; not contacts, real glasses with round black rims. For her age Joyce still looked pretty good. Time went by so fast. Harry had turned sixty-six two weeks ago. He was the same age as Paul Newman.

"You ever hear me tell anyone else?"

Joyce said, "I don't think so." And said right away, "If you want to tell it again, fine. It's a wonderful story."

He said, "No, that's okay."

They were in Harry's apartment at the Della Robbia on Ocean Drive listening to Frank Sinatra, Frank and Nelson Riddle driving "I've Got You Under My Skin," Harry speaking quietly, Joyce looking distracted. Harry all set to tell her about the time in Italy forty-seven years ago and then ask—this was the decision he'd finally made—if she would like to go there with him the end of January. Right after the Super Bowl.

But now he wasn't sure he wanted to take her.

For as long as he'd known Joyce Patton— Joy, when she was dancing topless—he had always wondered if he shouldn't be doing better.

Harry Arno was grossing six to seven thousand a week running a sports book out of three locations in South Miami Beach. He had to split fifty-fifty with a guy named Jimmy Capotorto—Jimmy Cap, Jumbo—who had a piece of whatever was illegal in Dade County, except cocaine, and he had to take expenses out of his end: the phones, rent, his sheet writers, various incidentals. But that was okay. Harry Arno was skimming a thousand a week off the top and had been doing it for as long as he had wiseguys as silent partners, going back twenty years. Before Jumbo Jimmy Cap there was a guy named Ed Grossi and before Grossi, going all the way back forty years, Harry had worked for S & G Syndicate bookies as a runner.

The idea originally was to get out of the business at sixty-five, a million-plus socked away in a Swiss bank through its branch in the Bahamas. Then changed his mind when the time came and kept working. So he'd quit at sixty-six. Right now the football season was in full swing and his customers would rather bet the pros than any other sport except basketball. Put down anywhere from a few hundred to a few grand—he had some heavy players—and watch the games on TV that Sunday. So now he'd wait until after the Super Bowl, January 26, to take off. Three months from now. What was the difference, retire at sixty-five or sixty-six, no one knew how old he was anyway. Or his real name, for that matter.

Harry Arno believed he was a hip guy; he kept up, didn't feel anywhere near sixty-six, knew Vanilla Ice was a white guy; he still had his hair, parted it on the right side and had it touched up every other week where he got his hair cut, up on Arthur Godfrey Road. Joyce now and then would arch her back, look up at him, and say, "We're almost the same height, aren't we?" Or she'd say, "What are you, about five seven?" Harry would tell her he was the height of the average U.S. fighting man in World War Two, five nine. Maybe a little less than that now, but in fairly good shape after a near heart attack, a blocked artery they opened with angioplasty. He jogged up and down Lummus Park for most of an hour every morning, the Della Robbia and the rest of the renovated Art Deco hotels on one side of him, the beach and the Atlantic Ocean on the other, hardly anyone outside yet. Most of the old retired people were gone, the old Jewish ladies with their sun hats and nose shields, and the new inhabitants of South Beach, the trendies down from New York, the dress designers and models, the actors, the stylish gays, didn't appear on the street before noon.

One day pretty soon now his players would

be making phone calls asking, "What happened to Harry Arno?" realizing they didn't know anything about him.

He'd disappear and start a new life, one that was waiting for him. No more pressure. No more working for people he didn't respect. Maybe have a drink now and then. Maybe even a cigarette in the evening looking out at the bay at sunset. Have Joyce there with him.

Well, maybe. It wasn't like there weren't any women where he was going. Maybe get there first and settle in and then, if he felt like it, send for her. Have her come for a visit.

He was ready. Had passports in two different names, just in case. Saw a clear field ahead, no problems. Until the afternoon Buck Torres told him he was in trouble. October 29, outside Wolfie's on Collins Avenue.

Wolfie's was the only restaurant Harry knew of that still served Jell-O. A friend of his at *The Miami Herald* said, "And with a straight face." There was a "Harry Arno" on the sandwich menu he couldn't eat anymore. Pastrami and mozzarella with tomatoes and onions, a splash of Italian dressing. Harry could eat deli and he could eat Cuban if he was careful, not load up on the black beans. What he couldn't get used to were all the new places that served tofu and polenta, pesto sauce on everything. Sun-dried cherries and walnuts on grouper, for Christ sake.

October 29, Harry would remember, he had vegetable soup, a few crackers, iced tea, and the Jell-O, strawberry. Stepped out into the sunlight in his beige warm-ups with the red piping, his Reeboks, and there was Buck Torres standing by an unmarked car, a blue '91 Caprice. Harry had been arrested by Buck Torres a half-dozen times or so; they knew each other pretty well and were friends. Not socially, Harry had never met Buck's wife, but friends in the way they trusted one another and always had time to talk about other things than what they did for a living. Buck Torres had never asked Harry about his business with Jimmy Capotorto, trying to get to Jimmy Cap through Harry.

This time was different, this October 29th afternoon. Harry could feel it. Torres said, "Man, you're looking sporty as ever. Get in, I'll drive you home."

Harry told him he had his car.

"That's all right," Torres said. "Get in anyway, we'll drive around."

They started south on Collins and pretty soon turned west toward Washington, not much traffic yet. By December it would be bumper to bumper down here. There was a stale cigarette smell in the car. Harry opened his window.

"What I'd like you to do," Buck Torres said, "is happen to take a look at the papers on the seat."

Harry already had.

A stack of legal sheets with the heading:

APPLICATION FOR WIRE INTERCEPT
OF WIRE COMMUNICATION

Addressed to the Circuit Court, Criminal Division, of the 11th Judicial Circuit in and for the County of Dade, Florida. Below that was the name of a judge and below the judge Harry saw the wording become personal, requesting authorization to hang wires on the telephone numbers of his three sports-book locations, "subscribed to by HARRY JACK ARNO," his name in there big.

He said, "Why're you going to all this trouble? Everybody knows what I do."

"It's serious this time," Torres said. "We've had pen registers on your phones since the beginning of football season. We know what numbers've been calling you and who you've called, twenty-four hours a day. Look at page fourteen."

"I believe you," Harry said.

"Last Sunday your phones had like a hundred and eighty incoming calls during action time, right before the pro games got started."

"I have a lot of friends," Harry said.

"Use that in court," Torres said, "you get a laugh and maybe a five-hundred-dollar fine. This's different."

Harry was still looking down at the legal papers.

He said, "This judge bets college games through a buddy of his, a lawyer. All Southeast Conference. He lays it on the hot side, the favorites, every time. He'll pick Florida, Florida State, and Miami, no matter what the line is."

"Turn to page twenty-eight," Torres said. "Look at the date and the signature."

"You already have me tapped?"

"The wire was okayed weeks ago. Those three numbers but not your residence."

Harry said, "Don't you know I record all my transactions? I could've given you my tapes, saved you the expense."

Torres turned right on Washington to head north past white storefronts that looked closed in the sunlight. The pastel colors and neon kitsch taking over South Beach not up this far yet. "It's a Bureau operation," Torres said. "They want Jimmy Cap, like they do every year or so, make a lot of noise. We do the legwork and they take what we come up with to a federal grand jury."

"What you're telling me," Harry said, "I could go down with Jimmy on a racketeering charge?"

He saw Torres glance over, Torres serious, and that began to bother him.

"That's how it started out," Torres said. "You go down unless you testify, help them put Jumbo away on a RICO indictment. I said to the agent in charge of the investigation, 'How you going to turn Harry Arno, hold six months over his head? He doesn't cross state lines. What he does is a misdemeanor.' McCormick, the agent in charge, goes, 'Yeah, he'd have to be desperate, wouldn't he?' So he thinks about it and he says, 'Okay, what if this guy Arno believes Jumbo wants him taken out?' "

Harry frowned. "Why would he?"

"Keep you from putting something on him."

"What do I tell, the guy's a fucking gangster? Everybody knows it."

Torres said, "You think I'm kidding?" No, he was serious, he was anxious, but took time now to pull over to the curb and park. He turned enough in the seat to face Harry and lay it out.

"The idea is to set you up. You think Jumbo

is going to have you whacked and you go running to the Justice Department for protection."

"What I've always wanted to be," Harry said, "a fink."

Torres said, "Listen to me. McCormick says, 'Or work it so Arno does get whacked and you bring Jumbo up on a homicide.' He says, 'What would be wrong with that?' He says after he was kidding, but I'm not sure. He thinks about it some more. Now the idea, he says, 'What if we put it in Jumbo's ear this guy Arno is skimming on him?'" Torres kept talking even though Harry was shaking his head. "'Jumbo makes a threatening move. Arno sees what's happening, he freaks and comes running to Uncle.'"

"Every wire room I know of," Harry said, "the guy operating it skims. It's expected, just don't be obvious about it. I can take a hundred a week off the top for expenses, Jimmy knows it. Long as he gets his cut he's not going to say a fucking word."

Torres said, "Yeah, but what McCormick is talking about, the idea, get Jumbo to think you're skimming on him big-time, big amounts." Harry was shaking his head again and Torres said, "You mentioned Jumbo's cut. What's that, half?"

"Right down the middle," Harry said.

"He knows how much you gross each week?"

"Sure he does."

"How's he know the exact figure?"

"I tell him," Harry said. "He doesn't believe me he can listen to the tapes anytime he wants."

"Has he ever?"

"You kidding? He's too fucking lazy."

Torres said, "Well, McCormick's had people monitoring all your action-time bets and running totals."

"Come on, they're listening to all that?"

"McCormick wants to know if what you make and what you tell Jumbo you make are the same thing."

"Guy's out of his mind," Harry said. "What about what my runners bring in? Hardly any of that's recorded. Or some players that're friends and call me at home? What about the different ways people who've come here from other parts of the country, Jersey for instance, place their bets? The language they use. A guy calls, he says, 'I like the Vikings and six for five dimes.' Another guys calls. 'Harry, the Saints minus seven thirty times.' He loses, what's the juice, straight ten percent? If they forget the juice they won't even get close to the gross. I keep the tapes in case there are any disagreements after, who owes who, or I go to collect and the guy claims he never made the bet. It rarely happens, because if there is any doubt about what the player is putting down I ask him. Guy calls up, he says, 'Harry, give me the Lions and the Niners twenty times reverse. Bears a nickel, Chargers a nickel. Giants five times, New England ten times *if* the Rams ten.' That's twice a day Saturday and Sunday I get straight bets, parlays, round robins, over and under, we got the NBA going into action, listen, I even get some hockey. You're telling me this Bureau guy's people are going to get a read out of that?"

Torres said, "Harry, we hear you talking to Jumbo, telling him the totals for the week, how you made out, all that. This one time we hear the two of you talking, we hear Jumbo ask you about a guy, this black dude in a suit, gold chains, that came up to him in the lounge out at Calder? Jumbo's having a drink between races. The black dude says, 'Man, you killed me last week.' Says he dropped ten thousand and paid another grand for the vig. We hear Jumbo ask you about the guy. You recall that?"

Harry took his time. "I told Jimmy it was news to me, right? You heard that? The guy was mistaken, he laid it off somewhere else. I said to Jimmy if he wanted to check my tapes he could."

Torres was nodding. "Yeah, but the black guy, Jumbo says, told him he laid the bet with *you*, nobody else. Ran into you at Wolfie's and you wrote it down."

"It never happened," Harry said. "I told Jimmy, 'Find the guy. Let him tell me to my face I took his bet.' I don't do business like that, with people I don't know. A player has to be recommended." Harry felt himself getting hot again, the same way he did on the phone talking to Jimmy Cap, all that coming back to him and realizing now what it was about. "I told Jimmy, 'This guy's setting me up, that's all, and I don't even know why.' Well, I do now."

"The guy's under indictment on a drug bust," Torres said. "He does what McCormick tells him and gets the charge reduced from Intent to Distribute to Simple Possession. See how he's working it? You can't prove the guy didn't put the bet down with you, right? And now Jumbo's wondering how many payoffs you might've skimmed on him. Okay, then another phone conversation we heard, Jumbo's discussing it with one of his guys. He says if the jig had the nerve to come up to him it must be true and tells the guy to handle it. This was yesterday afternoon."

Harry said, "Handle it. That's all he said?"

"He didn't say how he wanted it done, no."

"Who was he talking to?"

"Couple of times he called the guy Tommy."

"Tommy Bucks," Harry said. "Dark-complected guy. He came over from Sicily ten twelve years ago he was Tommy Bitonti."

"That's who I thought it was, Tommy Bucks," Torres said, getting out his pocket notebook. "He gives you that look, Don't fuck with me. Yeah, dark-complected, but the guy's a sharp dresser. Anytime I've ever seen him he has on a suit and tie."

"Like in the fifties," Harry said. "You went out at night to a club you wore a suit or a good-looking sports jacket. Tommy came over—the first thing he learned was how to dress. Always looks like a million bucks. That's where he got his name, Tommy Bucks, but he's still a greaseball." Harry watched Torres enter the name in his notebook. Tommy, Jimmy, like they were talking about little kids. Harry thought of something and said, "You must've wired Jimmy's place, too, if you heard him talking to other people." And saw Torres look up and then smile for the first time.

"You know his house on Indian Creek? Almost right across from the Eden Roc," Torres said. "We've had him under surveillance from the hotel. We see Jumbo out on his patio, he's wearing this giant pair of shorts—what's he weigh, three hundred pounds?"

"At least," Harry said. "Maybe three and a half."

"We're watching him, we notice he's always talking on a cordless phone. So we put some people in a boat that's tied to that dock on the hotel side of the creek? They use a scanner, lock in on his signal, his frequency, and monitor the phone conversations, whoever he's talking to. Portable handset, you don't need a court order."

For a few moments it was quiet in the car.

"What you pick up is in the air," Torres said. "You know, radio waves, and they're free. That's why you don't need authorization."

Harry nodded and it was quiet again.

He said, "I appreciate your telling me what's going on. I know you're sticking your neck out."

"I don't want to see you hurt," Torres said, "on account of this asshole McCormick."

Harry said, "Well, I'm not going to worry about it. If it was ten or twelve years ago and Jimmy told Tommy Bucks in those words, 'Handle it,' that would be a different story. I mean back when he first came over," Harry said. "Tommy's a Zip. You know what I mean? One of those guys they used to import from Sicily to handle the rough stuff. Guy could be a peasant right out of the fucking Middle Ages, looks around and he's in Miami Beach. Can't believe it. They hand the Zip a gun and say, 'There, that guy.' And the Zip takes him out. You understand? They import the kind of guy likes to shoot. He's got no priors here; nobody gives a shit if he gets picked up, convicted, put away. If he does, you send for another Zip. Guy comes over from Sicily, he's got on a black suit, shirt buttoned up, no tie, and a cap sitting on top of his head. That was Tommy Bucks ten, twelve years ago when he was Tomasino Bitonti."

"So you hope he's changed more than his suit," Torres said. He stared at Harry. "You don't look too worried."

"I can always leave town," Harry said.

Torres grinned. "You're a cool guy. I'll give you that."

Harry shrugged. Man, was he trying.

TWO

To Harry, Tommy Bucks would always be the Zip: a guy who was brought over to kill somebody, stayed, learned English and how to dress, but was still that person they imported.

He'd be coming anytime now. Or waiting somewhere. Harry, sure of it, was thinking, If you'd gotten out when you were sixty-five . . .

Someone had picked that age as the best time to quit whatever you were doing and Harry believed now it could be true. By forty you've lost a step, your legs aren't what they used to be, and twenty-five years later all your parts are starting to go. Something he'd never considered until last year when they stuck the tube up his artery, from his groin to his heart, and told him he'd better change his ways. If he had gotten out right after that, last year . . .

He thought about it not as a regret or with any feeling of panic, but as a practical notion. If he were no longer here he wouldn't have to worry about this Zip coming to see him, if that's what "handle it" meant. This primitive greaseball in a twelve-hundred-dollar suit, no education, spoke with a garlic-breath Italian accent—though not much of one, considering, and was not as dumb as most of the guys in Jimmy's crew, sitting around their social club. The Zip was coming. The only thing to wonder about, what was he waiting for?

Harry Arno packed a suitcase as soon as he got home that Thursday afternoon, October 29, not with the idea of taking off, not yet, but in case he had to. He packed going from the dresser with shirts and underwear to the suitcase on the bed to the front windows to look down at Ocean Drive three floors below. Every twenty minutes or so that afternoon he'd make a side trip to the bathroom, the idea of the Zip's arrival affecting his bladder. Or a combination of the Zip and a swollen prostate. He'd stand there taking a leak, imagine the Zip walking into the building and he'd shake it and hurry back to a front window. A couple of times he almost picked up the phone by the bed. But if he called Jimmy and told him what was going on, went into how he found out he was being set up . . . The way Jimmy would see it: "Oh, you're tight with this cop? They offered you a deal?" He could swear he'd never talk to a grand jury, it wouldn't matter. He'd be putting his life in the hands of a three-hundred-pound semiliterate slob who never smiled or had finished high school. Some things about Jimmy Cap you could anticipate. Harry knew that if he ever told Jimmy he was retiring Jimmy would have to say, "Oh, is that right? You quit when I tell you you can quit."

The Zip he didn't know well enough to anticipate. They had never been formally introduced or spoken more than a few words a year to each other. As far as Harry could tell, the Zip didn't talk much to anybody. The other guys in the crew seemed to stay out of his way. Women liked him, the semipros attracted to those guys, or they were afraid not to act as though they did.

Harry had a suitcase and a hanging bag packed now, put away in the bedroom closet. He stood at a window looking down at headlights in the dusk, dark shapes moving, wondering now if he'd forgot anything.

Bathroom stuff. What else?

Jesus, his two passports.

Someone knocked on the door. In the living room.

Harry felt himself jump, in the same moment remembering he hadn't packed his gun, the gun he'd used to shoot the deserter forty-seven years ago and he'd brought home as a souvenir. A U.S. Army Colt .45 sidearm. Wrapped in a towel on the shelf in the closet, not loaded, with the Zip at the door. Harry sure of it.

A black guy in a flowery blue-and-yellow sport shirt came in first, Tommy Bucks behind him in a sharkskin double-breasted suit, a white shirt against his dark skin and a maroon-patterned necktie. Harry stepped aside for them, the black guy looking straight into his face as he came in. The Zip put his hand on the guy's shoulder and gave it a shove, saying, "This is Kennet."

"Kenneth," the black guy said.

The Zip was looking around the room now. "It's what I said. Kennet." He turned on a lamp and stepped close to a wall of black-and-white photographs, saying, "Kennet, who is this guy here? Can you tell me?"

"Yeah, this is the guy," Kenneth said, looking at Harry. "I laid down five dimes each on the Saints and the Houston Oilers and paid him off on Monday, eleven grand with the juice, outside the hotel here. Was a friend of mine with me can testify to it."

Harry said to Kenneth, "You never saw me before you walked in this room," and turned to the Zip. "Ask Jimmy if I ever collect payments outside. My players know where to find me, and it ain't out on the fucking street." He said it again, "Go ask Jimmy," looking at the Zip hunched over studying a photograph.

"What is this one?"

Walking over to him Harry said, "The guy that used to own the hotel lived in this apartment. He was a photographer at one time." Harry looked at the photo. "That's a Georgia chain gang, nineteen thirties. You know, convicts." The Zip nodded. "That one, that's a turpentine camp, same period. The turpentine drips into those buckets? And then they boil it. The old man was commissioned by the government to take these pictures, during the Depression." Maybe the Zip knew what he was talking about, maybe not. Harry was showing the Zip he was relaxed. "Maurice Zola was the old guy's name; I used to know him. He married a woman about half his age who was a movie actress at one time. I've forgotten her name. You'd see her picture in the paper, appearing at a condominium opening. The old guy died, it was only about a year after they were married, and the movie actress sold the hotel to Jimmy Cap and moved away. So then Jimmy got rid of all the old women used to live here and brought in a bunch of hookers. It was like a girls' dorm in here for a while." Harry added a chuckle he didn't feel. "Broads running around with hardly anything on. Now there're only a few still here." Relaxed, talking to be talking, Harry keeping this between him and the Zip. Both on the same side.

"Was out in front I paid him," Kenneth said. "Saw the man at Wolfie's on Saturday and laid the bets down and paid him off on Monday. Out in the park they have there."

The Zip said, "What's this one?"

"You hear this guy?" Harry said. "He never placed a bet with me in his fucking life. I can name all the colored guys I know around here that're players and, believe me, this spook ain't one of them." He looked at the photo he thought the Zip was looking at. "That? That's an elephant on the beach. Used for some kind of a promotion."

The Zip said, "I know a fucking elephant

when I see one," turning his head to look at Harry next to him. "Not that picture. The one here."

This close he seemed all nose, the nose dominating his dark face, younger than Harry had thought, early forties maybe, his eyes not so dreamy as partly closed, heavy lids giving him a tough-guy look that worked.

"Those are Jamaicans digging drains in a canefield," Harry said.

"This one."

"Seminole Indians. Or Miccosukees, I'm not sure. Drive out the Tamiami, you'll see them. They give airboat rides."

The Zip walked into the bedroom.

"There're no pictures in there," Harry said. He turned to Kenneth standing by a window. "You know what you're doing to me? You're getting me fucking killed."

"You shouldn't have taken the money," Kenneth said over his shoulder. "Man, I can't help you." His head turned to the window again.

The Zip came out of the bedroom. He ran his hand over the smooth vinyl backrest of the La-Z-Boy recliner aimed at the television set.

"Ask this guy why he's setting me up," Harry said, watching the Zip slide into the recliner and begin working the footrest lever, raising and lowering it.

"I like this chair. Be good for watching TV."

Kenneth said, "I have me two of those at my house. Just like that with the Magic Ottoman."

"Goddamn it," Harry said to the Zip, holding on, not raising his voice too much, "ask him about the plea deal he made with the feds. You know what I mean by that, what he's doing?"

"Let me ask you one," the Zip said. "Why you have those suitcases in there full of clothes. You going someplace?"

There was no way to talk to him. The Zip decided it was time to leave and that was that. Harry wanted to tell him, Look, we're both on the same side if it comes to believing this colored guy or me. I go back twelve years with Jimmy Cap and another ten with the guy before him. But once the Zip was out of the chair . . .

Harry even thought of mentioning Italy, something else they had in common. Tell the Zip he'd spent fourteen months over there during WW II and loved it. Ask him if he'd ever been to Montecatini, not far from Pisa, where he'd spent a month and had a ball drinking wine, getting laid, at the time the Second Armored was broken up and his company was put in an infantry outfit, the 473rd, activated in the field. Tell the Zip his war story, how he shot the deserter, a black guy from the 92nd, the colored outfit. Tell it in front of Kenneth. How he had misjudged the guy, thought of the deserter as a GI who'd messed up, gone AWOL too long, that's all, and would do some stockade time, hard labor at the Disciplinary Training Center and be sent back to his outfit. Both of them on the same side. That was why he couldn't believe it when the guy grabbed the carbine and tried to kill him, both of them in a hallway, close, looking in each other's face as the guy raised the carbine to club him with it and Harry had time to use the .45 sidearm the lieutenant had given him. Blew the deserter off his feet with it, killing him. And didn't find out till later the deserter had nothing to lose, that he'd raped and murdered an Italian woman and was going to be tried by court martial and no doubt executed.

Ask the Zip if he'd ever been to the place where the condemned prisoners were hanged. Aversa? Something like that.

Ask him—what else? There was no time to say anything, find out where he stood. Once the Zip was out of the chair he waved Kenneth to come on and pushed him out the door. The only thing Harry knew for sure, the Zip thought the recliner would be perfect for watching TV.

Plan something for forty-seven years and all of a sudden you're out of time. Do it now, this minute, or maybe never get another chance.

He took the .45 from the shelf in the closet and cleaned it, stripped it and put it back together without too much trouble, and loaded the magazine. Harry hefted the automatic, three pounds of metal, stuck it in the waist of his pants, and walked around the room trying to get used to it.

He phoned Joyce.

"I have to talk to you."

"What's the matter?"

"Can you come over?"

"In about an hour. I just put my hair up."

"I have to talk to you now."

"Then come over here."

He had to think about it.

"Harry?"

"All right. Watch for me."

"Harry, what's wrong?"

He hung up.

It was less than a fifteen-minute walk to Joyce's apartment on Meridian, five blocks from the beach. This evening, though, Harry felt he should drive, not be walking along these streets at night. His car was in a lot on Thirteenth, behind the hotel: his '84 Eldorado he'd have to do something with before he left. Maybe sign it over to Joyce. She didn't do too bad as a catalog model, but it was seasonal and she had to work in between jobs as a cocktail waitress. In one catalog she'd be a young matron in sportswear; in the next, a swinger in gauzy lingerie, garter belts, her hair all curly. Harry would open a catalog thinking, Okay, which model would you most like to jump? He told Joyce, kidding, to guess which one nine times out of ten he'd pick. Her. He told her thinking she'd say he was sweet, but all she did was look at him funny.

Usually he ducked out the service door of the hotel that opened on the alley; the parking lot was right there. This evening Harry came out the front entrance past the rows of metal chairs to the street, Ocean Drive, and looked both ways, taking his time, noticing a good crowd at the Cardozo for a Thursday night, all the sidewalk tables occupied. He turned the corner and walked along the side of the hotel to the parking lot, a small one, two rows of cars squeezed in there, an open space down the middle, a streetlight at the far end. Harry paused in the alley; he pulled the .45 from his waist, racked the slide and slipped the pistol into his waist again, inside his sport coat. His car was toward this end, the third one in. He came to the Eldorado's white rear deck sticking out. The guy who ran the lot told Harry he'd buy the car whenever he wanted to sell it. He wasn't here at night.

No, but somebody was. A figure in the open space between the rows of cars. Coming this way now, a dark shape. It wasn't the guy who ran the lot, he was a little guy. This one was taller, over six feet. Harry wanted him to be cutting through the lot heading for Ocean Drive. Now this guy Harry had never seen before said, "That your car?"

About thirty feet away.

Harry said, "What, this one?"

"Yeah, is that yours?"

Harry stood at the Eldorado's right-rear fender looking across the trunk at the guy approaching. He felt the bulk of the .45 against his stomach and said, "What do you care whose it is?"

The guy said, "I want to be sure you're the right one." Saying then, "Your name Harry?"

Harry was telling himself as the guy spoke to pull the .45, do it right now, seeing the guy coming the same way the deserter from the 92nd

came at him with the carbine. That one, the deserter, didn't say a word.

This one did. He said, "What you doing,
taking a piss? Have your hands full?" He said, "I
got something for you, Harry," his right hand
going inside his coat, "from Jimmy Cap."

Harry brought up the .45 in both hands and
saw the guy stop and raise his hand that wasn't
inside the coat. He looked like he was going to
say something and maybe he did and Harry
didn't hear it, with the noise. He shot the guy
three times with that gun from the war and
watched the guy fly off his feet backward, throwing a cut-down shotgun in the air to clatter off
the trunk of a car and drop to the pavement.

Harry walked over to look at the guy. He was
white, about fifty, wearing a tractor cap still on
his head, an old suit coat over bib overalls, and
work boots. Some redneck from the Glades. His
eyes open, false teeth coming partway out of his
mouth, the cleanest thing about him in the streetlight. Harry didn't touch him or the shotgun lying on the pavement. He went back to his apartment and phoned Buck Torres at Miami Beach
police headquarters.

He wasn't there. Harry said it was urgent,
that Sergeant Torres should get in touch with

him right away. Waiting then, he felt he wanted a drink more than he ever did in his life, but held off. He thought of calling Joyce but held off on that too. Finally Torres phoned, not sounding in too good a mood. Harry said, "I just killed a guy. What do I do now?"

They talked for a few minutes and Torres told him not to move, not to do anything dumb.

"Like what?"

"Just don't do anything dumb."

Harry said, "Why do you think I called? If I was going to do something dumb, would I have called you, for Christ sake?"

He hung up and phoned Joyce.

She said, "No." She said, "You didn't. . . . Did you? You're putting me on and it's not funny."

By the time he heard the radio cars outside Joyce sounded like she believed him, asking what he was going to do and what she could do to help out. Harry told her not to worry about it, he didn't see a problem.

He wasn't thinking ahead yet. His mind kept looking at the scene and he'd feel pumped up at the way he'd known what to do and didn't panic, remembered to take a breath, hold it, let some out, remembered to squeeze the trigger, fired three times and hit the guy three times.

When he did think ahead he pictured Torres and some other detectives at the scene shaking their heads, commenting among themselves over the way he'd played it. Man, don't mess with Harry Arno. Blew the guy away before he could get off a shot. They'd go over the scene and then talk to him, ask him exactly what happened, maybe have him sign a statement. Ask him to stick around, in case they had any more questions. After that, what?

THREE

After they talked to him for two hours he spent the rest of the night in a detective-division holding cell. The next morning Harry told the Crimes-Against-Persons detectives it was just as easy to fix eggs the right way, over easy, for Christ sake, as it was to fry them till they were stiff as leather. One of the detectives let him know the eggs were from the Cuban joint down the street. Call them up if he wanted to complain.

Harry couldn't believe it, the way people he knew over the phone were treating him.

They transferred him to the Dade County jail, where he was booked and printed. That afternoon, at his first-appearance hearing in circuit court, he entered a plea of not guilty. The next thing he knew he was charged with second-degree murder and a bond was set at one hundred and fifty thousand dollars. He couldn't believe it. He said to his lawyer, "I understand this was a preliminary hearing, but you might've mentioned the shotgun the guy had."

His lawyer, actually the son of the lawyer who ordinarily represented Harry when he was brought up but was out of town, said, "What shotgun?"

"The one he was gonna kill me with. Doesn't anybody understand that?"

The young lawyer shook his head. "There's no shotgun mentioned in the Uniform Crime Report."

Harry said, "Did they look for one? You think I shot this guy I never saw before in my life for no reason? Or you think I was muggin' him, what?"

The victim was Earl Crowe, fifty-three, from the Glades, as Harry thought. Clewiston, up on Lake Okeechobee.

He said to Buck Torres, after, "Where were you last night when I needed you?" Meaning during the interrogation. "I have all these dicks ganging up on me."

Torres said it was a homicide investigation and he was with an organized-crime task force, Torres cooler than the last time they talked. He said, "You were nervous, right? Man, I can understand it. You thought sure this guy was coming for you."

"He *was*," Harry said. "He knew my name."

"You're a popular guy."

"He had a sawed-off pump-action shotgun, for Christ sake, he says from Jimmy Cap. He comes right out and tells me that so I'll know. From Jimmy."

"You had a loaded Colt .45," Torres said. "You want to talk about intentions?"

"I didn't *know* the guy."

"I hear he's got priors and state time going back thirty years," Torres said. "Maybe you can work a deal with the prosecutor's office, get it down to some kind of manslaughter. If you want you can talk to the feds about Jimmy Cap. Help your cause, if you know what I mean. McCormick asked me to mention it, that's all."

"They set me up," Harry said, "then offer to save my ass and I'm supposed to be grateful. If I say I'll tell stories on Jimmy, will they all of a sudden find the shotgun?"

Torres shook his head, saying he would never be part of anything like that.

"Yeah, well, I got no business being in jail," Harry said, "but if I'm out on the street I'm fucking dead."

"They'll look out for you," Torres said, "as long as you can do them some good. What else can I tell you? That's the way it is."

After the first-appearance hearing Harry was remanded to the Dade County Stockade in Miami, told by his lawyer he could be there as long as six weeks, until his arraignment came up. Monday, three days later, a woman from ABC Bail Bonds appeared at the Stockade with Joyce Patton and he was released on the one-hundred-and-fifty-thousand-dollar surety bond.

Not put up by Joyce, no way. In fact he didn't know a single person who'd be willing to put up the ten percent the bond would cost, fifteen grand in cash, and have the collateral to represent the value of the bond, the full amount that would be forfeited if he failed to appear for his court hearing.

"Please don't tell me," Harry said, "Jimmy Cap put it up. Okay?"

The ABC Bail Bonds woman said, "How about your wife in Palos Heights, Illinois?"

Joyce standing there taking it in.

"My ex," Harry said. "You're telling me she came down here and gave you a check for fifteen grand? The day I went in business for myself she stopped cooking, refused to go in the kitchen unless I got a real job. We ate out every night for the next nine years. When I couldn't live like that anymore I gave her the house, a four-bedroom Tudor in Palos Heights, outside Chicago, and came back here to live."

Joyce said, "You still eat out every night."

Looking for a fight because he had a wife at one time he hadn't told her about.

The ABC Bail Bonds woman, who was blond, maybe thirty-five and not bad-looking for someone in that business, said a man named Tomasino Bitonti had brought her the check and a quit-claim deed to the Palos Heights property as collateral, signed by Teresa Ianello, back to using her maiden name.

Now it made sense. Jimmy Cap wanted him on the street. He'd never use his own money, so he must have sent the Zip to intimidate Teresa, get her to put up the bond. What bothered Harry, How did Jimmy know he had an ex-wife up there? Unless they kept a file on him: knew he was from Miami originally, worked on the Beach in the fifties, got married and moved to Chicago, Teresa's home, following the Kefauver crime investigations in Miami. They'd know he came back in '71, without Teresa, and set up his sports book, because that's when they went into business with him.

He explained all this to Joyce driving back to the beach over the MacArthur Causeway: telling her general facts about his past and interrupting himself to say, Jesus, he could never do serious time. "There's nobody to talk to in jail you have anything in common with."

"I don't understand that," Joyce said. "You break the law every day of your life, you should expect to do some time."

Still peeved over finding out he'd had a wife. By the time they got to Harry's apartment, Joyce was asking direct questions about his ex. Where he'd met her. The Roney Plaza, Teresa down for the winter. How long they were married. Almost ten years. What she was like. An alligator. Harry wanting to know what difference did it make? No kids, that part of his life was behind him.

For the first time in over twenty years he phoned the house in Palos Heights and said to Teresa, as a courtesy, "I want to thank you for putting up my bond. I'll send a check for the fifteen thou as soon as I move some dough around. I sincerely hope it didn't inconvenience you any."

Teresa Ianello said over the phone, loud enough for Joyce to hear, "You coward, you two-bit bookmaking son of a bitch, you sent that muscle here to threaten me? You know what would happen to you if Papa was still alive? I say the rosary every night, praying they send you up and lose the fucking key."

Harry said, "Nice talking to you, Teresie," and hung up. He said to Joyce, "You think I could live with a woman like that? She had five o'clock shadow all day. She could teach a course in ball-busting to women that, for one reason or another, don't instinctively have the knack. Listen, all her life she believed her dad was in the pepperoni business. I had to get permission from him to divorce her. You know what he said? He said, 'Ten years, Christ, you have a lot more patience'n I would've.' "

FOUR

Harry's phone rang all day Monday and Tuesday, friends, players, calling to say what was this they heard or read in the paper, asking if he was okay, if he was still in business. A short piece in *The Miami Herald* said:

SOUTH BEACH RESIDENT

CHARGED IN FATAL SHOOTING

On page three, buried. That's all he was, a resident? Why not Popular South Beach Figure, or Personality? Christ, resident. He told friends and players it was all a mistake and would be straightened out before too long. When his runners and sheet writers called he told them to sit on their totals another day or so and he'd get back to them.

The Zip phoned late Tuesday afternoon. Harry wasn't ready for him. He heard the Zip say, "What're you doing, Harry, going around shooting people? You know who the guy was you capped? Earl? Jimmy's fish guide he always used, up on the lake. You gonna call Jimmy, tell him you're sorry? . . . Harry?"

He didn't know what to do. He couldn't play along, pretend he didn't know who sent the guy, Christ, Earl Crowe. So he hung up the phone.

It didn't give him any time at all to think. When the phone rang again Harry answered and the Zip said, "You hang up on me?"

"We were cut off."

The line was silent until the Zip said, "You know a reason we shouldn't be talking?"

Harry said, "You want to know if I'm wired and some people are listening? What do you think?"

"There's a guy sitting in your lobby," the Zip said. "I wondered was he a friend of yours. Somebody looking out for you."

"I haven't left the apartment."

"Haven't talked to people from the government?"

Harry said, "Not yet," and hung up. Fuck him.

He knew guys who punched walls in moments of frustration and some of them broke their hands. He could smash something, throw the telephone through the window. Kick in the TV set. What else? Thinking about violent things he might do calmed him down. He was leaving, putting his forty-seven years of planning into effect. So why get excited?

Later, Joyce came with Chinese. She set the dining table that was at one end of the living room, got the place mats and dishes from the kitchen. They started, Joyce using chopsticks, Harry a fork. He ate a piece of shrimp toast and then fooled with his Szechuan chicken, removing the peppers. He said to Joyce, "When you came in, was there a guy in the lobby? Like a federal agent pretending to be a normal person?"

Joyce knew how to handle those chopsticks. She said, "How about a guy in a cowboy hat? Not the kind country-western stars wear, a small one. Like a businessman's cowboy hat."

"I know what you mean, the Dallas special,"

Harry said. "That Stetson, the kind the cops were wearing when Jack Ruby shot Lee Harvey Oswald."

Joyce held her chopsticks poised and then nodded, no doubt seeing it. "That's the one. Light tan, or sort of off-white." She took a few moments to poke at her Gung Bo shrimp. "He's wearing a dark suit and tie, has a newspaper on his lap."

"All by himself?"

She nodded, but seemed to be thinking of something else. "He's the type, he's dressed up you might say, but looks like a farmer. You know what I mean? That weathered rawboned type. Probably around forty. I almost forgot, he's wearing cowboy boots, tan with sort of ivory wingtips. With a dark-blue suit."

"No style," Harry said. "I guess you did notice him."

Joyce looked up from her plate, thinking of something else. "You know what? He was there yesterday when we came in."

Harry shook his head. "Never saw him."

"Then last night when I left, there was another guy sitting in the same chair, near the elevator."

"My protectors," Harry said, "from some government law-enforcement body." He took a bite of chicken and vegetables and worked on his plate for a minute before looking at Joyce again.

"When you're finished, would you mind going down and ask the guy who he's with? I'm curious."

Joyce said, "Really?"

"Or, hey. Ask him if he could come up here for a minute. Tell him I'd like to meet him."

Joyce seemed to think it over.

"Why?"

"This guy could be risking his life for me. I'd like to shake his hand, that's all." He saw the way she was looking at him and said, "What's the matter?" Innocent.

Joyce said, "What're you up to, Harry?"

The first thing the man said, once he was in the apartment, was, "You don't remember me, do you?" with a slight grin, his head cocked looking at Harry. "I could tell yesterday when you came in. You walked right past like I wasn't there."

Harry tried narrowing his eyes, but it didn't help. Joyce had it right, he looked like a farmer: that stringy type with hollow cheeks, crow's-feet, and had the accent to go with it, not Deep South but from somewhere below Ohio. He touched the funneled brim of his Stetson with two fingers and held open his ID case in the other hand, showing his star.

He said, "Raylan Givens, U.S. Marshals Service."

The name was no more familiar than the face, that rugged outdoor type with a fighter's nose. Harry stepped up now and shook his hand, squinting to show he was trying to remember. Raylan Givens was nearly a head taller in his cowboy boots, tan ones, Harry had noticed, yeah, with a wingtip design. He kept nodding as he gripped Harry's hand, pumping it. Harry said, "It was in federal court," taking a shot. "Am I right?" He got free of Raylan's grip as the man shook his head.

"Almost," Raylan said. "I'll give you a hint. We took a trip together."

Harry said, "Right, we met on a plane one time," and saw Raylan shaking his head again, still with that grin, enjoying this. So he wasn't offended at not being remembered. A good-natured type.

"We made the trip together," Raylan said. "Started out from Miami International, got as far as Atlanta where we had to change?"

Now Harry was nodding. "On our way to Chicago." He said to Joyce, "I was subpoenaed to appear before a grand jury. It would've put me in about the same position I'm in now, getting squeezed."

"I was to see you got there," Raylan said, "but we never made it, did we? Least you didn't."

Harry said to Joyce, "This was about five years ago."

"Six years in February. We're hung up in Atlanta on account of the flight was delayed," Raylan said. "You were sore anyway 'cause you didn't want to talk to that grand jury. I mean you were good and ticked off."

"I had no business being there."

"If you had nothing to say, that would've been brought out in your testimony, wouldn't it? No, you had to pull a disappearing act on me after you gave your word." Raylan looked over at Joyce, in the kitchen now cleaning up. "We're in the Atlanta airport? I'm eating an ice cream cone, he says he's going to the men's and will be right back. The next time I saw him was yesterday, six years later."

Harry grinned, Raylan didn't. He said to Harry, "If you'd kept your word I'd be up in grade by now with the Marshals to a GS-Twelve 'stead of where I am presently and have been the past seven years. Nothing happened to you, though, did it? I thought sure the court would hold you in contempt and put out a fugitive warrant."

Harry, serious now, said, "If I had ever shown my face in that courthouse, I would have been seen by some people as far worse than contemptuous. It turned out the Justice Department didn't need me anyway." He narrowed his eyes at Raylan Givens and this time saw the two of them in the Atlanta airport, only a glimpse, but with enough recall in it for him to say, "I think you told me you're from Kentucky."

"Yes sir, Harlan County, in the eastern part of the state."

"You don't drink."

"Well, not too much."

"I don't drink at all anymore."

"Well, good for you."

"You said your goal, at least then, was to be a . . . revenue agent?"

"ATF," Raylan said. "That's Alcohol, Tobacco and Firearms, part of the Treasury Department. I still wouldn't mind it."

Harry glanced at Joyce. "Wants to stop people from drinking and smoking."

Raylan's grin returned. "That's what you said in Atlanta that time. I told you no, ATF goes after people who deal illegally in those items."

He looked over at Joyce. "On the plane he kept trying to get me to have a drink."

Harry watched Joyce give him kind of a smile, about to say something, but Harry beat her to it.

"Let me ask you, Raymond—"

"It's Raylan," the marshal said, and spelled it.

"Raylan, right. Can I ask you what exactly your duties are?"

"Well, we guard federal prisoners, see to their transportation. Work courtroom security, my least favorite assignment. We take care of forfeitures, property that's been confiscated."

"I mean what're you doing for *me*?" Harry said. "I'm not a prisoner."

"No, but you're likely to be called before a grand jury," Raylan said. "We're to see nothing happens to prevent your appearance."

"What if I don't want your protection?" Harry saw the man's puzzled look and said, "That's a theoretical question. I'm wondering about my rights."

"Our being around makes you nervous?"

It didn't seem worth getting into. Harry shook his head. "Let's forget I asked."

Raylan said, "We can stay pretty much out of sight except . . . Mr. Arno, could you do us a big favor? Don't go out at night, okay? And if you want to go someplace during the day, let us drive you."

Harry said, "This is for my protection."

"Yes, sir."

"Or so I won't run off on you."

"This's different'n that other time," Raylan said. "You jump bond you become a fugitive from justice." Serious about it.

Harry said, "I guess I wasn't thinking."

It seemed to satisfy Raylan.

Joyce was the one giving him the look.

He was at the window again where he spent half the day. Joyce watched him from the kitchen. She finished drying the dishes and crossed the room to put her hand on Harry's shoulder and stand close to him.

"Is he still outside?"

"In the park getting a cone. The U.S. marshal loves ice cream. You hear him say he's from some *county*? People from the South do that. Not in Florida so much, I mean people from the *south* South."

"I've heard of Harlan County," Joyce said. "You want to know what I think?"

"Tell me."

"He's not as dumb as you'd like to believe."

"I forgot you're from that part of the country. Nashville, was it? And you people tend to stick up for each other."

"We moved, Harry, when I was two years old."

"Yeah, but once a you-all, you're one for life," Harry said. "Look at him licking his cone."

When they were silent and it was quiet in the room they could hear faint sounds from outside, a car starting, voices raised. Out on the beach a photographer and crew were shooting a ninety-pound fashion model in after-swim wear, a girl fifteen or sixteen. Models now were babies. Joyce had three catalog jobs lined up for the winter and was pretty sure of doing aerobic outfits in the sexy underwear book. She looked okay as long as she could wear a stocking to cover her veins and bumps. She didn't mind Harry seeing them.

They went out weekdays during the football season, saw a movie and had dinner and sometimes she'd stay over. Harry became horny about once a month, always in the morning. Toward the end of his drinking days, a few years ago, he was horny every morning, especially hung over. But he was only normally horny, years before that, when she was dancing topless and he would take her out after to get something to eat.

He didn't seem to know what kind of attitude to have about her. Or he was self-conscious about being seen with her in public; though there was little chance anyone on the beach would recognize her. The clubs she worked were in Miami. Harry was prudish, while she didn't feel that dancing with her breasts exposed, when she was doing it, was that big a deal. She said to him once, "You wait for what seems like forever to see what kind of tits you're going to have. Then once you have them, whatever shape or size they are, you're stuck. Mine are o-*kay*, they're not showstoppers by any means, which is fine with me. I've never ever thought for one minute about getting them augumented, or envied girls who had big ones—no thanks, have to carry around the load some girls do. Of course, guys love big ones." At least guys who came to topless clubs seemed to. They'd ask why she wore glasses while she performed and she'd tell them so she could see where she was going and not fall off the stage. She told Harry the horn-rim glasses gave her a friendly rapport with the audience. Here was a girl being herself and they loved it, they could relate to her. "Like I was the girl next door." And Harry said, "Or their fifth-grade teacher they used to fantasize about, wonder what she looked like naked." There could be something to that. He asked about guys who ran these clubs hitting on her. She told Harry they weren't her type. As Joy she'd open her act with Led Zeppelin's "Black Dog," do funky moves to the intricate guitar riffs between the lyrics and get the room's attention fast. Her glasses would slip and she'd push them back up while she danced. The idea was not to look too professional. When she finally quit Harry said, "Well, you don't have to do that anymore." She told him she didn't ever *have* to do it, she liked it, all that attention. Harry told her she should be ashamed of herself. He didn't get it, because in his business the idea was *not* to call attention to yourself. They split up. She worked in the chorus aboard a cruise ship that toured the Caribbean, choreographed routines a couple of years, got into catalog modeling. About this time she began to hear her biological clock ticking and married a guy who sold real estate. He said he wouldn't mind a couple more kids. "I thought I was going to be a mommy," Joyce told Harry a few years later, when he was back in her life. "Until these two little girls he already had, not even in training bras yet, made him choose between them and me." Harry said, "You're not the mommy type, kiddo." Making it sound like a compliment. They'd go to movies, to Wolfie's, to Joe's

Stone Crab. Have Chinese in. . . . All those years, it was funny, she always felt she could do better than Harry Arno, twenty-five years older than she was, on Medicare. Though he never took advantage of the senior citizen's discount at the movies.

Joyce said, "You're getting ready to take off, aren't you?"

Looking out the window he didn't answer right away. When he did he said, "I've *been* ready."

She moved her hand across his shoulders, over and back again. "You know where you're going?"

"Of course I do." He said, "I may need your help to get started."

It surprised and scared her a little. "What would you want me to do?"

"I'll let you know." Another minute went by before he said, "I think tomorrow will be the day. Why hang around."

"But if you testify," Joyce said, "and they put Jimmy away—"

"It wouldn't matter, he could still get people to do a job on me."

"If you talked to him? Look at how long you've known each other."

Harry said, "I have bags packed ready to

run and I shot one of his guys. As far as he's concerned I skimmed on him, the same as stealing money, and there's no way to convince him otherwise."

"The FBI, they'll be after you, too, won't they?"

Still looking out the window he said, "I doubt it. They'd have to justify the expense and I don't think they'd be able to."

She said, "Can I ask where you're going?"

Harry turned his head and she was looking into his eyes, a bright clear blue with light reflecting in them through the window.

He said, "If I'm the only one who knows, I should be okay." He touched her face then, caressing at first, then fooling with her ear and the curly ends of her hair. "I'll tell you something I've never told a soul," Harry said, this time sure of it. "I actually have been skimming off those people over twenty years. You can't imagine how much money I've put away."

FIVE

After that business at the Atlanta airport, losing a federal witness in his care, Raylan Givens was assigned to the academy at Glynco, Georgia, where future marshals got their training.

He told Harry Arno, the two of them having an early dinner at Joe's Stone Crab, the training center was south of Savannah toward Brunswick and that guys applying as Treasury agents, ATF and Secret Service, also Customs, were trained there too. Raylan said what it was, you go through a Criminal Investigator course with the emphasis on PT, physical training. He was a firearms instructor. He said it wasn't a put-down to be assigned there; most guys liked the duty. It was just they knew he wanted field work, fugitive investigation, so he felt that in a way it was like a punishment.

"One thing they knew I could do without messing up was shoot. So I taught the care and use of basic firearms. Like that Army-issue .45 you used, developed about a hundred years ago to stop the fanatical Moros during the Philippine Insurrection. It stopped them too."

When Raylan said, "Hey, I'm doing all the talking," Harry Arno told him no, go on, it was interesting. Harry busy cracking those crab claws and dipping them into butter or a kind of mustardy sauce. The hash browns were good; everything was good here. Harry said to have the Key lime pie after.

Raylan said, "It wasn't too tough at the academy, but if you weren't used to it, it could be stressful. There was one trainee, he threw his suitcase over the fence and was climbing it when they pulled him off and asked him, 'What are you doing?' He said, 'I've had enough, I'm leaving.' They said to him, 'Well, why don't you use the front gate?' This trainee had the feeling he was in prison and to get out he'd have to escape."

"When you were a trainee," Harry Arno asked, sucking on a claw, "did you have that feeling?"

"No, I liked it," Raylan said. "I was in the Marines before that, so it wasn't anything new. I mean physical training." He said, "I had a roommate, though," and had to grin recalling the guy, "who couldn't wait to get out. He'd sit there in the room looking at a map of the United States he had Scotch-taped to the wall? He'd say, 'This is how I'm going home, this road here and this one,' showing me how he'd get to St. Louis, Missouri."

Harry said, "Is that right?"

You could see he was interested and enjoying himself.

"Then the next time, the guy would ask me what I thought of the route, a different one. He had roads traced with a colored pencil that were like the straightest lines to where he wanted to go, but without taking interstates if they weren't direct routes. You know, that might be longer but would be quicker? It was like he was on the run, using back roads and such."

Harry touched his napkin to his mouth, put it on the table, and said, "Excuse me a minute, Raylan."

Raylan gripped his chair arms, ready to get up.

Harry said, "I'm just going to the men's. I'll be right back." He was up now but paused to smile.

And Raylan knew he was thinking about that time in the Atlanta airport. Raylan grinned back at him.

"It seems to me you said that once before."

Harry raised one hand, the way you might interrupt someone to say good-bye, and walked off around the tables—just about all of them occupied now—toward the men's room over on the other side.

Raylan was thinking that when Harry came back he'd tell him the other thing the map reader did. How he went to bed real early every night, around eight, instead of going into town for a few beers. Raylan would come back around midnight and if he was quiet, the roommate would be quiet the next morning when he got up about an hour early. But if Raylan accidentally made any noise at night when he came in, bumped into his locker or knocked something off the desk? The roommate would make the exact same noises the next morning.

He could tell Harry that one. He could tell

about guys he knew from his training he ran into in the field.

He'd ask Harry if he did any fishing. Explain how he'd only been in the Miami Marshals Office since last spring and had not done any fishing around here. Growing up he'd fished mostly for catfish in ponds and streams that were contaminated and had hardly any fish in them. Then, instructing at Glynco and living in Brunswick, Georgia, he'd fished in the ocean, out in St. Andrew Sound off Jekyll Island. Ask Harry about bonefishing down in the Keys; he might know.

Now he wondered if Harry had fallen in.

He hadn't shown Harry pictures of his kids yet, his two boys, Ricky, nine, and Randy, three and a half.

If he did, though, he'd have to mention that his wife, Winona, was still in Brunswick with the two boys, but not go into any detail unless Harry asked why they weren't with him. How did you answer that in a few words and not bore him with a long, involved story? Well, you see, Winona's divorcing me. I left to report here, she stayed to sell the house, see if we could get sixty-seven nine, what we paid, and fell for the real estate salesman who sold the house and didn't even get our price. Let it go for sixty-five five, took his commission and also Winona. Like I'd call her up during that time? "Well, how we doing, hon?" "Oh, okay." She wouldn't say much till finally this one time she goes, "I have some good news," meaning the house was sold, "and some I know you won't like, so I expect you're going to give me a hard time." That was how Winona talked, always a little smart-alecky. If Harry wanted to hear about it . . . Harry had been divorced and might offer tips on how to accept what you saw coming and not take a baseball bat to that real estate salesman up in Brunswick. The thing was, he didn't especially miss Winona. The two boys, yeah, but not Winona. Raylan put his napkin on the table, got up, and followed Harry's route to the men's room. Pushed open the door and went in.

Okay, he wasn't here. Nobody was, the doors to the stalls were partway open and no feet showed underneath.

He's around, though, Raylan told himself. He's having a little fun with you, that's all.

Boy, did he want to believe it.

Torres got to Joyce Patton the next afternoon and talked to her in her apartment, Torres looking around the living room as he asked her, "Why don't you tell me where he went? Save us a lot of trouble."

She said she had no idea.

Torres said, "You know I'm a friend of his. I don't want to see him become a fugitive. But if he's left town or fails to show up for his arraignment, that's what he is."

She didn't say anything.

"At least he can't leave the country. We made him hand over his passport."

She was composed, standing with her arms folded waiting for him to finish and leave. A good-looking woman, nice figure.

"They know him at Joe's Stone Crab," Torres said, "he's been going there, what, twenty years? The hostess said he left about ten to six, as they were starting to fill up. A few minutes later the marshal he was having dinner with came looking for him. The valet parking kid told us Mr. Arno came out and got in his car. He didn't drive it there, the marshal who was with him drove. But it was his Eldorado pulled up on the other side of Biscayne the exact moment Harry came out the door. He walked across the street, got in, and the car left. The valet kid didn't notice who was driving."

"I don't know anything about it," Joyce said.

She looked right at him, Torres thinking, Like she might have prepared herself for this knowing it was coming. He said, "Wherever Harry went, he didn't drive. So I'm thinking he flew, but didn't want to leave his car at the airport." He waited a moment. "We're checking all the flights that went out yesterday." He paused again. "You understand I think you drove him to the airport and brought his car back to the lot where he keeps it."

She didn't move or say anything. If she had made up her mind to outwait him she was doing okay.

"I bet you have his car keys," Torres said, "in your purse."

Her expression changed slightly, eyebrows raising.

"That would prove I drove him to the airport?"

"It would to me."

She shook her head. "I can't help you."

"You mean you won't."

She said, "What's the difference?"

Raylan Givens was standing by as McCormick and another agent searched Harry Arno's apartment. They were casual about it, Raylan didn't think very thorough, though they didn't make a mess tossing the place. Raylan almost asked if they were looking for anything in particular, but decided to keep quiet. McCormick would sound like he was a nice guy, but underneath it was a snot-nose attitude he couldn't hide. He liked to make fun of people, especially with another agent to show off in front of. One on one, when you had business with him, he wasn't so bad. Then, he hardly paid any attention to you. McCormick was about fifty-five, heavyset, had his suit coat off to work in his shirtsleeves, his blue-and-yellow-striped tie pulled down.

Looking around the living room he would raise his voice to the other agent searching the bedroom, telling him that after he had the resident agent's job in West Palm he was ready to retire, take a job in corporate security, and should've instead of coming down to this Third World city. Talking about Miami. He said he worked an investigation once, a broad who lived in this same hotel tried to extort six hundred grand from the old guy who owned the place. They had her practically indicted and you know what happened? The old guy married her. His attitude: So she was trying to take him, he didn't give a shit, he wanted her. Not long after that he died of natural causes. She was a former movie star, Jean Shaw?

The agent in the bedroom said he'd never heard of her, but then asked where she was now.

"Who knows?" McCormick said.

Talking, they didn't seem too interested in what they were doing. Going through the motions. McCormick was in the kitchen now, bent over poking around in the refrigerator. Coming out to the living room he said to Raylan, "You wear that hat all the time?"

"When I go out," Raylan said, "yeah."

"You wear it when you sit down to eat?"

"Not usually."

"Some of you cowboys do. Never take your hat off. Watch country music awards on TV. You see all these bozos sitting there with their hats on, pretending they're cowpokes." He said, "Why don't you make us some iced tea? There's some instant in there."

It was the first time since they got here McCormick had spoken to him, and what was it about, his hat. Raylan fixed two glasses with ice cubes and lemon wedges he found and brought them out to the dining table. McCormick looked over from where he stood at a wall of pictures. Raylan thought he was going to ask to have his brought to him, but he came over to the table.

Raylan said, "You haven't found anything? Any clues to where he might be?"

"No, but I'll let you know if I do," McCormick said. He raised his voice to the other room saying, "Jerry? Raylan wants to know have you found any clues."

Jerry's voice came back, "Who?"

This was Jerry Crowder, a young agent who could learn a bad attitude, Raylan believed, hanging around McCormick. Basically he was a good guy, big and rangy, a former college football player. Raylan had backed him a couple of times making arrests.

McCormick had picked up his iced tea. He sipped it looking at Raylan and said, "I've meant to ask you, when Harry Arno gave you the slip, did he stick you with the dinner check?"

Giving Raylan a serious, interested expression now, waiting.

"Sixty bucks," Raylan said. "I paid it."

"I hope you don't put it on your expense account." Raylan didn't say anything and McCormick said, "What grade level are you?"

"GS-Eleven."

"For how long?"

"Seven years."

"Stuck, huh? That's a shame. I understand this is the second time you've let Harry Arno get away. Is he a friend of yours?"

"I've never thought of him as such, no."

"Didn't they teach you never let a prisoner out of your sight?"

Raylan said, "He wasn't a prisoner," and knew right away he shouldn't have. It was like talking back to the teacher.

McCormick said, "Well, you were watching him, weren't you? That's what we're talking about."

Raylan felt now he had to keep going and said, "You want to know how I see it?"

"How you see what?"

"This situation, with Harry."

"I sure would, but wait," McCormick said, and called out, "Jerry, come in here." Crowder appeared in the bedroom doorway, almost filling it, and McCormick motioned to him. "Have an iced tea. Raylan's going to tell us how he sees it."

Coming over to the table Jerry said, "How he sees what?"

"That's what we're going to find out." McCormick looked at Raylan. "Go on."

"Well, first of all," Raylan said, "I can't think of a reason why Harry would take off knowing he needs protection. Another reason, he's too smart to become a fugitive, have to hide out the rest of his life."

McCormick said, "You know Harry pretty well?"

"I was with him on two occasions. Both times we talked, shared experiences, you might say."

"If he realizes he needs protection," McCormick said, "and knows he'll become a wanted fugitive if he runs, then why did he?"

"Maybe he didn't," Raylan said. "Maybe he was abducted."

They hadn't thought of that, both of them turning enough to look at each other. "By who," Jerry said, "the bad guys?" And McCormick jumped in, asking, "What about the fact an eyewitness saw him walk out of the restaurant and get in his own car? Someone there to meet him."

"He could've been tricked," Raylan said. Damn, wishing he had thought this through and had answers.

It did stop them again, giving them something new to consider. McCormick said, "He comes out thinking it's a friend driving his car?"

"Somebody he trusts."

"But it isn't. Is that what you're saying?"

It was simpler in his mind. "Something like that," Raylan said.

"But why's he leave you sitting there and duck out? What would the plan be that he got taken in? You understand what I mean? Did a friend set him up?"

Raylan shook his head. "I don't know. I haven't figured it out yet. Right now it's a feeling I have."

"It would seem to me," McCormick said, "his idea was to take off. That's the feeling I get."

"Or somebody talked him into it," Raylan said, thinking hard.

"I'll tell you how I see it," McCormick said, straight now, not having fun with him. "You don't want to believe you twice blew your assignment and because of it you aren't going to get any higher in the Marshals than where you are. So you want to blame it on someone else, Jimmy Cap, the bad guys? You've told yourself this bookie you've come to know so well, he wouldn't fuck you over again, you trust him. Raylan, is that what you're thinking? You see yourself getting sent back to the academy as an instructor? Then retiring and living in Brunswick, Georgia, the rest of your life?"

McCormick put on his blank expression again.

"What's wrong with that?"

S I X

Transcription of a tape recorded 05 Nov., 2:20 P.M., monitoring the cordless handset of Jimmy Capotorto at his residence on Pine Tree Drive, Miami Beach, from the Eden Roc marina across Indian Creek. Jimmy Cap is in conversation with one of his aides known as Tommy Bucks.

TB: Jimmy? Tommy.

JC: Yeah . . .

TB: There's a problem here collecting from people, I don't know their names. Some of them go by numbers.

JC: Yeah, they use a number.

TB: In case on the phone if somebody's listening . . .

JC: Harry knows who those are.

TB: That's what I'm talking about. You know, does he have a list?

JC: What kind of list?

TB: Of the names. So I know who to look for.

JC: I don't know he's got one or not, maybe.

TB: You can't tell if the numbers that lost paid or didn't pay. His writers don't know shit. I talk to them, they say people are calling up asking where Harry is and who they should pay.

JC: So what's the problem? Get a guy to take his place. (Pause) Listen, you better come over. I don't want to talk about this on the phone. You never fucking know, do you?

At 3:10 P.M. on 05 Nov. Tommy Bucks appeared on the patio where Jimmy Capotorto was sunbathing. The two were observed in conversation for the next few minutes. Also present were Jimmy Cap's girlfriend, Gloria Ayres, 22, of Hallandale, and one of his bodyguards, Nicky Testa, 24, of Atlantic City, NJ, sometimes known as Macho or Joe Macho.

* * *

It drove the Zip nuts the way Jimmy told you things you already knew, or even things you had told him at one time and he forgot it was you. Right now he was lying on his stomach and you had to get down there close to his body to hear what you already knew he was going to say. Down close to his smell, his back soaking in the sun. He would turn his head. "Gloria? Where's Gloria?" And Gloria, with the string swimsuit stuck in her ass, would wait for Jimmy's bodyguard, Nicky, to wring out a face towel he kept soaking in ice water and hand it to her so she could wipe Jimmy down, cool him off. First his face as he raised his head, then she'd wipe down his back, Jimmy grunting and moaning while Gloria worked on him with the ice-cold towel, her tits coming out of the swimsuit. The second time she wiped him down Gloria looked this way, at the Zip hunched over in the lawn chair close to Jimmy, and winked at him.

It told the Zip Gloria was on some kind of drug or she wasn't as afraid of Jimmy as she ought to be. She didn't seem to care if Nicky, the punk bodyguard, saw her fooling around either. They were about the same age. Nicky had light-brown frizzy hair and liked to pose, show off his build he worked on with weights. The Zip would catch the punk and Gloria grinning at each other and was positive the punk was fucking her.

Sitting there in the sun, the Zip tried to imagine the girlfriend of any of the old-time bosses giving the eye to some guy that worked for them. Those people back then, Luciano, Costello, Joe Adonis, were respected because they had proved on the way up they were men and you better not fuck with them. Jimmy Cap was a different story: next in line to a boss that got shot in the back of the head. Whether Jimmy had it done or not, he was in the right place at the right time and now ran the show here. Extortion, shylocking, girls, some heroin, restaurant and bar supply companies, the same old stuff while the Latinos and the jigs were making all the money in South Florida. The Zip said to Jimmy one time, "Colored kids selling product on the street corners do better than your guys." He told Jimmy he should be moving crack as well as heroin and Jimmy said it wasn't his line. He said let the Latinos and the jigs kill each other over it. See? Nothing you hadn't heard before ever came out of him. Most of the time excuses, reasons to keep from having to get up off his butt.

Jimmy telling the Zip now, the Zip hunched down close so he could hear the man talking into his shoulder, "We have to get another guy to step in there and run Harry's book. Even so, we're going to lose some of his players, business Harry built up, personal relationships. There's nothing we can do about that."

It was as true as anything he ever said.

"Or find Harry. Either way you want to do it."

The Zip, perspiring, trying to protect the crease in his trousers, asked Jimmy what he knew about Harry Arno outside of he was from here originally and had lived in Chicago at one time. Jimmy didn't know much more than that. The Zip asked if Harry had a girlfriend and Jimmy said, "Yeah, talk to her, Joyce Patton. And go see the ex-wife again, she might know something."

"Once was enough with the wife," the Zip said. "I can see why Harry left her. She was Family up there at one time in Palos Heights. I'll tell you something, it's harder to check on anybody that lives in that place now or used to, that Palos Heights, than anywhere I ever been. No, the main thing," the Zip said, and paused. "First I want to know, you giving me the sports book to run?"

"What I said was I want you to handle this matter. That's all I said."

"And I want to know, I'm in this, I get it

straightened out, are you giving me the sports book or not?"

"Okay, handle it and you can run the book."

"You said before to handle it and you send this guy catches *fish* to do the job. Guy from the Lake."

"Hey, Tommy? Handle it, okay? It's yours."

"And I have the sports book?"

"Jesus Christ—yeah, it's yours."

"People in that business," the Zip said, "they gonna see what happens they try and skim on me. Harry's gonna be found dead. Found dead in the ocean or in the swamp or he runs away someplace, to Mexico, I don't care where he is, Harry's gonna be found dead. Am I right?"

Jimmy said, "What?" into his shoulder.

"I say he's gonna be found dead."

Jimmy raised his head to squint at the Zip's face. "Your nose is getting burnt." He kept staring and said, "You got a big fucking nose, you know it? I mean looking just at your face." He said, "Gloria? Come over here. Tell me who Tommy looks like."

Gloria stood close to Jimmy Cap's lounge, hands on her hips, looking down at the Zip. "I don't know, who?"

"It's what I'm asking *you*."

"You mean like a movie star?"

Jimmy said to his bodyguard, "Hey, Joe Macho. Who's he look like?"

This punk Nicky Testa with his ponytail, his shirt off to show his body, stared at the Zip and said, "He looks like some of those outfit guys you see pictures of from the old days. Some of those guys, they look like they just got off the fucking boat."

Jimmy Cap was grinning, nodding his head, so the punk was grinning, his attitude not showing any respect at all. When the Zip called him Joe Macho, which wasn't too often, he said it in a way that let the punk know he thought the name was a joke. Otherwise he saw him as just Nicky and called him that.

Jimmy said, "Where's that picture you showed me? The one you cut out."

The Zip shook his head. "I don't have it no more." He did, but wasn't going to show it to this punk.

It was a photo of Frank Costello taken in the 1930s that had appeared in a news magazine last year. The Zip showed it to Jimmy Cap who looked at it and said, "Yeah, what?" Finally he caught on, seeing the resemblance, raised his eyebrows, and gave the Zip a nod.

The Zip cut the picture out and took it to his

tailor in Bal Harbour, an Italian guy in his seventies. He waited for the tailor to say, "Who is this, you?" or something like that. "This you or your brother?" But he didn't. The Zip said to him, "This is what I want, a buttoned-up look just like this. Dark-blue almost black double-breasted cut to fit close. Six buttons in front, right? Count them. Buttoned up high to show some white shirt and a pearl-gray tie with it. What do you say?"

The tailor said, "Sure, if that's what you want."

The Zip asked him, "You know who this is in the picture?" The tailor said no, so the Zip told him, Frank Costello.

The tailor said, "I made a suit for Meyer Lansky one time, way back. I was down on Collins then in the McFadden-Deauville. Made him a beautiful suit of clothes and he stiffed me. You believe it? With all his dough?"

The tailor, there was a guy old enough to know better and even he didn't show any respect. What did Nicky, a punk like that, know about it? Or Gloria, aiming her bare butt at the Zip while she cooled Jimmy down with the cold towel. The Zip reached over, gave her a pat, and watched her wiggle her butt at him. Like saying he could have some if he wanted. The Zip was thinking he could have it all, anything Jimmy Cap owned, if he wanted. Why not? He had already taken over his sports book.

SEVEN

Raylan had decided he needed to talk to the Zip to clear something up. Originally he'd thought of him as Tommy Bucks because it was what the Bureau guys called him. But then had started thinking of him as the Zip because that's what Harry called him and Raylan liked the sound of it.

The way he got on the Zip's tail was to wait till he showed up at Jimmy Cap's and then hang on to him after that. The Zip was in there only fifteen minutes, got in his Jaguar and cut through streets to head south on Alton Road, Raylan thinking he was going home and would find out where he lived. The Jag got to Fifteenth and turned left, went past that little park there and turned right onto Meridian. When the spiffy dark-green car all of a sudden pulled to a stop across from the Flamingo Terrace apartments Raylan realized, Jesus, the guy was going to see Joyce Patton. There was no way they could be friends. No, it had to be the Zip was going to question her about Harry, get her to tell him things she might know. Use force on her if he had to. Beat her up. Maybe do worse than that. All this was in Raylan's mind as he drove past, U-turned at Eleventh, the south end of the park, and pulled up in front of the Flamingo as the Zip reached the stoop of Joyce's terrace apartment and rang the bell. Now, Raylan out of the car and starting up the walk, the Zip was banging on the door with the edge of his fist. Raylan didn't think at this moment it was going to open. Maybe it wasn't, until Joyce looked out the peephole and saw him coming up behind the Zip, the man too intent on what he was doing to be aware of anyone behind him. So that as the door started to open Raylan was moving up fast on the Zip, and as the door came wide open and Joyce appeared and saw she had to get out of the way, Raylan hit the Zip from behind, grabbed him around the shoulders, and took him down hard on the living-room carpet. The Zip landed on his side, twisted around to lie faceup and now had Raylan astride his chest, pinning his arms to his sides. He didn't ask Raylan who he was or what he was doing, not with that furious look on his face. No, he started to buck and twist and didn't calm down till Raylan had his nine-millimeter out and was telling the Zip, "Keep still, or I'll shoot your nose off your face."

Joyce watched Raylan, sitting on the man, look over and touch his hat brim with two fingers. This U.S. marshal she had never seen without his cowboy hat. The man beneath him wore sunglasses, a pearl-gray tie with his dark suit. He wasn't moving a muscle now, Raylan holding the gun on the man's chest, the tip of the barrel resting on his chin. She heard Raylan say, "What'd you come here for?"

The man under him said, "Get the fuck off me."

With a gun in his face.

Two guys on her living-room floor in dark-blue suits talking to each other.

"I was looking to ask you," Raylan said to the man under him, "if you know where Harry Arno is, but I 'magine you came here to ask the same thing." He looked up again. "You know who this is?"

Joyce, standing away from them, shook her head. She held her hands in front of her twisting a ring Harry had given her as a birthday present.

"He works for Jimmy Cap," Raylan said, and looked down at the man in the sunglasses again. "I'm going to shoot his nose off he don't answer me. What'd you come here for?"

"Talk to her, say hello."

"About what, Harry Arno?"

"About *her*. I see her around. You know, so I want to get to know her."

Raylan looked up at Joyce again. "What do you think?"

She shook her head. "I've never seen him before."

"Mr. Tommy the Zip," Raylan said. "I'd say he came to ask if you know where Harry's at. I think we can all agree on that." He said to the Zip, "I wondered if you had him. I didn't think so, but I wanted to be sure. So, you don't know where he's at or have any idea. Is that right?"

Joyce moved closer to them. She heard the Zip say, with an accent, "No, I don't know."

"Well, the lady here, she don't know either. So she don't need a bozo like you coming around. You understand?"

"Okay."

"Don't bother her no more."

The man didn't move or say anything.

"You hear me?"

"Yeah, okay."

Raylan brought his ID case out of his inside coat pocket and held it open in the Zip's face.

"Can you read, partner? It says I'm with the U.S. Marshals Service. You ever come around here again I'll be all over you like a bad smell. You understand me?"

"Yeah, okay."

Joyce saw Raylan look up at her again.

"Anything you want to tell him?"

She shook her head.

"I'm letting you off easy this time," Raylan said, rising to his knees and then pushing up on one of them to stand up. Stepping away he said, "Are you packing? Roll over on your tummy for me."

Raylan stooped now to feel around the Zip's waist, Joyce watching the two men in dark-blue suits.

Do you believe this?

Roll over on your *tummy*? Raylan sounding more country today than he did before, in Harry's apartment.

Now he was helping the Zip to his feet and

the Zip was giving him a look because he didn't get it either. He was calm now behind his sunglasses, straightening his suit coat, pulling it down and smoothing it over his chest and stomach, putting his ego back together, Joyce detecting a touch of arrogance: the Zip looking about the room as he brushed himself off, looking absently until he came to her and stopped. He removed his sunglasses and held them, still looking at her with a sleepy expression he had to believe was cool, and it wasn't bad, really. Showing her he was in control of himself, allowing this to happen.

Raylan stood by the open front door now, suit coat unbuttoned, his gun put away. He said, "Here's the way out, Mr. Zip, and don't come back."

Mr. Zip.

She watched him pause to look at Raylan again before walking past him, Raylan much taller in his hat and cowboy boots. Mr. Zip was about Harry's size—now that she thought of it—both of them, by today's standards, little guys.

Raylan was thin and looked tall standing alone by the door. He watched Mr. Zip walk out to his car and the Jaguar drive off before he turned to Joyce.

"What if he comes back?"

Joyce shook her head. "I don't know where Harry is. Really, I can't help him."

"Maybe not, but what if Mr. Zip doesn't believe you?"

She said, "Are you trying to cheer me up?"

He left saying he'd see what he could do about her situation.

Joyce made herself a drink in the kitchen, Club and water, and brought it out to the living room to stand at a front window looking at the park across the street. At the park and at her options. Leave town. Stay with a friend. Count on Raylan to arrange some kind of protection.

He was a weird guy. He was funny and she wondered if he meant to be. There was no affectation about him, nothing put on. He sat on the gangster, told him to keep still or he'd shoot his nose off, and politely touched his hat brim and nodded to her. Mindful of his manners—sitting on the guy on the floor and telling him to roll over on his tummy. He did look like a marshal in a Western. He could be a lawman or a cowboy with that stringy look and his Kentucky drawl. She wondered what he looked like with his hat off and wondered again if he knew he was funny.

* * *

It was only a block to Miami Beach Police headquarters on Washington Avenue. Raylan's plan
was to talk to Buck Torres, get him to put Joyce
under some kind of protective surveillance.
Torres would say no, because he couldn't spare
the men. Not because she was uncooperative, everyone believing she knew where Harry was.
Torres wasn't that kind. He'd say to Torres,
"Look, I'm with you. Sure, I think she knows. I
think she helped him get away. So what are you
going to do, punish her? Let the Zip get hold of
her and do what he wants?" Torres would say he
still didn't have the men. So the next step would
be, try to get Torres to go to McCormick to get
McCormick to request a surveillance team from
the Marshals Service. Protect an innocent woman
who got trapped in a deal the Bureau put together and wasn't her fault. He could hear Mc-
Cormick come back with "Why don't we let the
Zip have her and then pick him up for assault
with intent? What's wrong with that?" With his
innocent look, to make you think he was kidding.

Raylan came to Washington Avenue and
turned left to park across the street from the Art
Deco police headquarters, which Raylan thought
of as some kind of religious temple with its
round front rising up four stories. Crossing the

street he was about run over by a girl with long blond hair riding a bicycle. There were all kinds of girls around here with long blond hair, long black hair; he had seen some on motorized skateboards cutting through crowds on Ocean Drive. South Beach was not too much like Brunswick, Georgia.

Inside, the lobby rose three floors wide open to show railings and rows of office windows up there. It was a modern new building, the holding cells with aluminum toilets, a sally port around on the side street where they brought in prisoners. Raylan approached the information counter and told the officer there he'd like to see Sergeant Torres and gave his name.

If you went in the holding-cell area you had to surrender your weapon. It was the cleanest city jail Raylan had ever seen in his life.

Up on the wall here they had an American flag framed in behind glass.

There were not too many visitors, a few civilians waiting around. Maybe a witness asked to come down and look at a lineup. A woman asking if this was where her husband was being held.

Buck Torres had come out of a doorway and was already crossing the lobby when Raylan saw him. Torres holding what looked like a computer printout sheet.

He also seemed like he had something to tell, but was going to let his visitor go first.

"I'd like to speak to you," Raylan said, "about Harry's friend Joyce Patton. I know you think she knows where he is, as do others. You know what I mean? Like Jimmy Cap, and that's a problem I see facing us."

One thing, he could talk to Torres, Torres never giving him the feeling he was wasting his time.

"We know where he is," Torres said.

It stopped Raylan, coming like that.

"Harry?"

"He went from Joe's Stone Crab to Miami International, got on a British Airways flight at seven-fifteen, and landed at Heathrow the next morning, Wednesday, November fourth, at eight-thirty."

Raylan said, "Harry's in England?" squinting at Torres. "Wait a minute, you took his passport."

"That's why we didn't check international flights right away," Torres said. "Soon as we did we find out a man named John Arnaud, A-r-n-a-u-d, booked the British Airway flight through a travel agent on Lincoln Road. We show the travel agent Harry's picture and he says yeah, that's John Arnaud, a customer he'd had for years. We look into this a little deeper," Torres said, "we find out John Harold Arnaud is Harry's real name. He has a birth certificate to prove it, so he's able to get a passport in that name and renew it whenever he has to. In seventy-one, when he moved back here from Chicago, he changed his name legally to Harry Jack Arno, same pronunciation of the surname but a different spelling. Don't ask me why he did it, outside of it gave him a passport in each name."

"So he's in England," Raylan said.

"The same day he landed," Torres said, looking at the printout, "he took off from Heathrow at eleven-thirty on British Airways five sixty-six. The flight arrived in Milan at two-twenty P.M. He stayed at the Hotel Cavour three nights and checked out on the eighth of November, a Sunday morning."

"You don't know where he is now?"

"As far as we know he's still in Italy."

Raylan frowned thinking about it, until his eyes came open and he started to nod, saying, "So Harry's back in Italy," as though his being there wasn't a bad idea.

* * *

One time the Zip and Nicky Testa got in an argument over the punk having only a few words of Italian and didn't care that he couldn't speak what the Zip called his mother tongue, the Zip saying he should learn it out of respect. Nicky said, "The only reason you can speak the language, you're from the old country, so don't fucking give me a hard time, okay?"

This punk twenty-four years old talking like that because he was close to Jimmy Cap and felt he was privileged.

Once in a while the Zip would call him *mammoni,* meaning a mama's boy, or *bambolino,* a doll, or the worst thing the Zip could think of to call an Italian male, *frocio,* a guy who was queer.

Nicky would say, "Okay, what's that mean?"

And the Zip would say, "You don't learn how to speak it, what do you care?"

The afternoon of the day following the visit to Joyce Patton, the Zip arranged to have a talk with Nicky and brought him out to the lanai, the open sitting room that faced the patio, saying, "Follow me, *stronzo.*" This time calling him an asshole.

"*Stronzo,*" Nicky said, fingers caressing his bare chest, "what's that mean, strong? Like referring to how I'm built?"

"Something like that," the Zip said. This guy was so dumb you could say anything you wanted to him. Now he seemed restless, looking out at the patio where Gloria was sunning herself, lying on her stomach topless, while Jimmy Cap was upstairs taking his afternoon nap.

"You waiting for her to turn over?"

The punk didn't bother to answer.

"Tell me something. You go to bed with her?"

This time the punk turned his head to his shoulder. He said, "Jimmy's right, you got a big fucking nose," and turned his head away again.

At that time Nicky wore his hair in a ponytail. The Zip reached over and took hold of it, brought it with him as he turned away and swung the punk screaming to hit the end of the sofa and land facedown on the tile floor. The Zip, still holding the ponytail, planted a knee on him, brought a switchblade out of his coat pocket, released the blade, and sliced up with it in a single motion to sever the ponytail. The Zip rose. He kicked the punk now, getting him to roll over, and showed him the hank of hair in his hand.

He said, "You want to learn a word? *Minchia*. It means a dick. That's the Sicilian word. You say *cazzo* you're from someplace else. So, look. I would have your *minchia* in my hand instead of this hair if I was Jimmy. You understand? I'm not like him, a *cornuto*, wearing the horns. You know what I mean? I don't let people think they can do things behind my back. You going to be working for me now and see what I mean. No sitting around feeling yourself like you do, showing your body."

"Who says I work for you?"

The kid with all those muscles, getting some of his nerve back. Or he saw Gloria watching them, sitting up now on the lounge, not bothering to cover herself as the Zip looked over.

"I say it, *stronzo.* I have something for you to do and Jimmy says okay."

"Like what?"

"Watch this woman for me, see where she goes. Harry Arno's girlfriend."

"Why can't you handle it?"

The punk lying on the floor, looking right at him past the knife in his hand. It meant Gloria was watching too. This time the Zip didn't bother to look over. She was there if he wanted her.

He said to Nicky, "Man, that attitude you have," making a face that was kind of a puzzled frown. "While I have the knife, maybe I should cut your *minchia* off anyway. How do you think about that?"

EIGHT

The ABC Bail Bonds woman's name was Pam. She had worked with her husband and then taken over the business when he was shot and killed by one of their clients. Pam explained this to Raylan when he asked what an attractive young woman like herself was doing in the surety business, mixing with undesirables. This was after he had shown his ID and marshal's star and she seemed impressed.

ABC was in a storefront on NW Seventeenth in downtown Miami, two blocks from the Justice

Building and the courts. A message in gold paint on the window outside said:

GETTING YOU OUT IS
EASY AS ABC!

There was an old guy working here part-time, a former licensed bail bondsman who chewed his cigar and looked right at home in this kind of office. And there was a stocky black guy named Desmond that Raylan met who went after offenders who missed their court dates. Pam told him one out of every three defendants she wrote never showed up in court when they were supposed to. Raylan didn't ask many questions, he knew how the business worked. He noted that Desmond did not appear qualified to go after Harry Arno. The cigar-chewer surely wasn't going to and it didn't seem likely Pam would, since she was running the business.

Raylan felt sorry for her, the poor woman working in this rat hole and trying to appear attractive. He judged her heavier than his wife, Winona, who went about one thirty. This woman had a rounded figure in her white V-neck outfit, black beads and earrings and a black velvet bow in her blond hair, a feminine touch, or else it was holding her swept-up hairdo together.

He got around to the subject of Harry Arno, asking if she had heard.

Yeah, someone from Miami Beach PD had called her to say a fugitive warrant had been issued. Pam shook her head. "That's all I need, a hundred-and-fifty-thousand-dollar forfeiture."

"He hasn't missed his appearance yet," Raylan said. "And you even have time after that, don't you, before you have to pay the court?" Showing her he knew how the system worked. "Up to as long as a year after, you only stand to lose ten percent."

"That's if I get him back," Pam said. "And if he's over in Italy or some goddamn place it doesn't seem too likely, does it?"

Raylan said, "You want me to go get him for you?"

She said, "Yeah, sure."

He said, "Ma'am, look at me." When she did he said, "I'm serious. You want me to go get him?"

Now she had to reconsider.

"But you're working." She gave him a suspicious look then. "Are they sending you over there anyway? They're extraditing him?"

"He skipped on a state charge," Raylan said. "I'm federal. I've checked, Miami Beach PD has no plans to bring him back."

"This would be on your own?"

"My own time. I have some coming and I can get off if I want."

Now she was busy thinking of all the reasons she believed it wouldn't work—without telling him any of them.

"Don't you know," Raylan said, "that fugitive investigation is one of the main duties of a U.S. marshal? Rounding up offenders and taking them to court?"

Pam stared at him for a minute, he believed entertaining the idea of using him.

"I imagine it would cost me an arm and a leg."

"His ex-wife," Raylan said, "signed a contingent promissory note, didn't she?"

"You better believe it."

"Guaranteeing if he skips she'll pay the expenses to get him back."

"I'm not worried about expenses," Pam said. "I want to know what you'd charge as a fee."

Raylan held up his hands, showing her his open palms. "Nothing. Pay my way and I'll bring him back for you."

"Why would you do that?"

"I need to prove I can. You give me airfare and I'll use my own money for hotels and meals till I get back and you reimburse me. You get a U.S. marshal for two weeks, though I doubt I'll need more than a few days over there."

She hesitated, as though being careful about what she'd say next. "All they know is he's in Italy somewhere. How do you expect to find him?"

"Because one time he said to me . . ." Raylan paused. "This was six years ago but I'll never forget his exact words. We're spending some time together waiting for a flight, talking, he's having a few drinks. He says, 'Raylan, I'm going to tell you something I've never told anybody before in my life.' He said then, 'On the tenth of July, 1945, I killed a man in the town of Rapallo in Italy. Shot him dead.' "

Pam said, "Yeah? You mean that's where he is?"

"I'd bet every cent I have," Raylan said, "he's over there taking it easy, right this minute sipping coffee at a sidewalk café—he doesn't drink anymore—pretty sure nobody'll ever find him."

The woman seemed confused again.

"He's gone back to this place 'cause it's where he *killed* somebody?"

"You could say that," Raylan said. "Except there's more to it."

NINE

The woman Harry sat with Saturday afternoon at the Gran Caffè Rapallo looked like Gina Lollobrigida. Well, somewhat. That type, with short dark curly hair and a full figure, big ones; Gina Lollobrigida in her forties. They sat among palm trees and potted plants beneath an orange awning on Rapallo's Via Veneto. The woman said her name was Maura.

"Maura," Harry said, "that's a nice name."

The woman said, "Not Mawra. *Mau*-ra, like you say ow. You know how to say ow?"

She spoke right up in a voice that was

hoarse, maybe from talking so much. She had large thighs in stone-washed jeans, her legs crossed at the table. Maura told Harry she was from Genova. Not Genoa, Genova. She was part owner of an industrial film company in Genova, where her husband had died of a heart attack in the editing room two years ago. Maura had an apartment here, up the hill where people from Genova and those stuck-up Milanese have bought places for weekends and for retirement. She asked if he had seen the Lina Wertmüller film *Swept Away*. She said the stuck-up rich woman in it—that was the way the Milanese spoke, trying to sound better than everyone. She said she came here every weekend—Genova less than a half hour away on the *autostrada*—except in the winter. This would be her last visit until spring.

"But it's still warm," Harry said, believing the weather here much the same as South Florida's. It seemed tropical, all the palm trees, flowers in bloom.

"Wait till next month," the woman said.

She had worn a fur jacket, coyote or lynx, Harry wasn't sure, draped over one shoulder when he first noticed her on the cable car this morning, descending from Montallegro, and then later, Maura strolling along the seafront promenade, hips working in the tight jeans. The jacket now hung over the back of her chair.

When she asked why he had come to Rapallo, Harry said it was his fifth visit in the past forty-seven years and this time he had made up his mind to stay. Last year he had bought a car, he'd found a place up in the hills . . . Harry sounding at peace.

"Why on earth," Maura said, "you pick this town? Why not Roma? Sit at a café on the real Via Veneto, the center of the world."

"I've been there," Harry said. "I like it here because it's off-center, off the beaten track. You don't see tourists everywhere with cameras. The only tourists, as you say, are from Genova, Milan, I suppose Turin? This is your Riviera and it appeals to me, the tropical setting, the olive trees. I like the promenade along the seawall where everyone strolls."

He heard himself speaking, sounding like someone else.

She told him it was called the *lungomare*, not the promenade, and said, "Are you hiding from someone? Your wife?"

Harry smiled, patient with her, approaching this woman with care. He said he liked the old castle sitting out in the water. He liked the palm trees and the color, the wooden shutters on the

buildings, clotheslines four stories up, underwear hanging to dry. He thought of the words
picture postcard and *quaint* but didn't use them.

Maura said, "Are you serious? Why?" She
said the buildings, the hotels and apartments
along the seafront, were crumbling with age. The
ones up the hill, where people from Genova and
the stuck-up Milanese had their apartments,
were much better, with air-conditioning.

Harry said, "I have a villa."

He believed he had stopped her, because
she looked surprised and was quiet for a moment. She sipped her wine. Harry, in no hurry,
finished his espresso. He liked espresso and
wished there was a way to make it last. Two sips,
it was gone.

Maura said villas, unless you had the money
to modernize, fix them up, were all right to look
at from a distance, but were drafty and damp in
the winter.

Harry told her he had central heating. He
had leased it furnished and was looking for a
cook and a maid.

That did stop her. She said, "Oh."

He didn't tell her he was living at the Hotel
Liguria and hadn't moved into the villa yet. Two
weeks now. He would go up there and stroll
through the rooms, the grounds, look out at the

view. The villa needed a comfortable chair and a good firm bed, lamps with hundred-watt bulbs. Also someone who knew how to use the kitchen.

"This morning," Harry said, "I saw you on the cable car coming down from Montallegro."

"The *funivia*," Maura said.

"The *funivia*. If I don't drive," Harry said, "I take the *funivia* to Montallegro and then walk down the hill to my villa. It's near Maurizio di Monti."

He had gone up this morning to check for leaks following a heavy rain the day before.

"I have my car here," Maura said. "I much prefer to drive from Genova than take the train."

"You were smoking on the *funivia*," Harry said, wanting to stay on the cable car.

She was smoking a cigarette now with her glass of wine. She seemed always to be smoking, blowing it out in quick gusts, as though in a hurry to finish. She said, "Yes?"

"There was a sign in the *funivia*, I believe it said no smoking."

"I didn't see it."

"A man kept waving his hand in the air and saying in a loud voice—I think he was saying— 'There's no smoking in here.' Very upset. And you said something to him."

"That one," Maura said. "I told him to mind

his own business. Listen, I was in Barcelona during the summer to see the Olympics. I'll tell you something if you don't know it. Everyone smokes in Barcelona."

"I quit last year," Harry said.

She inhaled and blew a stream of smoke at him as she said, "So, you saw me on the *funivia*. All the years I come here, when my husband was alive and now, I never visit the Santuario di Montallegro. So I went there today." She stubbed out the cigarette and sat back against her fur jacket.

"The Sanctuary of the Holy Virgin of Montallegro," Harry said. He paused and said, "At first, when I came back here to visit, I thought I wanted to live in Sant'Ambrogio. You know where it is?"

"Of course. Not far from here."

"Where the poet Ezra Pound lived."

Maura nodded. "Yes, I heard of him."

"During the war, in 1944, the Germans made him move out of his apartment, number twelve Via Marsala. There's a plaque on this side of the building." Harry pointed. "Down there, near the bandstand. He was living there with his wife."

"Yes?"

"The Germans were fortifying against the American Army coming up the coast from Rome. And they made Ezra and his wife move in with Ezra's mistress, Olga Rudge, in Sant'Ambrogio."

"You serious?"

"She had a house there. Olga did."

"His wife and his mistress under the same roof?"

Harry was nodding, yes, that's how it was.

"It could never be," Maura said.

"I don't imagine it was easy."

"The wife," Maura said, "did she kill the mistress or her husband? Or both?"

"They made do."

"I don't believe it."

"The house in Sant'Ambrogio also has a plaque on it that says Ezra Pound lived there. Last year when I was looking for a place the house was being renovated, fixed up, painted. . . . It was raining the day I saw it."

"You wanted to live in this house?"

"I thought it might be possible. The first time I saw the house was in sixty-seven, but I wasn't looking to buy it then. Ezra Pound was living here again and I came to see him."

"He was someone you admired?"

That was a good question. Harry said, "I did

meet him the first time I was here, during the war. It was in 1945. I was between here and Pisa, back and forth, and I got to meet him."

"Ezra Pound," Maura said. "I know the name, but I don't think I read any of his poetry."

"At the time I met him," Harry said, "they had him in a cage. They called it the gorilla cage. He was being held on a charge of treason. For making radio broadcasts in Rome during the war."

"Yes? What did they do with him?"

"He was brought home. . . . It's a long story. But, I met him. I talked to him. I saw him here again in sixty-seven. Then last year when I looked at the house in the rain . . . It was in August and it rained most of the time I was here. The next day I went up to Montallegro for the first time and decided to look for a house around there instead."

Harry paused. The woman was waiting for him to continue and he didn't know what to say, how much he wanted to tell her.

"So you bought a villa?"

"I leased it for two years."

"You rather live where the Virgin Mary appeared to a man four hundred years ago than where this poet lived with his wife and his mistress and somehow wasn't killed. I don't blame you."

Harry saw he was going to let her go, not waste any more effort on her. She was too big for him. Joyce was as tall as Maura but slim, without those tremendous thighs. Still, he asked Maura if she would like to see his villa, not sure why he did. She seemed to think about it, as though she might accept his invitation, then shook her head and said, "Not today." So after that he stopped trying to make conversation and pretty soon the woman from Genova picked up her fur jacket and left the café.

Harry wondered about her, a disagreeable woman. He could imagine her husband in the industrial film business having an affair with an attractive dark-haired actress who demonstrates electronic devices and Maura finds out about them. Catches them on a dark set or in the editing room. If the husband hadn't died of a heart attack Maura might have killed him.

Maybe she did.

The woman discounted or disagreed with everything he said. He was glad she didn't want to see his villa; he didn't feel much like going up there, riding the *funivia* with the woman. Then feel he should ask her to have dinner with him and ride back down again.

As soon as he returned to his suite at the Hotel Liguria, Harry called Joyce and saw her living room in late morning sunlight as he listened to the phone ring.

TEN

He told Joyce right away, "I don't want to say too much over the phone."

"But are you okay?"

"I'm fine. Listen—remember when I told you that story I've never told anyone else in my life?"

"That's where you are?"

"Yeah, but don't say it. Are you busy?"

"Am I *busy*? Right now?"

"I mean are you working?"

"The end of the month I'm doing a German

catalog, right here. Everybody in the world's using South Beach."

"How would you like to take a trip instead?"

She paused. "You sound different."

"I'm trying not to say too much, just in case. I'll tell you, though, I'm standing here looking out the window. . . . I think you'd like it."

There was a silence as she paused again.

"I don't know if I can. I have to make a living."

"Don't worry about that for now, just think about coming. You wouldn't need anything dressy, but bring a coat. It's cooler than Florida."

"How do I get there?"

"Don't worry about that either. I'll work something out."

She said, "I think I'm being watched."

This time Harry paused.

The Hotel Liguria, on a hillside above the road that followed the coast to Santa Margherita and Portofino, was high enough to give Harry a clear view of Rapallo from this far side of the bay: centuries of gray and sand-colored houses and buildings against steep green hills, palm trees along the seafront, an old resort city more Victorian now than medieval. Learning to live here, he hadn't thought of what he might have left behind.

He said to Joyce, "You mean the police?"

And heard her say, "I hope so." And then say, "I've had visitors, friends of yours and someone who isn't a friend. They all seem to think I know where you are."

He was careful, saying, "Was it Tommy who came to see you? You know who I mean?"

"He tried to. Raylan ran him off. But I don't think it's Raylan who's watching me. He's a pretty nice guy."

Harry said, "I didn't mean to get you involved." Heard himself and knew it sounded lame. "I'm really sorry. I can understand if you don't want to come."

She said, "No, I want to." Sounding sincere.

He said, "You don't think maybe we should wait awhile?"

And she said, "Do you want me to come or not?"

He liked her voice, the familiar sound of it, just then with an edge; but he felt they were talking too much. He said, "Are you nervous?"

"A little, yeah."

He said, "I miss you, I want you to come more than anything. Listen, I'll figure out how to work it and get back to you." Harry paused. He said, "Joyce? You know the after-shave I like?"

"Yeah?"

"Bring me a couple bottles. Okay?"

She said it again, "You sound different."

He said, "I know I do."

Harry stood looking at his view of Rapallo beyond the marina on this side of the bay and the statue of Christopher Columbus, anxious to show Joyce his villa. He believed that with a good pair of binoculars he would be able to pick out the villa from here. Tomorrow was Sunday; he'd look for binoculars on Monday. This evening he could stroll down to his favorite fish restaurant or stay in, have dinner in the hotel dining room with its sterile white tile and potted palms. Hotel literature said the English loved the Liguria. At least at one time they did. Built more than a hundred years ago the hotel became popular with English tourists just after the First World War. The restaurant in town or the hotel dining room . . . Harry hated eating alone. The woman this afternoon, the way she smoked, sucking deeply on her cigarettes, had made him want one. He'd almost taken a Salem from her pack on the table. He had told Joyce he wanted her to come more than anything, and it was true as he said it. Right now what he wanted more than anything was a drink, a Scotch over ice. It was that time of day and he was far enough from home that it would be safe here. He wouldn't be drinking and talking, telling stories—the way he had most often gotten in trouble in the past, overdoing it—there wasn't anyone he could hold a conversation with here and not sound as though he was explaining a joke.

He had imagined himself strolling in the evening along the seafront promenade, the *lungomare*, where Ezra Pound had strolled more than a half century ago and again a few years before he died, and where Harry had actually watched him stroll in '67. Pound with his style, his cane, his black hat with the wide brim that was like no other hat, the long points of his shirt collar outside his black overcoat. Harry would imagine Ezra Pound returning from his stroll to have a drink with his mistress at the Gran Caffè. Harry had seen Olga Rudge also in '67, gray-haired, but still a knockout. Most people would probably consider his wife, Dorothy, better looking. Maybe, but in one photograph she appeared pigeon-toed and to Harry that indicated a tight-assed personality, little or no sense of humor. He was convinced Olga would have been more fun, or else why get involved in that kind of situation?

He had never thought of Joyce as his mistress, but now liked the idea as he explored ways of getting her here without being followed.

He could call his travel agent, charge Joyce's fare to his account. It seemed the likeliest way. Work out a few details. . . .

There were North Africans here from Tunis, Benghazi, from places in Algeria, who were called "wannabuys" in English and something else in Italian. They sold cheap watches and jewelry on the walk along the seafront: laid out their goods on blankets and called in low voices what sounded like "Wannabuy?" and waited for the people strolling past to notice them.

Harry stood looking out at the bay, at power boats skimming past the sixteenth-century castle that sat out past the seawall; it was connected to the shore by a concrete ramp, like a driveway, and was much smaller than Harry had imagined castles would be. Four-thirty Sunday afternoon there were only a few people on the beach, some old men playing boccie ball. Harry had taken his blazer off and wore it draped over his shoulders now without putting his arms in the sleeves. He believed he might be taken for a real Italian.

Lately he'd been thinking he might have to learn the language.

About ten feet from him one of the North Africans had unrolled a straw mat and was now laying out a display of umbrellas, the collapsible kind in a variety of dark colors. The black guy paused, bringing the umbrellas out of a plastic trash bag, looked this way, and Harry felt himself being sized up, judged, the guy about to spring some Mediterranean con on him. The man was slim, his T-shirt hanging loose on his body; he wore a mustache, a tuft of beard under his lower lip, rings and a gold earring, sandals, a pleasant-looking guy actually, smiling now. He said in English:

"I'm not going to sell you an umbrella today, am I? You made up your mind you not going to need one."

With an accent that was Caribbean, British colonial.

Harry said, "Where're you supposed to be from, the Bahamas, Jamaica, or Tunisia?"

The guy said, "You caught me, huh?" Now in American English without the hint of an accent. "I can get away with it talking to Italians, they don't detect the, you know, the nuances. I should've known, man like you would pick up on it."

"I still don't need an umbrella," Harry said. "Day like this, why would anybody want to buy one?"

"It's the way I look up at the sky. See?" He raised his gaze as Harry watched. "Like I know something from my native intelligence, in my genes, I can tell when it's going to rain."

"Being, they think you're from North Africa, the Sahara, and know all about rain."

"They don't put that together. The sun can be out, it don't matter. I sniff the air. Like that, smell it coming. See, I knew I wasn't going to sell you a umbrella. I can also tell when I ought'n try to bullshit the person."

"You didn't think I was Italian?" Harry said.

"Uh-unh, not even you wearing your coat like that, like Fellini. You from somewhere on the East Coast. New York?"

"Miami. The Beach most of my life."

"You could be Italian, yeah, but not from around here the way you're dressed. Well, you could come from Milan, I guess, close by. But to look all the way Italian, man, you got to have the suit with the pointy shoulders and the pointy shoes with the little thin soles. You staying here on your holiday?"

"I've got a place," Harry said, and then

came right out and told him, "a villa. I'm making up my mind if I want to live here."

"Rapallo? Man, this is all there is to it. You hiding out?"

"Do I look like I am?"

"I've run into all kinds of people over here hiding from *some*thing—the only reason I ask. I don't *care*, you understand. I see a man like yourself come to a place like this? Pretty much strictly for locals? I have to wonder, that's all."

"You live around here," Harry said, "don't you? Or you come over from Africa with your umbrellas?"

"Where I came over here from was Houston, Texas. Man, a long time ago, after doing Vietnam and not finding things at home to my liking: everybody from up north down there trying the oil business. I came over to the Mediterranean, did Morocco, the Greek islands, Egypt. For a while I became an Islamic brother, named myself Jabal Radwa after a mountain in Saudi Arabia. But then, you know what I finally did? I went to Marseilles and joined the Foreign Legion. I did, I'm not kidding, under the name Robert Gee. And you don't believe me, do you?"

Harry shrugged. "Sure, why not?"

"Influenced by a former legionnaire," Robert Gee said, "I knew when I was in Saigon, a

Frenchman that stayed over there from the fifties —you know when I mean?—married a woman there and became part of that life. He kept telling me what I should do was stay, get me a cute woman like he did. . . . But I couldn't see myself going Asiatic. You know what I'm saying? So I come over here instead and join the French Foreign Legion, full of mercenary-type motherfuckers had been fighting in wars in Africa, for pay and also the chance to shoot brothers. And here I am in the same outfit, sleeping and marching with these racists."

"And if I happen to lean that way," Harry said, "too bad."

"You might. Though I don't think you lean too much one way or the other. Or give a shit what I think especially."

Harry let him believe what he wanted. He said, "How long were you in?"

"The whole five years, made corporal and got my jump wings. Served in Corsica, where they train, and in Djibouti on the Gulf of Aden, over in East Africa. I got out, found myself after a while in Kuwait before Desert Storm and got a job as this sheik's bodyguard and driver. I was the only one he trusted to drive his stretch in some of the capitals of Europe. Pretty soon, though, I had enough of the sheik and his ways. I quit being Jabal Radwa and changed my name back to Robert Gee for the second time."

Harry said, "I've got a couple of names."

It brought a smile, Robert Gee saying, "I thought you might. Running some kind of game and they caught up with you, huh?"

"I retired," Harry said.

"Well, I'm semi," Robert Gee said. "I sell umbrellas sometimes or can get you whatever you might need, or your imagination allows. You want American cigarettes, Scotch whisky? A pistol, shotgun? For sport or whatever your reason. I can get you some pretty good hashish. Smoke it watching American sitcoms on TV. Andy Griffith talking Italian. Cocaine, you have to go someplace else."

"What kind of pistol?" Harry said.

It got another smile from Robert Gee.

"Beretta. We in Italy, man."

"You hire out?" Harry asked.

"To do what?"

"Hang around. See if anything comes up."

"Sounds like bodyguarding."

"Drive to Milan and meet a lady who's flying in. Bring her back here?"

"I could do that. Tell me how much you paying for these services?"

"Why don't you put your umbrellas away," Harry said. "We'll step over to Vesuvio's or the Gran Caffè and talk about it." He said, "You don't by any chance cook, do you?"

ELEVEN

Jimmy Cap was having his dinner, some kind of fish baked with the head and tail and a plate of linguini, it looked like, with clam sauce. His tongue was moving around in his mouth in search of something that shouldn't be in there as the Zip came into the dining room with Nicky Testa, brought him in, sat him down at the table opposite Jimmy Cap and stood behind him. Jimmy Cap pulled a fish bone out of his mouth. The Zip, using the heel of his hand, popped Nicky in the back of the head.

"Tell him."

Jimmy Cap worked his tongue around. He pulled out another fish bone and said, "Fucking snapper."

The Zip popped Nicky again. "I said tell him." Nicky hunched his shoulders as the Zip said, "He's watching Harry Arno's girlfriend. This afternoon five o'clock—go on, tell him."

Nicky leaned against the table, away from the Zip. He said to Jimmy Cap, almost in confidence, "I don't need this kind of shit."

"Tell me," Jimmy Cap said, "what you're suppose to tell me."

"Tell *him* to keep his fucking hands off me."

"Work it out between you," Jimmy Cap said. "Now talk to me, what?"

"I followed this lady," Nicky said, "from her apartment to a travel agent's on Lincoln Road."

Behind him the Zip said, "What was she driving?"

"She was driving Harry Arno's Cadillac. She comes out of the travel agent's, gets in the car, and takes the Julia Tuttle and One-twelve over to the airport and parks in the long-term place there. I'm right with her. I get out of my car, I ask can I give her a hand with her suitcases. She's got a big one and two smaller ones."

Jimmy Cap sucked in linguini and said,

"The Macho man. Never sees a broad he don't make a fucking move on her."

"Hey, come on, this one's old."

The Zip popped him with the heel of his hand. "Tell him what happened."

Nicky hunched his shoulders and then straightened slowly, staring at Jimmy Cap sucking in linguini, Jimmy ignoring him.

"Tell him," the Zip said, "what you talked about."

"I start a conversation with her, tell her I'm meeting somebody, my mother. The idea, get her so she don't think, you know, I'm trying to find out anything."

"But he never asked her," the Zip said, "where she was going."

"I didn't have to. We go in the terminal right to British Airways. Where do they go? They go to fucking London, England. I asked her there at the counter, you going to England, huh? She says yeah, she is. So what do you want?"

Jimmy Cap looked up at the Zip as though asking the same question.

"Half the people that get off in London," the Zip said, "go on to someplace else. They stop off there. So we don't know where she went because this *stronzo* wouldn't ask her."

Jimmy Cap said, "Ask the travel agent."

"Yeah, that's what I have to do."

"So, what's the problem?"

"I got to wait till tomorrow, when the guy opens. Lose a whole day."

"You don't know she's going to meet Harry."

"She drove his car," the Zip said. "Watch and see somebody turns out to be a friend of his picks it up tomorrow." The Zip, standing behind the chair, looked down at Nicky. "The woman's going to meet Harry and I'm going to be a day late because of this *stronzo*."

Nicky hunched his shoulders, waiting to get popped.

Thursday, November 26, Raylan Givens had coffee with Buck Torres in a Cuban joint down the street from Miami Beach police headquarters. Raylan had a plate of beans and rice too; he'd missed lunch. He asked Torres if they were going to get Interpol into it, try to locate Harry and have him extradited. Torres said they might do that if he had shot an upstanding citizen and not some lowlife ex-con who was known to have worked for Jimmy Cap. He said as a favor to Harry he was on the lookout for sawed-off shotguns. One had been picked up at a dope house the past week and they were checking it out.

"The reason I ask about extradition," Raylan said, "I leave tomorrow. I'm going over there and look for Harry."

Torres didn't seem surprised. He said, "Going on your own?"

And Raylan nodded. He said, "Nobody cares about him, huh? I think they're even dropping Jimmy Cap's investigation anyway."

"You can count on it," Torres said. "But you're going over there? Italy's a big country."

"I know, I been looking at maps."

That was all Raylan said about Italy. Nothing about where Harry might be, not with extradition still a possibility.

"Twice now he's ducked out on me," Raylan said, without any show of emotion. "I owe it to myself, you might say, to go look for him." He poked at the black beans with his fork, not as hungry now.

"It's too bad," Torres said, "you didn't leave yesterday. You know the flights Harry took, here to Heathrow and then on to Milan? That information I got from Harry's travel agent?"

"I remember, sure," Raylan said.

"First thing this morning," Torres said, "a guy comes to see the travel agent, the same one. He says, 'I want to know where Joyce Patton went yesterday besides London.' Doesn't give him a story or anything why he wants to know. The guy looks the travel agent in the eye and the travel agent tells him."

"Tommy Bucks," Raylan said, "the Zip. The travel agent knew he was serious."

"Knew he didn't want to get hurt," Torres said. "We show him pictures and he picks out, you guessed it, Tommy Bucks. So now, we checked, he's going over there too. Leaving this evening, seven-fifteen, the same flight Harry and then Joyce took. The Zip and a guy named Nicky Testa."

"You're not going to pick him up, huh?"

"What do I charge him with? He asked the travel agent where Joyce Patton went."

"No intimidation of any kind?"

Torres shook his head. "Outside of the guy himself, the way he looks? Not a word. You know him."

"I only had that one run-in with him," Raylan said. "See, first I had to get the time off. Which I did, only I can't leave till tomorrow. By the time I get there . . . What if the Zip's called one of his friends over there to meet Joyce's plane in Milan?" Raylan looked at his watch. "Getting in just about now, as a matter of fact. They'd follow her, see where she goes. The Zip gets there tomorrow." Raylan paused. "I doubt

Harry will have her come directly to where he is, Harry'd know better'n that." Raylan took a few moments to think about it some more. "What I have to do is get to him before the Zip does."

"You have an idea where he is you're not telling," Torres said.

Raylan didn't say yes or no. He was anxious now, wishing he could leave tonight. Get on the same flight the Zip was taking. Watch him. Except the Zip and this other guy would be up in first class while he was back in coach.

That Thursday, Joyce took a taxi from the Milan airport to the Hotel Cavour on Fatebenefratelli. They were ready for her at the reception desk, cordial, English speaking, the clerk saying, "Yes, and a message for you, please," as he handed her a sealed envelope. She opened it right away. Handwritten on hotel stationery the note said:

Harry sent me. I'm the Afro-looking person in the suede jacket sitting across the lobby from you. Look if you want but don't come over.

She did, looked up and saw the black guy in a suede jacket sitting, as he said, across the lobby from the desk. He stared back, raising his hand to fool with the tuft of hair on his chin. She looked at the note again.

Go up to your room and I will call you in about 30 minutes, after I see if anybody comes in looks unfriendly. My name is Robert.

When she looked over at him again, Robert was reading a newspaper. Joyce went up to her room.

It was small but okay, moderately priced modern. Outside were the traffic sounds of a big city, the view from the window the building across the street. She waited, wondering if she should unpack; if Harry was here in Milan; if he had really sent the black guy, Robert; if her electric curlers would work in the bathroom outlet.

When Robert called he asked what everyone did when you've just arrived somewhere: how was the flight and was she tired and would she like to rest awhile. He could call back later.

Joyce said, "First you check to see if I was followed and then you ask if I want to rest. Does it seem to you under the circumstances I'd want to take a nap?"

"It's what you say," Robert said. "You don't want to rest, that's cool, but we ain't going anyplace till tomorrow. Some people, two guys came in after you went up and they're still hanging around, but I can't tell nothing about them."

"Are you still in the hotel?"

"I'm someplace else now. What we going to do, in about an hour, go on over to the trattoria across the street from the hotel, down just a bit, and I'll meet you there. Go through the front to the back part. I'll see if anybody follows you."

"How could anyone know I'm here?"

"We'll talk about it, okay?"

She said, "Just tell me where Harry is."

"We'll talk about everything. In an hour."

Friday, November 27, right before they landed in Milan, Nicky couldn't believe it: Tommy the Zip goes in the lavatory with his carry-on bag and comes out wearing a clean white shirt and a different tie. He has the stewardess get his suit coat out of the closet and help him on with it. There were different things like that he'd tell Gloria and a couple of the guys when they got back. How Tommy hardly ever spoke unless it was to tell him to do something. How they walked through Customs, never opened a bag, into the terminal, Tommy the Zip stops, puts his hands out but with his elbows, you know, tucked in against his sides the way he does? And these two Italian guys come up and each one puts his arms around him and gives him a kiss on both cheeks, Tommy dressed up, the two guys looking like they slept in their fucking clothes, cheap suits, no ties, both guys kind of fat. Nicky would tell how they spoke Italian to each other nonstop and Tommy never fucking once bothered to introduce him. Okay, then how they drove to a hotel in Milan, the Plaza on Piazza Diaz, where there were more people waiting to put their arms around Tommy and kiss him. A guy tried to take Tommy's picture and the fat guys smashed his camera and threw him out of the hotel, two cops in front watching the whole thing. The cops with white belts and holsters.

He'd tell how they went up to the suite reserved for Tommy, got out a few bottles and some ice and had a party, Nicky hanging around watching, listening to them speaking nothing but Italian till he said fuck it and went to his room down the hall. He stood at the window looking down at these orange streetcars going by the park. Or maybe they were buses.

He'd tell how Tommy called him up, said to come to his suite, Tommy alone now, empty glasses and full ashtrays all over, and ate him out for insulting his friends, walking out on them like that.

Nicky thought he was kidding. Come on—

nobody says a fucking word to him since he steps off the plane and he insulted *them*? This was some more of Tommy's bullshit from olden times, always talking about respect. Atlantic City, he had grown up on North Georgia, the same street where Nicodemo Scarfo lived, and had seen his guys all the time in the social club on Fairmount Avenue where he worked and made his first connections. The guys there had respect for Scarfo, naturally, but they didn't make a big fucking deal out of being Italian like Tommy did. There were people who worked for Jimmy who had no use for the Zip and had said in so many words they wouldn't mind seeing him taken out. The guy, it was like he was from another fucking planet.

Nicky said to him, "You gonna tell me what's going on or what?"

Tommy opened an athletic bag one of the Italian guys had brought and took out two Beretta nines and a couple boxes of cartridges and laid them on the table.

He said, "Harry's girlfriend came here yesterday and stayed one night at the Hotel Cavour. She ate dinner with a colored guy, an American, that Harry must have sent to meet her. The colored guy tried different ways to see if anybody was on her. Like he had her walk out of the hotel and then watched to see did anybody follow her. Then he drove around to the back of the restaurant and went in that way. Driving a gray Lancia my friends found out is registered to Harry Arno. He bought it last year and it's got a Milano plate on it. This other friend of mine, Benno, followed them this morning from here to a town south of Genova on the coast. Its name is Rapallo. Benno called my friends here, he said the colored guy left her at a hotel and took off. So far nobody's come to see her. Benno's going to watch the hotel and meet us in Rapallo tomorrow. The lady is at the Astoria. If we have to be there a day or two we going to stay in an apartment they have for me; it's more private. So, okay," Tommy said, "we get a car and go there a hundred miles an hour on the *autostrada*. We find Harry and I let you pop him. How you think about that?"

"I thought you're the one," Nicky said, "with the hard-on to do him."

"I'm giving him to you, Macho man, see how good you are."

"You think I can't?"

"That's what we find out."

The same as saying he didn't think Nicky had the nerve. That's what it sounded like and it pissed Nicky off. He began to imagine a setup where he could do Harry, turn around, and do Tommy. Pop him, ask him how he fucking thinks about it, and pop him again. Pull that off, it could get him made. He could see Jimmy Cap grinning. Hey, Joe Macho. Jimmy getting up out of his chair to give him a hug and a kiss on both cheeks.

Saturday, November 28, Raylan Givens stepped out of a taxi in front of the Central Station in Milan and thought the driver had made a mistake. It looked more like an art museum than a railroad station: the biggest one he'd ever seen, all marble and statues and full of different kinds of shops. Across the street was a Wendy's.

It was in this station Raylan got his first look at a pair of carabinieri with their swords, their shiny black boots, light-blue pants with a red stripe up the side, not looking too much like cops but that's what they were, in a military kind of way. Raylan walked over to them, took out his ID, and held it up to show his star. They looked at it, both of them taller than he was, without any kind of recognition or acknowledgment that he was in law enforcement the same as they were. Or more so.

"The Marshals Service," Raylan said. "I'm a

deputy United States marshal. The same kind they used to have out in the wild West."

Both the carabinieri nodded at the star but didn't seem too impressed. But then with those swords and boots, why would they be?

Raylan said, "You guys ever use your swords? I wouldn't imagine, though, you run into too many offenders you can have sword fights with, huh?"

So much for trying a little humor. They didn't have any idea what he was talking about. Raylan touched the curved brim of his Stetson and went across the street to Wendy's to get a couple of burgers for the trip.

On the train there were three guys in the same compartment with him arguing about sports, a soccer game it sounded like, with a lot of emotion, waving their arms around. One had the sports section of a newspaper open and would read from it every now and then, it looked like to make his point. Raylan thought for a while they were going to end up in a fistfight. If they did, he'd stay out of it, leave the compartment if he had to, knowing he had to keep his nose clean. He'd brought along his Smith & Wesson Combat Mag, the gun he was most accurate with, also a snub-nosed Smith 357 he wore sometimes in his right boot, both down in the bottom

of the suitcase he'd checked through on the
flight. He'd left his Beretta at the office.

Looking out at the countryside he didn't see
anything growing this time of year, the soil a
color that reminded him some of Georgia,
though not quite as red. There were more
cornfields than he'd expected, rows of stubble.
Dusty-looking olive trees with nets spread on the
ground underneath. Lot of olive trees. The train
would pass through tunnels in the hillsides and
come out to more hills covered thick with trees,
cypress, poplar, some oak, different kinds of
palm trees. He saw his first aqueduct on the trip:
it came down out of high country, stopped at the
tracks and the *autostrada*, the freeway, and then
picked up again, built most likely two thousand
years ago. He had read about olive trees in Italy
going back hundreds of years, villages up in the
hills that hadn't changed much since the Middle
Ages. It was an interesting, good-looking country with history you could look at, the old and
the new, cops standing around with swords,
some others at the airport with submachine
guns.

They stopped in Genoa at suppertime and
Raylan ate his two Wendy's while they sat there.
Rapallo was next. If they ever got the train mov-
ing again it wouldn't take long to get there. It

was already dark out, so he wouldn't see much tonight. A picture of Rapallo in his travel guide to Italy showed date palms along the beachfront and sidewalk cafés, a resort town of thirty thousand said to be popular summer and winter. He had picked out the Hotel Liguria—named for the region Rapallo was in—as not too expensive and phoned from Milan to make a reservation; at the last minute but no problem. Still, he didn't like getting in so late. The last one to arrive. Joyce would have come in yesterday, the Zip sometime this morning. So about a half hour from now, Raylan was thinking, everybody would be in Rapallo.

TWELVE

Sunday, Raylan found out it was a city with commercial streets and residential neighborhoods up back of the postcard front it put on for tourists. Photos in the *Guide to Rapallo* he bought at the hotel showed date palms and flower gardens on the Via Veneto, coleus in bloom, young potted palms he wasn't sure were sabal or livistona. But there were city buses, too, traffic, and that big pink train station he came in at, all lit up last night.

Raylan had walked past the marina—his guidebook called it the Tourist Harbor—and the statue of Christopher Columbus before moving away from the beach to the Piazza Cavour he judged to be near the center of downtown, where the main church was located. (Only Nashville, he believed, had more churches than towns in Italy.) And came down to the beachfront again at the south end of the postcard bay where the cafés and crowds began to thin out: down where his guidebook said "the beaches were renowned for their elegant bathing establishments." He must've missed them. The book said that "in the antique quarter" you could "participate with enthusiasm in the daily life of artisan workshops." He must've missed those, too, or else they weren't open on Sunday.

Today he was more confident of finding Harry because when he asked at the hotel, by any chance was a Harry Arno registered there, the clerk said no, Mr. Arno had checked out Friday. Raylan was so surprised he said, "You serious?" and got a surprised look from the clerk. Harry, he found out, had been at the Liguria two weeks, up till just the day before yesterday. The clerk didn't know where he went. No, he hadn't said anything about leaving town. Raylan called hotels then and found Joyce Patton registered at the Astoria, but no Harry Arno. The operator, thinking he wanted to speak to her, connected him with her room. Raylan heard Joyce say "Hello?" in a quiet, tentative voice, and he hung up the phone. Then wondered if he should call her back, tell her to look out for the Zip. Sure the Zip was here by now. But when Raylan checked the hotels again he didn't find a Tomasino Bitonti or a Nicky Testa registered anywhere. He didn't recall this kind of situation being covered at the Glynco training center.

Raylan tiptoed around town hoping to run into Harry, find him buying *The New York Times* or having his breakfast somewhere. No luck. So now he'd have to walk along the Via Vittorio Veneto, the postcard part of town, where everybody was parading around or having their Sunday-morning coffee, sitting at sidewalk tables with their coats on. It was chilly, only partly sunny, somewhere in the high fifties, no one in swimming and only a few hardy souls on the beach.

He came to a garden, a bed of red salvia set off by a pair of black cannons and a couple of park benches. A plaque said it was the Ezra Pound Garden and it gave Raylan another boost of confidence, knowing Harry was around here, remembering Harry talking about Ezra Pound that time in Atlanta, part of his story. Part of the reason Harry was here; Raylan convinced of it.

He got a book of Ezra Pound's poetry from the library after being with Harry that time and tried reading it, tried hard, but couldn't make sense of what the poet was trying to say. *Cantos,* with different numbers. He wondered to this day if Harry understood them.

He came to another plaque, this over the entrance to the Alle Rustico, a passageway through the building where, the plaque said:

HERE LIVED EZRA POUND AMERICAN POET

in English and in Italian, here from 1924 to 1945 and with a stanza, it looked like, from one of his poems. Something about "To confess wrong without losing rightness" and some more that made even less sense. Raylan thinking, I don't know; maybe it's me.

He felt himself out in the open, easily spotted. Harry could see him first and hide, good at ducking out. But if he was going to be where people were, check what looked like the popular cafés, he'd have to risk it. He looked in at Vesuvio's then ahead to the next place, the Gran Caffè Rapallo, Raylan in the shade of the postcard buildings now and wishing he'd worn his raincoat over his suit, his light-tan one. A wind came up off the bay that felt moist and Raylan paused, turned his head, and set his Stetson down closer on his eyes. It was when he looked up again, ready to continue on, he saw Joyce Patton sitting at a table, a number of rows back, well underneath the awning. It was darker in there, but it was Joyce all right. She was watching the cars creeping by. Now she turned her head this way and Raylan saw her looking at him. Moments went by and she kept staring. Almost as though he had a light on her and she sat there fixed to the seat, not able to move.

That Sunday morning Robert Gee told Harry if he was going to live up here on top of the world the one thing he needed besides food was a telephone. Harry said, "If nobody knows where I am, they can't call me anyway. And anybody I want to call I can do it in town."

"Except you go down this time to phone," Robert Gee said, "you may as well go to the hotel and see her." He waited while Harry thought it over before he said, "Or, you sure you want to do it, take the chance, I'll bring your lady friend up here."

They were in the library of Harry's villa, three walls of books in Italian, the front wall French doors that opened on the garden: a view of privet hedges and plants in decorative clay pots, a few young orange trees, nothing but sky beyond a concrete railing. Harry, wearing a raincoat today, was pacing.

"You said nobody followed you."

"I said I didn't *see* nobody follow me. There were cars behind us all the way here from Milan. To put your mind at ease you say, well, that's what they do on the *autostrada*, they come here from there, nobody following anybody."

Harry moved in his pacing, hands in the raincoat pockets, to the open French doors, Robert Gee watching him.

"I should get you a cellular phone. You can stay up here and call anybody you want in the world. In the meantime," Robert Gee said, "do I pick up Joyce or not?"

Harry stood looking out at his garden now and the sky full of white clouds, waiting to catch a glimpse of the sun. He knew that weather could affect your disposition and he wasn't going to let it.

"She's going to be, lemme see, sitting in the Caffè Rapallo at noon. Ezra Pound Garden at three, Vesuvio's at five. What we worked out." Robert Gee looked at his watch. "It's coming on noon. You want me to get her, you have to let me know in the next few minutes."

"I've had forty-seven years to make up my

mind," Harry said, "if I want to live here. And now I'm not sure."

"We back to that," Robert Gee said. "Or, it's the question everything else is all about. Without even giving it a chance, you saying it's not like you thought it was going to be." Robert Gee looked up at the ceiling. "I don't see any leak where you said. There might've been one two, three hundred years ago, the way it's stained, but it's dry now. This is villa living, man. You have to get in the right frame of mind for it. Dig architecture, history, art, different related kinds of shit like that. You know what I'm saying?"

He looked over. Harry was gone, in the garden now. Robert Gee followed him out to the concrete railing where Harry was taking in his view of Rapallo on the bay: way down there about fifteen minutes on the *funivia*, and all the green countryside in between, spots of tan that were villas and farms, twin holes like a shotgun muzzle in hillsides where the *autostrada* tunneled through.

"I imagined myself sitting here in the evening," Harry said, "watching the sun go down, the red glow sliding into the sea."

"That from one of Ezra's?"

"He didn't write that kind of poetry." Harry

turned all the way around to face his villa. "What color would you say that is?"

Now Robert Gee turned. "Your house? Kind of a hot mustard with a red tile roof. You don't like it, change it. But leave the white stone around the windows, that's cool."

"I lease the place last year, I'm here two weeks even before last Sunday, when you tried to sell me an umbrella."

"I believe I said at the time, I knew you weren't going to buy one."

"Two weeks in a hotel while this place is sitting here," Harry said. "You know why? I felt like I was in first gear all the time, couldn't seem to get going."

" 'Cause you weren't able to talk to people in your own style," Robert Gee said, "like you want."

Harry was nodding. "That's part of it."

"You sounded okay to me."

"Yeah, well, that picked me up, talking to you, but now . . . I can't get used to this place."

"You been here two days."

"It's damp, it's cold. . . ."

"It is today, yeah, a bit chilly. Got to turn the heat up, get a fire going in your main room. Man, you can walk into that fireplace."

"It's cold other ways," Harry said. "All that

old furniture. I need a bed, a comfortable chair. Some lamps. It's dark in there."

"Have to decorate it the way you like," Robert Gee said. "Nothing wrong with the kitchen, though, it's nice and big. You got enough supplies to last you awhile, I packed the freezer." Robert Gee hesitated. "Now, if you like how I cook, least that'll be taken care of."

He waited for Harry to comment, say something about the pasta carbonara he made and left for him, full of bacon and rich cream, Harry's first meal in his villa.

"I didn't tell you," Harry said, touching his chest, "I got a hiatus hernia. It acts on you like heartburn and you have to watch what you eat. Nothing too spicy. Otherwise, yeah, the pasta was great."

Robert Gee watched Harry turn to look out again at his view. "Joyce cook any good?"

"She's okay, nothing fancy."

"Maybe that's why you anxious to see her."

Harry was staring at Rapallo, way down there on the bay, church spires sticking up, the tourist harbor full of boats. "I wish I knew if they followed her," Harry said. "It's possible, but did they? The Zip would have friends in Italy he could get to help him. Maybe he's not here but found out Joyce was coming, called one of his friends to follow her when she got off the plane. Are they watching her? Is the Zip here? If I knew . . . The thing is, forty-seven years I've been planning, working on coming here, dreaming about it, and now I got all this going on. I have to decide something in two minutes." He looked at Robert Gee. "You know what I mean?"

"You're saying you don't want nothing to happen to you," Robert Gee said, "till you find out for sure if you like it here."

Harry stared at him for several moments.

"Yeah, something like that."

Raylan said to Joyce Patton, "You know what I'm going to ask you." Raylan sitting with her now at the Gran Caffè Rapallo, five rows back beneath the awning, his guidebook lying on the table. Joyce wore a navy wool coat and held her coffee in beige wool gloves.

She said, "I still don't know where he is. I'm not even sure he's here."

"But you're waiting to hear from him."

Joyce said she wasn't even sure of that and asked Raylan how he'd known enough to come to Rapallo. When he said, "You may not believe this, but Harry told me a story one time—" Joyce stopped him right there. She said, "One he'd never told another living soul—I believe it."

Raylan ordered coffee, then sat there rubbing his hands together. He said it seemed colder than fifty-eight degrees out, didn't it? He said they went by centigrade here. But all you had to do to convert to Fahrenheit was multiply the centigrade by one-point-eight and add thirty-two. Joyce said, "Is that what you're going to do, talk about the weather?"

Raylan opened his guidebook and read her the part where it said "Rapallo offers to its guests magnificent surroundings and various plants for leisure time activities in whatever period of the year." He asked her what she thought they meant by "various plants." Joyce shrugged in her navy coat. He showed her a photograph in the book of the new auditorium and the caption that said it "disposes of 340 seats."

When she didn't smile Raylan closed the book. He put it on the table next to Joyce's purse, saying to her, "I want to talk to Harry. Get him for his own good to go back with me."

Joyce said, "He won't do it," shaking her head. "Not if he has to go to prison."

"It's better than getting shot."

Joyce said, "Your job's worth that much to you? You'd shoot him?"

"I hate to tell you this," Raylan said, and told about Tommy Bucks, the Zip, and another guy with him flying to Milan, following the same itinerary she did.

Joyce was quiet for a minute, hunched up in her coat. Her gaze moved past him to the street, then came back and she asked if he knew for certain they were here.

"I suspect they are." Raylan watched her and said, "I wish you knew where Harry was."

She didn't say anything, staring out at the street again. A dark-blue Mercedes sedan was holding up traffic, cars behind it blowing their horns. Raylan turned to look over his shoulder. He said, "I don't know which makes the most noise, the way people over here lay on their horns or all those motor scooters flying around. Man, they're loud."

They watched a boy about twelve years old step out of the shrubs and palm trees separating the street from the seafront walk on the other side. The boy crouched behind the Mercedes to light a match out of the wind. They saw him touch it to something in his hand, drop it on the rear deck of the car, and run off as a string of firecrackers began to explode, sounding to Raylan like low-caliber gunfire.

He said, "I just read in my book they love fireworks here. They have what they call pyrotechnic matches between different neighborhood clubs, see who's best at lighting up the water-front. You ever hear of anything like that?"

Joyce didn't answer. Raylan turned again to look at the Mercedes. The rear door on this side was open and a young guy in a leather jacket was getting out. The Mercedes didn't move, horns still blowing, raising a racket as the young guy came across the street toward the café.

"I thought he was going to chase after that kid," Raylan said. "Didn't you?"

He watched a heavyset guy in his shirt-sleeves, a white shirt, get out from behind the wheel of the Mercedes and start toward the back of the car. The horn blowing died off and then stopped.

The young guy was in the aisle now looking this way. Raylan noticed how his shoulders filled that leather jacket; zipped up, it reached almost to his hips. The young guy was coming toward them now, to their table, his eyes on Joyce, his hands hanging free; big hands. He reached them and the tips of his fingers touched the edge of the table next to Raylan, that close to him.

Raylan said, "What can we do for you?"

The guy didn't bother to look at him. He said to Joyce, "There's a friend of yours in the car wants to see you. That Mercedes."

Joyce said, "Oh?" glancing toward the street. She said, "What's my friend's name?"

The young guy said, "He wants you to come over to the car."

Joyce said, "Tell me who it is first."

The young guy motioned with his hand. "You'll find out. Come on, let's go."

Raylan said, "She wants to know who this friend is. Don't you understand that?"

The young guy looked down at Raylan for the first time. He said, "I'm not talking to you."

"She still wants to know who it is."

The young guy said to Raylan, "Stay the fuck out of this," and turned to Joyce again. "You want, I'll pick you up and carry you."

Joyce was looking toward the street. When she got up all of a sudden Raylan said, "Wait now," putting his hand out to stop her. She brushed past him, past the young guy, and Raylan turned to watch her. He said, "Joyce?" seeing a gray car at the curb now, on the near side of the street, that blocked his view of the Mercedes, the two cars pointing in opposite directions. Raylan started to get up, again calling to Joyce, and the young guy shoved him down in the chair and held him there with one hand, pressed against the table. Raylan didn't move, except for his right hand. It reached down his leg beneath the table, down into his boot to touch the grip of his Smith 357 wedged in there. He paused then, still intent on Joyce, seeing her walking toward the gray car and expecting her, about now, to go around it to the Mercedes. But she didn't. No, the door on the passenger side of the gray car swung open, Joyce ducked inside, and the car was down the street before the door slammed closed.

There was a pause then, Raylan surprised, taking a few moments before he finished his move: pulled the 357 out of his boot as the young guy let up on him, turning to leave, and jammed the stubby barrel into his groin. The young guy grunted.

Raylan said, "My turn," and told him to have a seat.

Horns were blowing again on the Via Veneto. The Mercedes had come to life, trying to U-turn in that narrow street: backed into the parkway, into shrubs and flower beds to come flying out of there, but now traffic was lining the café side of the street, blocking the way. The Mercedes tried its horn for a while and gave up. A door opened.

Raylan watched the Zip step out and come toward the café, the Zip wearing his dark suit, his sunglasses. Finally, there he was and it was strange, to watch him coming and feel a sense of relief, in a way glad to see him, or glad to see him in plain sight, in the open. The Zip seemed to be staring back at Raylan until he reached the table and stood with his hands on the back of a chair. Now he looked down at the young guy, ignoring Raylan.

"What's the matter with you?"

The young guy looked surprised. "What?"

"What're you doing sitting there?"

"I asked him to," Raylan said. He sat close to the table, his hands out of sight.

The Zip looked at him, no more interested than before, and turned to the young guy again.

"You see her walk off, whyn't you go with her?"

The young guy said, "I can give you the long version or the short version. The short version is he's got a fucking gun he pulled on me and now prob'ly has it pointing at you. So you tell me what you want to do. I don't even know who the fuck he is."

The Zip didn't say anything, not until he pulled the chair out and sat down, ignoring the young guy now. He said to Raylan, "Okay, what're you doing with Harry? You over here to extradite him?"

"I'm on my vacation," Raylan said. "How 'bout yourself? You been here before?"

The Zip kept looking at Raylan but didn't answer; he seemed tired, maybe feeling jet lag, all dressed up but not too happy.

"You're wasting your time," Raylan said. "All you can do here is get in trouble." He looked at the young guy. "You must be Nicky Testa, sometimes called Joe Macho? I'll stay with Nicky. I've read your sheet." Raylan shrugged. "I've read a lot worse. All I can say is you better keep your nose clean over here or they come at you with swords. I mean it. Go on up to carabinieri headquarters on, I think it's Via Salvo D'Acquisto, and you'll see what I'm talking about."

Nicky turned to the Zip. "Who the fuck *is* this guy?"

"You want to know?" Raylan said. "Well, I'm the law, that's who the fuck I am, a deputy U.S. marshal. You want to see my star I'll show it to you. But *he* knows, your boss. I'm going to advise the both of you to go on home and forget what you *think* you have against Harry Arno, 'cause it ain't true. That story about him skimming on you was made up so you'd do something dumb and we'd come after you. I'm telling you the truth. There's no reason for you to per*sist* in what you're doing, since Harry never did nothing to you." Raylan paused. "Well, outside of shoot that scudder you sent to do *him*. But you can't fault him for that, can you? He still has to answer to it in court and that's where I come in. In other words you can put your head on your pillow, not have to think about getting back at Harry. How's that sound to you?"

The Zip sat there staring at him for what seemed the longest time. Finally made up his mind about something and said, "You act like Harry's your pal and you're looking out for him. That's what you're saying to me, that you and him are on the same side. Only you don't know where he is, either, do you? I can see that." The Zip nodding. "So who you think's going to find him first?"

He got up from the table, looked at Nicky, turned, and walked out to the street.

Raylan watched Nicky take time to stare at him with a fairly cold look, meant no doubt as a threat, like saying, *Just wait.* Raylan said, "You want to look mean, squeeze your eyes closed a little more." Raylan grinned at him then and said, "Go on, boy, I won't hurt you. 'Less that's what you want."

He watched him walk off before he noticed Joyce's purse, on the table with his *Guide to Rapallo.*

* * *

They drove around looking for the gray Lancia, Benno at the wheel of the Mercedes doing most of the talking, glancing at Tommy in the front seat next to him. Telling him, Nicky believed, some story why he didn't recognize the car after following it all the way from Milan, for Christ sake. The other genuine Italian, Fabrizio, in the backseat with Nicky, sat hunched forward so he could listen and put in his two cents, all three of them talking Italian a mile a minute. Benno had come up from Naples. Fabrizio was from Milan. Nicky had asked him this morning what *stronzo* meant and found out it didn't mean strong. He listened to them, the car creeping from street to street, until he'd had enough of all this Italian shit, not knowing what was going on, and yelled out, "Hey, talk fucking English, will you!"

It did the job. There was a silence, the Zip and Benno looking at each other. Nicky said, "You want me to get out of the car? You want, I'll go home. Say the word, I'm outta here. I'll tell you something, though, before I leave I'm gonna do that guy, that marshal. I'm gonna find out where he's staying and I'm gonna fucking take him out." Looking right at the Zip's profile. "I'm telling you that now so you'll know."

The Zip said something to Benno in Italian and Benno pulled the Mercedes to the curb in front of an apartment building. The Zip turned in the front seat now to look at Nicky, Benno and Fabrizio watching him.

"You say you want to whack this guy," the Zip said to him. "I'm going to tell you something, Joe Macho. If that guy had pulled on me, or on Benno or Fabrizio, we wouldn't be in the car saying I'm going to take him out. You know why? Because he would be dead. We wouldn't, any of us, we wouldn't walk out of that café and leave him sitting there. We would shoot him and put one in the head, here," the Zip said, touching a spot on his temple, "when he's laying on the floor, to make sure. Okay, then it's done, no more to talk about."

Nicky saw Benno nodding as the Zip spoke.

"Maybe you don't understand something," the Zip said then. "Why bosses send for us. Benno and Fabrizio have both been to the States. I went over and I stayed. They send for us because the guys they have at home to do jobs are punks who don't have the nerve. Pussies, afraid to use the gun. They sit around in the social club and talk about what they going to do, but they don't do it. What you do, Macho, you insult us. Here we are in Italia, my country, and you say speak English. Then we suppose to listen to you tell us you want to whack this guy you let pull a gun on you, that, and we suppose to believe you going to do it." He said to Benno, "Is that right?" and then looked at Fabrizio.

Both of them nodded.

"I *am* gonna do it," Nicky said, careful now as he tried to remain calm. "I give you my word."

Benno said something in Italian. Fabrizio laughed, the Zip smiled. He said to Nicky, "Benno wants to know if we can watch. Maybe learn something."

THIRTEEN

Harry looked different. He seemed smaller. Or it was the high ceilings.

She couldn't get him to stand still and talk.

He led the way, showing off his villa. The yellow drawing room, full of chairs from different periods; the study, with framed portraits Joyce guessed were from the thirties and forties, black-and-white and sepia photos of mostly men with small mustaches; the library walled in leather-bound books and more portraits, men from the early 1900s.

All the rooms with sixteen-foot ceilings, at least.

Harry talking nonstop, telling her the place was frayed, cracked, flaking, smudged here and there with two-hundred-year-old stains; not what you'd call cozy, but villa living, you weren't looking for cozy. Harry putting on kind of a casual strut, acting cool. Telling her it needed lamps more than anything else. Light. Lamps and a new heating system. Harry wearing a wool scarf with his sport coat, the bookmaker turned landed gentry. Telling her he had just over twenty-five hectares, enough for a nine-hole golf course, except it was almost all downhill.

Joyce said, "Harry."

He said, "Ten-thirty we turn on the TV and watch *Colpo Grosso*, a nudie game show, *Wheel of Fortune* with tits. There's all kinds of nudity here, on TV, in the advertising, on magazine covers. I mean even on the news magazines, *Panorama*, *L'Espresso*." He said to her, "You could've made a lot of money here in your day."

"My day," Joyce said.

"You know what I mean. When you didn't mind taking your clothes off."

They were in the formal garden now, as frayed as the inside of the house, waiting for a good soul to rake and prune. Joyce saw a way to keep herself busy if they were stuck here. She followed a path of crushed stone to the concrete railing at the edge of the yard. Harry reached her as she looked down at Rapallo crowded around the bay, at terraced farmland, the *autostrada* coming out of holes in the hillside, the road winding up from Rapallo that they'd taken. Three kilometers as the crow flies, Robert Gee had told her on the way—Robert most of the time looking at his rearview mirror—but close to twelve kilometers following the scary curves without railings and the long, sweeping switchbacks. They passed through a village Robert said was San Maurizio di Monti and approached Harry's place from above, looking down at red tile roofs, the villa and several farm buildings close by. Robert Gee said, "Home at last," and Joyce said, "Wow," impressed. There was even a swimming pool, but no water in it. Robert said it leaked, needed work. He pulled the car into the structure nearest the house, a long shed with heavy wooden doors, its earth-colored stucco chipped and crumbling to show bricks underneath. Harry brought her out of the car saying, boy, was he glad to see her, taking her in his arms saying everything was going to work out now. She got to say, "Harry, they're here," and that was it until he was ready to, what, listen and accept the facts? She wasn't sure what his game was; he didn't give her time to think. He said, "You're here and that's all that counts." She told him she didn't have clothes with her, her luggage was still at the hotel; and she'd left her purse with her passport, all her money, at the café. He told her not to worry about it. She said, "How do I get home if I don't have a passport?" He told her she could stay here with him. Harry was different: trying to act unconcerned, or believing that if he didn't think about those guys or talk about them they'd go away.

They were in the garden, not one of the high-ceilinged rooms, and he still seemed smaller.

Joyce watched him.

His gaze moved from Rapallo. He said, "Sant'Ambrogio is over that way, just past the edge of town. Remember my telling you about it? Where Ezra Pound lived for a while?"

She kept looking at him as he stared into the distance.

"Harry, there are people here who want to kill you."

He didn't say anything right away and she knew she had him, trapped against his view. So he took his time, coming around to look at his villa for a moment before, finally, he turned his head to her and she could see his eyes.

"Who's here?"

"There's a young guy with muscle, broad shoulders, he looks like a bodybuilder."

"It sounds like Nicky Testa, Jimmy Cap's bodyguard. You didn't see the Zip?"

Joyce shook her head.

"I suppose he could've sent Nicky," Harry said, "told him to pick up some guys over here." He thought about it and shook his head. "No, Nicky's too dumb. He wouldn't be able to communicate. The Zip was told to handle it, so he's either here or he's coming."

"There were three other men in the car," Joyce said. "I'm sure of that. And there's Raylan."

"You brought a whole convention with you," Harry said, "didn't you?"

That sounded more like the old Harry, who could piss you off without even trying. "Raylan's here," Joyce said, "because you told him a story one time you'd never told another soul in your life."

"I did?"

"In Atlanta, that time at the airport."

"I might've told him."

Not ready to admit it. Joyce let it go. She

said, "What about Jimmy Cap? Did you tell him?"

Harry shook his head. "I'm positive I didn't. Or the Zip. I've never sat down with those guys where I'd tell them any kind of story. You know, we were never sociable. Raylan, I don't know. Maybe I told him."

"He came up to me," Joyce said. "He was there, he saw those guys and they saw him."

Harry waited. His eyes didn't move.

"He wants to talk to you."

"I bet he does. He have court papers with him?"

"He's here on his own."

Harry shook his head. "He's a weird guy."

"He wants you to go back with him."

"I hope you set him straight."

"I told him you wouldn't," Joyce said, "but it's different now. I don't mean you should go back, but talk to him. You might need him."

Harry hesitated, then grinned. "He have his cowboy hat on? No, I don't need him. 'Cause I don't see how they're going to find us." His gaze moved past her as he spoke.

Joyce turned enough to see Robert Gee coming through the garden. She waited and said, "Harry doesn't think they'll find him." Speaking to a friend she'd gotten to know on the ride here from Milan, a man she trusted.

"I was about to mention," Robert Gee said, "I think you all ought to be in the house. There's a stretch of road up there where you can see right down to where we're standing."

"They have to look for me in town," Harry said, "before they ever come up that road. I know where you mean. You can see the garden, but it's like that"—Harry snapped his fingers—"for a split second. You'd have to know where to look, and you'd need a pair of binoculars to identify anybody."

Robert Gee said, "You want my advice?"

"Okay, what?"

"Go on in the house. The only time you come out here is after it's dark."

"My bodyguard," Harry said to Joyce. "And my cook. The one keeps me alive and the other tries to kill me with pasta carbonara."

Joyce was watching Robert. Neither of them smiled. Robert said to Harry, "I'm not fooling. Maybe you're thinking, your age you can act brave, like you don't give a shit what happens to you. Or I'm wrong, I don't know where your head's at and shouldn't try to guess. But I'm here too. You understand? I'm here and now Joyce is here. We saw those people Joyce say want to kill you. I know they serious. You understand? So *we* have to be serious. They ever come in here with guns they gonna shoot everybody they see. You know them. Am I right about that or not? How these people are."

Joyce watched Harry, frowning now like he was squinting into the sun. Overdoing it.

He said, "What're you trying to say?"

As though he didn't understand. Putting on an act.

And Robert seemed surprised. "What I just said. I didn't make it clear enough for you? I'm trying to get you," Robert said, "to be serious about this and come in the house, do what I tell you. See, you not thinking about anybody else here, like Joyce and myself, if these people find out where we are and come in the house, like I say, with their guns."

Harry kept frowning at him.

He said, "You know a certain amount of risk goes with the kind of job you have. It's why you carry a gun. Am I right in assuming that?"

"Always," Robert said. "I understand sticking your neck out for pay there's risk. What I don't like is having to stick it out farther than I'm getting paid to stick it out."

Harry grinned.

"Now we're getting to it. What you're telling me is you don't think what we agreed on, five bills a week, is going to do it. You want to renegotiate, on account of you see now you might actually have to earn your money. And if you don't get what you want, you take a walk. Is that how it is? I'm asking," Harry said, " 'cause I guess I don't know you as well as I thought I did. You take these other people now, that kind I've known all my life. You pay them to do something, they do it. You can take their word."

Robert was shaking his head now. Joyce thought he seemed tired as he said, "You're missing the point, Harry," and she was sure he was right. He said, "Maybe you're missing it on purpose, wanting to argue. Wanting to act like you aren't scared, so you talk tough, like you don't care. I can understand that, Harry, the tendency why you do it. But I ain't gonna stick around if you keep it up, 'cause then you're not careful and it gives those guys more of a chance. You know what I'm saying to you?"

"I know," Harry said, "exactly what you're saying. It's like the price of umbrellas goes up when it rains. Right? I don't meet your price, you take off, you're a free agent."

Joyce wanted to hit him.

Robert was shaking his head again saying,

"Harry, money's got nothing to do with it. It's all how you're acting."

"You can shop around," Harry told him, ignoring what he'd just said. "Go see those guys that're looking for me. . . . Maybe they'll pay your price."

Robert said, "Man, you're worse off than I thought." He turned to walk away.

And Joyce said, "Wait." She said, "Harry, you're drinking again, aren't you?" She watched him turn to her taking his time, getting his answer ready. Now he cocked his head.

"Why do you say that?"

Giving her his serious, interested look. Robert Gee was waiting to hear too.

She said, "Well, I know you are."

He said, "Wait now. Whether I am or not, I want to know why you said it."

She said, "Harry, for God's sake, because you're serious and trying to sound logical, pretending to be clever, and it's not you. I can tell by now when you're acting."

"You're not saying I'm drunk."

"No, you're what you used to call maintaining, drinking just enough to take the edge off, keep your central nervous system from getting out of hand. Remember when you used to say that?" Her expression turned almost to a smile.

"I'm not saying you shouldn't be drinking, I'm only saying you *are.*"

"I did have a few last Sunday," Harry said. "I was having trouble, you know, talking to people, I couldn't get going, so . . . I didn't have any martinis, just plain Scotch and water. They don't know how to make martinis here anyway. That was Sunday. Since then, during the past week I haven't had more than two on any given day and a couple glasses of wine with my dinner. Ask Robert. I was my old self again after going through a—what would you call it?—a period of adjustment, settling in?"

"While you were being your old self," Joyce said, "did you happen to tell anyone where you live?"

FOURTEEN

Sunday evening Raylan went in the hotel lounge for a drink, not knowing what he wanted. He had learned already they didn't have Diet-Rite or Dr Pepper or had ever heard of them. Mountain Dew either. They had Coke, Pepsi-Cola, and 7-Up. Raylan sat at the old dark-wood bar seeing himself in the mirror and asked for a Pepsi, no ice, poured a glass, drank it half down, and felt his eyes water with the sting. He was tired.

He'd shown the front-face half of Harry's mug shot at all the cafés on the Via Veneto and got a few waiters to nod, yes, the American. The assistant manager of the hotel said, "Yes, the American with the same name as the river in Tuscany, though spelled a different way in his passport."

No one recalled Harry saying anything in particular and it surprised Raylan, knowing Harry to be a talker. He hadn't asked anyone in the bar, since Harry didn't drink. But then thought, Well, you *hardly* drink and you're in here. So he showed the mug shot to the little guy behind the bar and right away got a nod.

"You know him, huh?"

"Yes, of course, Sr. Arnaud."

"Same name," Raylan said, "as the river."

"Yes, he was here, oh, three weeks I think. Come in here every afternoon for the tea. That was the first two weeks. The third week, no. He change to whisky." The little guy smiled. "And became a more friendly person."

"Harry was drinking hard stuff?"

"Sr. Arnaud, yes, Scotch whisky."

That didn't sound good.

"You know what happened to him? Where he went?"

"I think to stay in his villa." The little guy turned, pointing to a window across the room and said, "Up the mountain," waving his arm now, "by Montallegro. Drive up in a motorcar or ride the *funivia*. You know the Santuario, where it is?"

No, but Raylan sure intended to find out. First thing in the morning he'd rent a car. The bartender didn't know if Harry had bought the villa. If he did, there would be some record of ownership in a government office. Wouldn't there? The bartender said the villa was between Montallegro and Maurizio di Monti, a big place you see far off from below and then close from above. He said the reason he remembered it was because Sr. Arnaud had drawn a map on a napkin to show where the villa was located and how you could see the orange trees in the garden if you went by on the road above slowly. Oh, and a persimmon tree. Two or three turns in the road above Maurizio di Monti, that was where you looked down. The bartender said Sr. Arnaud was very proud to have this villa. Raylan asked then why wasn't he staying in it before? The bartender didn't know the answer to that one.

Raylan thought of something else. He said, "I've seen orange trees growing around here. Some out in front of the hotel."

The bartender said, "Yes?"

"But you serve canned orange juice in the morning."

He went to his room and tried calling Buck Torres, forgetting it was Sunday afternoon in Miami Beach. Torres had given him his home number, so he tried that and ended up leaving a message on the policeman's machine, self-conscious doing it, talking to a person who wasn't there. He had supper and was back in his room before Torres got home and called, wanting to know first of all where he was, insisting.

Raylan said, "I know you can find out anyway from the number," and told him he was in Rapallo, as was the Zip, the guy with him, and some friends from here, it looked like, but there was no sign yet of Harry.

Torres said, "How do you know he's there?"

"I give you my word he is," Raylan said. "The reason I'm telling you all this, I wonder if you'd call the local cops, the city police, not the carabinieri, and tell them the situation, that a man is gonna get killed if they don't do something about the Zip and his guys. See, if I tell them," Raylan said, "by the time they got done interrogating me Harry's liable to be dead. The other thing, while you're talking to the cops, ask them to find out if Harry owns property here. Under his real name. I'm no good at stuff like that. Okay? And let me know as soon as you can? I spoke with the Zip. I told him Harry was set up, that he never skimmed in his life. The Zip don't care, he still wants him. Can you tell me why?"

"Try and figure those people out," Torres said. "Listen, you remember I told you we found a sawed-off shotgun? Was in a dope house. We got the guy who brought it in and sold it for twenty bucks' worth of crack, two bottles. The guy said he picked it up in a parking lot in South Beach, behind the Della Robbia. He said a guy in overalls was laying there; he thought he was asleep."

Raylan said, "Can you put the gun in the hands of the victim? What's his name, Earl Crowe?"

"We're pretty sure it's his. It's got his prints on it. I think it's going to be enough for the state attorney to turn Harry loose. I know he wants to."

"I can't wait to tell him," Raylan said. "If I can find him."

They were winding down.

He said, "The emergency number here is one thirteen instead of nine eleven. In case you wondered."

Torres said, "What's he doing in Rapallo? Why there?"

"A friend of his lived here on and off," Raylan said. "You ever read Ezra Pound?"

Torres said, "Who?"

They got Nicky a red Fiat and gave him Fabrizio as his driver. The guy's stomach touched the steering wheel. He was okay though. Quiet, Nicky thought, for an Italian. He told Nicky he'd lived in New York, actually Brooklyn, a couple of years, but didn't like it too much and returned to Milano. Talking to Fabrizio, asking what different words meant, Nicky found out the Zip had been calling him a mama's boy, a pussy, an asshole, a queer—the Zip's idea of being funny. Fabrizio said, "So what're you gonna do about it? Forget it."

They found out Raylan Givens was staying at the Liguria and were at the hotel by eight o'clock Monday morning. Nicky went in hoping to catch the marshal in the dining room having breakfast. Walk up to him and say, "Now it's my turn," the same way the guy had said it when he shoved the gun in his groin. Have him looking up from the table, put three nines into him, one in the head and walk out. Only the marshal wasn't in the dining room or up in his room. Shit. The desk clerk said he had asked directions to the Avis car rental office and left the hotel only a short time ago.

Fabrizio knew where it was, on della Libertà, not far. So, okay, if he couldn't nail the guy at the table eating he'd do it on the street, a drive-by, only making sure the guy saw who it was.

Fabrizio said, "You do this before?"

Nicky said, "Don't worry about it."

Fabrizio said he'd do it if Nicky wasn't sure. He said he had killed five people when he was in New York, three of them with a pipe bomb. If Nicky wanted to use a bomb they were easy enough to make. Throw it in the guy's car. Nicky said he was doing this one himself, no help. He looked at Fabrizio, man, what a slob, wearing the same ugly gold sport shirt three days in a row. Nicky, wearing his black leather jacket with a white T-shirt next to his body and pressed jeans, couldn't believe how some guys didn't care what they looked like.

Fabrizio spotted him. He said, "There, you see him? Wearing the hat. A cowboy, uh?"

Walking along the left side of the street ahead of them. Wearing a dark suit today and the hat, always wearing that hat. Nicky said, "That's him," getting excited. "Go around the block so you're coming back the other way."

Fabrizio didn't get it. "Go around the block?"

"So I'll have him on my side of the car. I don't have to shoot past you."

"Get in the backseat."

"I'd still be shooting across the street. I want him close." Nicky got a good look at the marshal as they drove past him, Jesus, wearing that hat and cowboy boots with it. They were coming to an intersection.

"Via della Libertà," Fabrizio said. "The street where Avis is, to the left."

Nicky said, "Go past it and make a U-turn and come back. So we get to him before he gets to the corner."

He leaned forward to reach around with both hands and pull the Beretta stuck in his waist, pressing against his spine, as Fabrizio gunned the Fiat through the intersection and into the next block before he braked; then had to wait for cars to pass before making the U-turn. Nicky racked the slide on the Beretta. He was ready. But as they crossed the intersection again Fabrizio said, "Where's the cowboy?"

And Nicky said, "There he is."

Already walking up della Libertà. They saw him for only a second. Fabrizio turned right at the next intersection and again at the next one, bring them around the block to della Libertà.

Raylan was nowhere in sight.

Nicky said, "Where's Avis? He must've gone in the office."

"It's up the street more, behind us," Fabrizio said, creeping the Fiat along close to the sidewalk, his gaze moving from one side of the street to the other. He stopped the car. "You have to get out and look for him. Find out where he is. I go around two blocks this time and come back for you."

"I want him," Nicky said.

Fabrizio nodded, impatient. "Yes, all right. You told me. Now you going to get out?"

Nicky was on the sidewalk, the Fiat moving away before he'd thought this out, looked at it good and saw what he'd do once he located Raylan. He still had the Beretta in his hand and had to quick stick it in his pants and zip the jacket over it. He started walking, passing store windows, restaurants, a place to get ice cream, and came to a street called Via Boccoleri that seemed more like an alley. Narrow and dark in there with doorways to what looked like shops. Nicky unzipped his jacket as he started in. There was a cross street not too far ahead, another alley. He half turned as a motor scooter came up behind him and shot past with that noise, that high whine, Jesus. Yesterday, riding around in the Mercedes, Benno would drive up behind motor scooters and nudge them off the road, into parked cars, into ditches, up on the sidewalk. Not all motor scooters, just the ones he said annoyed him. What he meant was smart-ass kids on motor scooters who came too close to the car, or gave Benno the finger going past at the way he was creeping along. When they were looking for the gray Lancia. They had brought more guys down from Milano and had them at the airport, the train station, and roads leading to the *autostrada*; they'd paid gas station guys to call a number if they saw the Lancia. Benno said one more day they'd find it. Fucking Benno, bored driving around so he had some fun with the motor scooters. Nicky grinned thinking about it, Benno bumping the motor scooters, nudging them and watching the kids driving lose control. Nicky half turned again hearing another motor scooter on della Libertà. He waited. This one went whining past the street. Nicky turned to continue on, stopped in the same motion, and felt himself jump.

The marshal was standing about ten feet in front of him wearing that dark suit he saw now had a vest: the marshal with his thumbs hooked in his belt, his hat down more on one eye than the other.

He said, "Nicky, you looking for me?"

Raylan saw Nicky's hand touch the front of his jacket at the waist and hesitate there, the boy catching himself in time. Now his other hand came up to fool with the thumbnail, it looked like, of the hand already there.

Raylan said, "Well?"

Nicky still didn't answer. Though he'd narrowed his eyes, maybe getting into the game, Raylan wasn't sure. Narrowing your eyes wasn't that hard to do. He said, "You didn't want to talk to me yesterday either. Told me to stay out of it. So I have to wonder why you're looking for me. I see you drive by and come back. I see you get out of the car with a pistol in your hand. . . . So I guess what you're wondering, if you can get it out again before I get mine out. Am I right?" It wasn't the kind of question likely to get an answer, so Raylan said, "What we might have here is the kind of situation you see in real life out there. Like it was a contest, who could pull the faster." Raylan shook his head. "If you wanted to shoot me, Nicky, for some personal reason you might have, would you walk up and tell me? Or would you wait to catch me unawares?"

Raylan paused now. "You're not telling me what you think about this. What's wrong?"

"I'm trying to figure out," Nicky said, "what the fuck you're talking about."

"You know but don't want to let on," Raylan said, seeing Nicky's hands right there at his waist, the boy still in the game, "waiting to see if you have a move. Well, I'll tell you something. Shooting at a person is not the same as shooting out on a firing range. Even if you're a dead shot, it don't mean you can look a man in the eye and be able to pull the trigger. I know this for a fact, partner, cause I taught the use of firearms at the training academy."

The way Nicky kept staring at him Raylan was dying to know what was going on in the boy's head. He believed some confusion, as the boy didn't seem to know what to do. Scratched his jaw. Shoved his hands flat down in the pockets of his jeans. Raylan could see the blue steel grip of the automatic against his pants. It looked as though it was going to stay there this time. Raylan raised his chin and nodded toward the street.

"Your car's out there." He waited until Nicky turned and was walking away before he said, "Nice talking to you."

* * *

The Fiat was parked now on della Libertà across the street from the Avis car rental office.

"I'm trying to understand this," Fabrizio said. "You didn't say nothing to him?"

"What was I suppose to say?"

"You know he had a gun?"

"Sure he did."

"You saw it?"

"I did yesterday."

"But you don't know he had it today."

"He has it 'cause he's a U.S. marshal and they pack. The son of a bitch, he knows I'm going to kill him I get the chance."

"What was that, before?"

"What was what?"

"When you were talking to him. Wasn't that a chance to do it?"

"He was waiting for me."

"You think so?"

"He knew I had a gun, he saw it and told me he did. So I knew he had one. He wouldn't have stopped me if he didn't. He was waiting, hoping I'd touch my gun."

Fabrizio said, "Yes?" He was going to ask why he didn't, but saw Nicky's expression change and it was too late.

"There he is," Nicky said, sitting back, not as anxious as he was before.

Fabrizio looked across della Libertà to see the cowboy with the Avis man, the cowboy taking the keys from him and a folder and then getting into a blue Fiat sedan standing at the curb. Fabrizio waited for Nicky to tell him to follow the marshal.

"Okay, follow him."

He made a U-turn and trailed behind the blue Fiat almost to the seafront, della Libertà to Via Gramsci, where the car turned right and then right again into the courtyard of the Astoria Hotel and stopped facing the entrance. From the street they watched Raylan get out of the car and go inside. Fabrizio waited for Nicky to say it.

"That's not his hotel."

"It's the woman's."

"What's he doing in there?"

"I don't know," Fabrizio said. "But maybe it's a good thing you didn't shoot him."

Raylan had the key to Joyce's room he'd taken from her purse, the one she'd left on the table in the café and was now in his hotel room.

He turned the key in the lock and entered knowing her room might have been tossed already and it was, her clothes everywhere, her bags open on the bed, empty. They would have been looking for something bearing a Rapallo address or phone number, the name of a hotel maybe, no one believing Joyce didn't know where Harry was.

Raylan assumed they didn't find anything worthwhile or that boy with the muscles and no brain wouldn't be outside waiting for him. He pushed open the shutters covering the window and looked out from the second floor past a magnolia tree to the red Fiat in the street. The magnolia surprised him. Beyond the red car were date palms, and the walk along the beach: a better view than his room at the Liguria offered. He'd keep her things there with his until this business was settled. Which meant he'd have to pack her bags.

Doing it gave him a strange feeling, touching her clothes, her skimpy underwear, her bras, folding and arranging them as neatly as he knew how inside her nylon bags, nothing that looked like Winona's and everything in smaller sizes. He found it wasn't possible to handle a woman's things, even her slacks, sweaters, and jeans and not have a feeling about the woman and wonder about her. She had T-shirts, too, with Florida scenes on them. Wherever she was he bet she missed having her clothes. He remembered Joyce hunching her shoulders in that navy wool coat sitting in the café. It took nerve for her to come here, hook up with a guy who'd jumped his bond. He wondered if she loved Harry or was just used to him. She had curlers in the bathroom and all kinds of beauty aids that went into a smaller plastic bag and then into her carry-on. He wanted to be able to say to Joyce, once he found Harry—that had to come first—"Oh, I brought your things," and she'd know he was thinking of her while this was going on. See what she thought of that.

Raylan turned the key in at the desk. He didn't even mind putting her bill on his credit card. She would insist on paying him back and he'd say don't worry about it. Something to that effect. It was another scene he could play in his mind waiting for it to happen.

They watched him come of the Astoria with luggage in both hands, a bag hanging from his shoulder. Fabrizio said, "Right now would be a pretty good time, uh?"

In Bay Ridge, Brooklyn, they remembered Fabrizio as Ladykiller. Of the five people he had taken out during his tour in the States, four were women. One he shot sitting in a car with her husband, who was the target, and three in the dry-cleaning establishment when the pipe bomb

came through the plate-glass window and ex-
ploded.

Nicky had hold of the door handle.

They watched Raylan set the luggage on the
pavement, open the back door of the Fiat, and
begin to load the pieces inside.

"It's still a pretty good time," Fabrizio said.

Nicky opened the door of the red Fiat and
moved to stick his leg out just as Raylan closed
the door of the blue Fiat and turned to face the
street. Nicky hesitated and Fabrizio helped him
out.

He said, "But if the cowboy knows where
they are, since he's picking up her baggage? . . .
You better wait, uh? Not kill him yet."

Fabrizio having some fun with this *stronzo*
from the States. He waited.

And Nicky said, "So we follow him."

FIFTEEN

Raylan noticed the Zip preferred Vesuvio's as his hangout, there yesterday and again today. A couple of his guys were eating, it looked like, while the Zip had only an espresso cup in front of him. There weren't as many people here as Sunday, so it was easy to keep an eye on him. Which is what the Zip was doing, facing this way at his table.

Tuesday, December 1, some of the tourist places along the Via Veneto, like the ice cream parlor, were now closed for the season. People here loved ice cream, so there were other places to get it. That was something he could mention.

So he did, sitting at the Gran Caffè with coffee and a plate of pasta with meat sauce, writing postcards to his two boys in Brunswick, Ricky and Randy.

That part of South Georgia had about the same weather as here. He'd already mentioned that on a postcard. He'd told them the spaghetti here wasn't like the spaghetti their mom made with tomato soup, and that they put all kinds of things on top of their spaghetti here. Like octopus, honest. He'd told them people liked to eat outside here even when it was kind of chilly.

What else?

He could tell them he'd rented a car yesterday, a blue Fiat, and was driving around. That maybe today he'd drive up into the mountains that were actually like hills in eastern Tennessee, up in the Smokies, but with different kinds of trees on them, not so piney as back home.

The Zip was getting up from his table.

Tell them about the olive trees on hillsides with the nets under them. So you wouldn't have to chase a mile after the olives that dropped on the ground.

The Zip looked like he was coming this way. Alone.

Tell about the Doris Day movie on TV last night, Doris flying a plane for the first time after the pilot had a heart attack, it looked like, and landed the plane getting instructions from the tower. In Italian. Doris talking Italian back to it.

The Zip was standing by the table now. He said, "I know you haven't found him. After you go to all the trouble to come here?"

"You either, huh?" Raylan said. He broke off a piece of bread and mopped his plate with it.

The Zip, watching him, swallowed. He brought a wad of currency out of his inside pocket, straightened and smoothed the bills, and dropped them on the table. It made a pile of money.

Raylan looked at it and took a sip of coffee. "How much is that?"

"Thirty million lire. Pick it up, it's yours."

"I mean how much in dollars?"

"Twenty-five thousand."

"You think that's my price?"

"This is between you and me," the Zip said, "nobody else. So why don't you take it, uh? Go to Rome and get laid, get drunk, have a good time, spend it all and go home. Sound good?"

"Or what?" Raylan said.

"No or what. Take it, go on, and spend it."

"Only do it," Raylan said, "someplace else. I

understand what you're saying, only I'm not going anywhere. So where does that leave you?
That's what I mean by 'Or what?' "

"Well, you could disappear," the Zip said.
"You not scared of Nicky? Okay, somebody else
can do it."

Raylan said, "Am I talking to him?"

The Zip said, "I think you could put me in
that business again," nodding, as if considering
it.

Raylan said, "It's hard to imagine you in a
pair of Big Ben overalls, like that scudder you
sent to do Harry. I'm told they found the shotgun he carried that night and somebody walked
off with. Soon as they put it on him, Harry's
home free. Does the fact he shot your guy in self-
defense move you any?"

"To begin with he wasn't my guy," the Zip
said. "Even if he was, this is between me and
Harry, nobody else. The same as this money's
between me and you. Uh, what do you think?
You can't do everything by yourself. Take it,
have a good time."

Raylan waited and said, "Tell me why you
want Harry."

"It's not your business."

"He didn't skim on you."

"How do you know he didn't?"

"You're using him as an example," Raylan said.

The Zip shrugged.

"Only he hasn't *done* anything."

"I want to talk to him," the Zip said. "See if he'll go home with me. It's the same thing you're doing. You told me you're here by yourself? You don't have any court papers, nothing asking the police to help you. Okay, but you're in my way; so, I offer you something to step aside. How do you think about that?"

"I already called the police on you," Raylan said. "Pretty soon they'll be asking what you're up to. You can bet they'll keep an eye on you."

The Zip said, "You think so?" giving Raylan a faint smile, like telling him he didn't know what he was talking about. He said, "Okay, this is how you want it," turned, and walked off around the tables.

Raylan picked up a postcard and looked at it: a view of that worn-out castle on the edge of the bay. He turned the card over and wrote:

Hi Boys. Remember that castle we saw at Disney World? This is what a real one looks like. People lived in it till they got tired of getting soaking wet every time they stepped out the door, so they rented an apartment in town.

What else?

Ask the boys if they could believe there wasn't any Dr Pepper in Italy.

He might've mentioned that already.

Tell them there didn't seem to be any dryers here? People hung their clothes out the window on lines, even four and five stories up.

He raised his gaze enough to see the Zip on the sidewalk now in front of Vesuvio's. The Zip motioned and Raylan saw the red Fiat standing at the curb. The young guy in the leather jacket, Nicky Testa, and the fat guy who drove the car were getting out. The fat guy went over to the table where the two guys were eating. Nicky went to the Zip's table—about a hundred feet from Raylan watching them. He saw the Zip say something to Nicky and now Nicky turned and was looking this way.

Going to be sent over, Raylan thought. But for what?

"So you had two chances to take him out," the Zip said. "On the street, Fabrizio tells me, and in front of the hotel."

Nicky said, "What?" frowning, acting more confused than he was. "He told me *don't* do it, Fabrizio did. The guy rents a car and picks up the broad's luggage? What's that look like? He knows where they are, he's bringing her stuff to her. Right?"

"He don't know nothing," the Zip said. "He never did and he still don't."

"What's he doing with her bags then? They could've called him, couldn't they?"

"What I'm telling you," the Zip said, "he don't know nothing. You believe me?"

Nicky wanted to go over to the other table, sit down with those guys talking Italian, he didn't care, have some pasta and a beer.

The Zip said, "You believe me?"

"Yeah, I believe you."

"He don't know nothing."

"Right." Christ, like repeat after me. "He don't know nothing."

"So," the Zip said, "you want to take him out?"

Nicky wanted to tell him to keep his big fucking nose out of this.

"Do you?"

"Yeah."

"Haven't changed your mind?"

Shit, he could see it coming. He said, "I have to set it up first."

The Zip motioned toward the cowboy hat at the café next door, dim in there but the hat easy to see.

"He's set up. He's sitting there waiting for you." The Zip said something in Italian to Benno, Fabrizio, and another guy with them at the next table, and right away they were quiet, all three of them turning to look at Nicky. Now the Zip said, "You going to do it or not?"

Raylan watched him approach the table: man, those arms and shoulders of his filling that leather jacket. He'd be a hard one to take down 'less you hit him with a ball bat. Raylan brushed crumbs from the green tablecloth, dropped both hands to his lap, and sat back in his chair, ready for Mr. Testa.

He said, "Mr. Zip sent you ever here, didn't he? Well, it couldn't be to tell me anything. I think it's all been said. He offered me money— did he mention that to you?—thirty million lire, which sounds like a lot more'n it is, if I'd go away and quit bothering you people. To me, that was an insult. Not the amount, you understand, but that he'd entertain the idea I might take it. A man like him thinking everybody has a price. Well, there was a time he could've had me for fifteen dollars a day—hell, less'n that—when I was a boy working in the coal mines. Anybody ever asked what was my price, that would've been it, fifteen a day. I've worked deep mines, wildcat mines, I've worked for strip operators, and I've sat out over a year on strike and seen company gun thugs shoot up the houses of miners that spoke out. They killed an uncle of mine was living with us, my mother's brother, and they killed a friend of mine I played football with in high school. This was in a coal camp town called Evarts in Harlan County, Kentucky, near to twenty years ago. You understanding what I'm saying? Even before I entered the Marshals Service and trained to be a dead shot, I'd seen people kill one another and learned to be ready in case I saw a bad situation coming toward me."

Raylan bent forward a moment, brought his right hand up from his boot, and laid his 357 snub-nose on the table. He watched Nicky's eyes lock on the gun and stare like he might never look away.

"In other words," Raylan said, "if I see you've come to do me harm, I'll shoot you through the heart before you can clear your weapon. Do we have an understanding here?"

SIXTEEN

Fabrizio watched Nicky walk away from the
cowboy, out to the sidewalk. Now he was coming this way, toward them. He saw Tommy at
the next table watching Nicky, Benno watching,
everybody watching and wondering what Nicky
was going to say to Tommy. The kid wasn't looking this way or showing any kind of expression
on his face. Tommy wasn't either. Tommy
showed pleasure, anger, contempt, all the same
way.

Nicky—wait a minute—was walking past
them, going past the café.

Tommy turned his head this way and said, "Where's he going?"

So Fabrizio called to him, "Hey, Nicky, where you going, man?"

Tommy said, "Get him."

Fabrizio saw Tommy turn his head to look back at the cowboy, who was standing now, walking away from his table at the Gran Caffè, and Tommy said it again, "*Get him,*" louder this time, still meaning Nicky.

So Fabrizio got up from the table and went after him, because the cowboy was his and Nicky's responsibility. Only it was getting to be tiresome. If Nicky didn't take the cowboy this time, Fabrizio believed he would have to. Man, to get it over with.

Raylan's idea was to have them in view but looking the other way when he made his move. He left money on the table, picked up his revolver and his postcards, and got out of there, over Via Veneto to the corner and then up to where his car was parked off the Piazza Cavour. He drove through downtown streets in light traffic, working his way around buses, hoping to get some space between him and them, sure they'd be on his tail in a matter of a few minutes. He found the road that curved around the perimeter of the city and the turnoff where the sign pointed to Maurizio di Monti and Montallegro. A guy wearing sunglasses, his arms folded, leaned against his car at the side of the road. Raylan watched him in his rearview mirror, expecting to see the guy jump in the car and come after him, but pretty soon he was out of sight and the road remained clear. Raylan felt somewhat relieved, but not much.

Coming up out of the plain the hill became steeper and the switchbacks longer, straightaways that extended close to a quarter of a mile between curves: different from eastern Kentucky, though it was still mountain driving and Raylan had done enough of it to last him. The trees were different too: there weren't any cypress that he knew of in eastern Kentucky, or olive trees. They made the land here seem older, from an ancient time, a way he had never looked at the land back home.

There was hardly any traffic in either direction, letting him get a good look up and down on the straightaways. Some of the homes were right smack on the road or behind low stone fences. Get through the curve to the next straight section of road and he would be looking down at the same houses and see farmyards and outbuildings. Going through Maurizio di Monti he passed a cluster of houses built close to the road and came to a car parked at an intersection, another one with the guy standing outside, watching the world go by, this one smoking a cigarette. Raylan passed him. Then in the rearview mirror saw the guy throw away his cigarette and reach into the car through the window. Now he saw the guy with a hand radio, speaking into it, telling somebody about the blue Fiat he'd just seen whiz by, the guy getting smaller and smaller in the mirror. It reminded Raylan of an old Waylon Jennings number, "When You See Me Getting Smaller." One of his favorites when he was still home in Kentucky. On the same record as "You Picked a Fine Time to Leave Me, Lucille," the one he thought of right after Winona told him she was getting a divorce and he was alone in Miami Beach without his family. Without his boys anyway; the real estate guy could have Winona. He thought of Waylon and wondered if there was such a thing as Italian country music. He remembered reading somewhere that Clint Black was half Italian, his mother being full-blooded.

Raylan kept glancing at his mirror, but nothing seemed to be coming after him. Somebody would, though, before too long. Right now he'd concentrate on locating Harry's villa. Some-

where, the hotel bartender said, between Maurizio di Monti, which he'd just passed, and the
church at the end of this road, the Sanctuary of
the Holy Virgin of Montallegro. Driving north on
straight stretches of road, he'd look for houses
above him. Then around a curve and driving
south, he'd try to look down the slope, at places
directly below him, without going off the road.
There weren't any guardrails to speak of. Seeing
vegetable patches cut out of the slope reminded
him of home, people scratching to have enough
to eat. He wondered if they had food stamps
here.

The thought vanished from his mind as he
jammed on his brakes and the Fiat skidded to a
stop close to the shoulder. Raylan backed up until he was looking directly at the villa, a plain
square structure, kind of a dirty yellow in color,
a gravel drive that needed to be weeded leading
up to it. He backed up some more and now had a
view of the garden behind the villa with its
hedges, its plants in concrete pots, orange trees,
four of them, and a persimmon tree. Raylan put
the car in drive and crept past the house, noting
a building, back and to the side, with wooden
doors that might be a garage. Out beyond were a
couple more farm buildings, all the structures
with red tile roofs. Raylan glanced at his mirror

and right away pressed his foot down on the accelerator. A car flashing red in the sunlight was coming fast out of the hairpin behind him.

"As I pass his car," Fabrizio said, "you shoot him. How does that sound? Stick your gun out the window and pop him. Where's he going to hide? You have him."

Nicky had his Beretta in his hands, ready. He'd already racked the slide. All he had to do was put the gun on the marshal and pull the trigger. He liked what Fabrizio said about where was he going to hide. He liked it when he could see ahead of time what was going to happen. Where's he going to go? Nowhere. He'll see the gun pointing at him and try to duck. Guess when the piece was about to go off and then duck, try to, keep from getting shot and the car from going off the road. So the guy would duck —okay, wait for him to come up and *bam.*

He said to Fabrizio, "Hurry up if you're gonna get next to him. Goose it."

"After the turn coming up. We get through, I'm going to put it on the floor. Come up on him, he'll be two feet away. You think you can take him?"

Fucking Fabrizio having a good time. All of them, the genuine Italians, thinking they were pretty funny, the things they said about him. Asking if they could watch and learn something. Nicky held on going through the hairpin curve and still got bounced around. They came out on the straight and . . . Shit, where was he?

"Where'd he go?"

Fabrizio didn't answer, looking around and then looking at his rearview mirror.

"Could he have gotten behind us?"

Fabrizio still didn't answer. It meant he didn't know. They both kept quiet now, looking around. No sign of the blue Fiat. They kept going. Two more turns and a long stretch with only a few bends in it and they were approaching the Sanctuary of Montallegro, a pretty big church.

"You know why they built this?" Fabrizio said. "Four hundred years ago the Virgin Mary appeared to a man who lived here, a poor man. She told him she would grant favors to the people who came here and prayed to her. You know, to ask for different things, money, a husband. . . . All the cars, it means a service is being held in there. You want to go in?"

"Yeah, light a candle," Nicky said.

"No, I mean it," Fabrizio said. "Ask the Virgin Mary to help you find the cowboy. And then if you do, grant the miracle that you shoot him and don't think of an excuse why you can't."

"Fucking comedian," Nicky said.

Fabrizio drove past the parking area so they could look over the cars, then stopped and got his radio off the top of the instrument panel. He spoke into it in Italian and a voice in Italian came back to them.

When he was finished, Fabrizio said, "That was the man in Maurizio di Monti. He says the cowboy didn't come back that way. It means he has to be still up here somewhere. Maybe turned off one of the roads that don't go nowhere, waiting for us to leave. So, we go back that way and sniff, uh? See if we can smell him, this cowboy."

They had gone no more than a half mile when Nicky said, "There he is," excited now, seeing the blue Fiat standing a short distance up a side road, pointing away from them. They came to the road and turned in and the Fiat took off, topped a rise, and was gone.

Fabrizio said, "Now what's he doing?" sounding puzzled. "He was waiting for us."

"We had him set up for a drive-by," Nicky said. "Now he's thought of something and he's setting *us* up."

"How does he do that?" Fabrizio said, hunched over the wheel now. "There two of us, one of him."

"I don't know," Nicky said, "but I'm telling you that's what he's doing, setting us up."

"I better do this one," Fabrizio said. "I think you starting to come apart again."

Raylan brought them to high ground, an open field of scrub on what he would call a hogback ridge that sloped to valleys choked with brush.

He turned the car around to be facing them when they came over the rise, took out his revolver, and checked the loads, spinning the cylinder to hear the sound of it, Raylan getting the feel of the weapon again in his hands. Nicky hadn't seen this one yet, his Smith & Wesson 357 Combat Mag, stainless steel with a six-inch barrel. He watched for them now, expecting the red Fiat to come flying over the crest of the ridge, then brake hard and fishtail as they saw him waiting, and that was how it was. The car stopped about a hundred feet away, maybe a little less, and sat there.

Deciding how to do it, Raylan thought. You go at him from over there and I'll go at him from over here. Why didn't he drive up close?

'Cause it's show-off time, Raylan thought. The Italian gun thug is going to show the boy how it's done. What do you bet?

* * *

"We're going to walk up to him," Fabrizio said. "You leave the car and walk toward him, but out that way. You understand? I do the same on this side. Go toward him but out, so he has to turn from me to you. You understand? We have our guns in our hands. No cowboy stuff. Okay? But don't say nothing to him."

"You gonna say something?"

"As we going toward him, yeah, keep him busy."

"What're you gonna say?"

"Don't worry about it. It's not important what I say. But you keep quiet. And don't shoot till I do, when I see we close enough. You understand? Then you can shoot all you want."

"He's an expert with a gun," Nicky said, "a dead shot."

"Yeah, who told you that," Fabrizio said, getting out of the car, "him?"

Raylan watched them come out of the red car, both with pistols in their hands, making their intentions fairly clear. Fine. If they didn't have them out now they would soon enough, the fat guy having decided, Raylan believed, to have this business done.

See? You could tell by the way he moved. Confident, running the show now, Nicky along to help out. Pick up the body after and chuck it down the slope. Raylan asked himself if he was sure of that, the fat guy running the show. Yes, he was. He slid out of the Fiat and stepped one stride away from the door, leaving it open. The fat guy, the real Italian, was almost directly in front of him but moving a little to his right, while Nicky was over to the left. Their plan, to spread out as they came for him. What other way was there, outside of stay in the car and drive up to him?

When they were about eighty feet away Raylan said, "That's good, right there."

He saw Nicky look over at the fat guy, who kept coming, so Nicky did, too, until Raylan raised his left hand to point it at Nicky. He said, "I'll take you first," and Nicky stopped. The fat guy, looking over, stopped too.

He said to Nicky, "You listen to him or me?"

It seemed a hard question. Raylan saw the boy didn't know what to do, even with those big arms and shoulders on him and a pistol in his hand.

Now the fat guy waved his pistol at Nicky, saying, "Come on," and started toward Raylan again, getting a sincere look on his face as he said, "We want to talk to you, man. Get a little closer, that's all, so I don't have to shout."

"I can hear you," Raylan said.

The fat guy said, "Listen, it's okay. I don't mean real close. Just a little closer, uh? It's okay?"

Getting within his range, Raylan thought. If he knows what it is. The guy was confident, you could say that for him. Raylan raised his left hand, this time toward the fat guy.

Then lowered it saying, "I wouldn't come any closer'n right there. You want to talk, go ahead and talk."

The fat guy kept coming anyway, saying, "It's okay. Don't worry about it."

"You take one more step," Raylan said, "I'll shoot you. That's all I'm gonna say."

This time the fat guy stopped and grinned, shaking his head, about sixty feet away now. He said, "Listen, I want to tell you something, okay? That you should know." He took a step. He started to take another one.

And Raylan shot him. Put the 357 Mag on him, fired once, and hit him high in the gut. Raylan glanced at Nicky standing way over to his left, Nicky with his pistol about waist high. Raylan put the Mag on the fat guy again, the guy with his hand on his gut now, looking down like he couldn't believe there was a hole in him before looking at Raylan again, saying something in Italian that had a surprised sound to it. When the guy raised his pistol and had it out in front of him, Raylan shot him again, higher this time, in the chest, and this one put him down.

The sound echoed and faded.

Raylan turned his head.

Nicky stood facing him, holding his pistol in both hands in a stiff-armed pose the way Raylan used to teach it—sort of; his feet weren't right—and the way they did it in movies. He looked frozen, like a plastic toy figure, G.I. Joe. There were G.I. Joes all over the house in Brunswick.

Raylan said, "Use it or throw it away." Watched and saw the boy didn't want options, he needed to be told what to do. So Raylan told him to toss his gun aside; go on, do it. Then go over and kick the fat guy's out of the way. He said, "Then I want you to pick him up—you can do that, huh? You're a weight lifter, aren't you? Think of your friend there as a big dumbbell, 'cause that's what he was. Wouldn't listen. Okay, so pick him up and put him in your car. Take him to where you all're staying and ask Mr. Zip what he wants done with him. Can you remember all that?"

Raylan had his supper at the hotel, went back to his room, and called Buck Torres. Torres said he

was waiting to hear from a cop friend of his in
Rome who was checking with the Rapallo police
for him.

"You tell them it's urgent?"

"Call me tomorrow," Torres said.

"I'm checking out in the next ten minutes,"
Raylan said. "If all goes well I'll call you from
Harry's villa."

SEVENTEEN

Benno and some others hanging around the apartment came down to look in the car at Fabrizio sitting in the front seat, his head against the window. They'd hunch down and stare at his eyes and ask Nicky why he hadn't closed them. He said, "You want to, go ahead." But no one did. They'd hunch in close with their hands in their pockets. It was getting cold again as the sun went down. Benno asked what happened. Nicky told him the version he'd made up and Benno said not to bother Tommy, he was in his room with a woman, relaxing.

Nicky stood by the car to wait. He didn't know what else to do.

On his twenty-first birthday he drew two years at La Tuna Correctional in Texas on a drug-related concealed weapon charge. This was while he was trying to work his way into the Atlantic City crew, hanging out at the social club, packing a gun for somebody when he was asked to. A guy he met at La Tuna was with Jimmy Cap's crew in Miami Beach. Nicky looked him up after doing his time and that was how he got to meet Jimmy Cap and went to work for him: picking up Chinese takeout, lighting his cigars, getting him young girls, generally serving on an ass-kissing basis at first. Until one time: Jimmy Cap in the backseat of his Cadillac, Nicky in front with the driver, at a service station getting the tank filled with free gas, Jimmy said, "The schmuck owns this place is two weeks behind in his payments." He said to Nicky, "How would you get him to pay up?" Nicky said, "You mean the guy pumping gas?" A Cuban. Jimmy said no, the Cuban worked for the guy owned the station. Nicky got out of the car, took the gas nozzle away from the Cuban guy, and hosed him down with super unleaded. Jimmy liked it, his eyes lighting up as Nicky took out his Bic, the one he lit Jimmy's cigars with, and held it ready to flick and set the Cuban guy on fire. Jimmy asked him, "You'd do it?" Nicky said, "You want me to?" He said, "You can't do it to the guy owns the place. How's he gonna pay you if he's dead? But you light this guy up, the one owes you money will see what can happen to him." He said, "You want this guy lit up or not?" Jimmy Cap hesitated, then shook his head and told Nicky, "Not this time." His smoke-glass window slid closed and the show was over. Later on Nicky asked himself if he would've set the guy on fire if Jimmy wanted him to. The answer was yes, without giving it another thought. You saw a chance to step up, you took it.

What happened, he became Jimmy Cap's bodyguard as the tough kid from Atlantic City without ever having beat up, set on fire, or shot anybody. All he had to do was get a certain look in his eyes and walk around with his shirt off.

It worked, except with the Zip.

The Zip said to him, after that time at the gas station, "You were going to set this guy on fire? Standing between the pumps and the car, crowded in there, gas fumes in the air, you're going to light your lighter?" Nicky didn't say anything. "Everybody around there and also the car and anybody in it," the Zip said, "would've gone up in a ball of fire." Nicky said, "Jimmy liked the idea." The Zip said, "Then you should've done it."

Nicky had always wanted to shoot some-body, see what it would be like. He still did, and he wanted to shoot that fucking cowboy. What he shouldn't have done was talk about it, give the Zip and the genuine Italians something to needle him with. So now the Zip would give him a hard time as usual, ask him a lot of questions. Where was he when Fabrizio was getting shot? And so on.

Nicky's story was the cowboy surprised them: said he wanted to talk and shot Fabrizio as he got out of the car; then made him bring Fabrizio's body here so everybody could see the two bullet holes in him. Like a warning, what can happen if they come after the cowboy. Nicky told it to Benno and then to the Zip standing on the sidewalk, after he came downstairs with his whore, a woman who looked to Nicky like she took in washing. The woman went off down the street in a ratty yellow fur jacket and white shoes. The Zip told them to get rid of Fabrizio and took Nicky to a trattoria around the corner.

"I don't give a shit what you think," Nicky told him. "It was how I said. He was waiting for us and came over to the car."

"Up in the hills."

"Yeah."

"Fabrizio, he let him walk up to the car?"

Nicky hesitated. "He didn't come real close, no. He yelled out he wanted to talk."

"Fabrizio got out of the car . . ."

"Yeah, and walked toward him."

"And you walked toward him?"

Nicky used the salt and pepper shakers on the table. "Fabrizio's here and I'm here. Fabrizio told me not to shoot till he did. I could've, but that's what he said so I didn't. It looked like we were gonna have a talk. He said to Fabrizio, 'Take one more step and I'll shoot.'"

"Yes?"

"Fabrizio took a step and he shot him."

"How many times?"

Nicky hesitated. "I guess twice."

"From how far away was he?"

Nicky paused again. "I don't know—twenty yards?"

"What did he have? What kind of gun?"

"Revolver, with a stainless finish."

"Cowboy hat and a six-shooter," the Zip said. "Why didn't you shoot?"

Nicky hadn't said if he did or not. The Zip surprised him, speaking so quietly. They were the only ones in the place; waiters setting tables around them, rattling dishes and silverware.

"I told you, Fabrizio said don't shoot."

"I mean while he was shooting Fabrizio. It would be okay then, wouldn't it?"

"What would?"

"To shoot him."

"I didn't have time. I'm about to, he's already aiming at me. What'm I supposed to do?"

"But he didn't shoot."

Nicky shook his head.

"Why not?"

"He told me, drop the gun."

"So, it's in your hand? He sees that, why didn't he shoot?"

"He wanted me to put Fabrizio in the car and bring him down here, show him to you. That's what he said."

"What did you say to him?"

"Nothing."

"I mean when he was pointing his gun at you."

"I didn't say nothing."

"You didn't ask him not to shoot you?"

"No."

"Beg for your life?"

"I'm telling you I never said a fucking word

Check Out Receipt

McAlester Public Library
918-426-0930
seolibraries.com

Tuesday, February 6, 2024
10:32:33 AM

Item: 50792556341262
Title: Pronto
Material: Book
Due: 2/27/2024

Item: 50792531543818
Title: Road dogs
Material: Book
Due: 2/27/2024

Item: 50792000590787
Title: Riding the rap
Material: Book
Due: 2/27/2024

Item: 50792531834118
Title: Djibouti
Material: Book
Due: 2/27/2024

You just saved $95.97 by
using your library. You have
saved $506.83 this past year
and $506.83 since you began
using the library!

Thank You!

to him. If I had seen any chance at all to shoot him, I fucking would've. Jesus—okay?"

The Zip wouldn't let it go.

He said, "You both have a gun in your hand looking at each other?" Still speaking quietly and taking his time, maybe picturing the situation.

Nicky shook his head. "It wasn't like what you're thinking, like either one of us could've fired and let's see what happens. It wasn't like that."

"No? What was it like?"

"He *had* me. If I moved I was fucking dead."

Now the Zip began to nod, maybe still picturing it, Nicky wanting him to hurry up and get this over with. The Zip was different than at any time before, here or at home. Nicky wondered if his getting laid had anything to do with it, if it actually had relaxed him. The Zip was quiet for about a minute. He nodded again.

"You have your gun in your hand . . ."

Jesus Christ. He would *not* let it go.

"I explained it to you. Didn't I explain it?"

The Zip waved his hand in front of his face as he shook his head. "What I want to ask you, where's your gun now?"

"Where do you think it is?" Nicky said, wanting to reach over, take the Zip by his hair, and smash his face down on the table, bust his fucking nose. "It's up there on the fucking mountain. He said drop it, I dropped it. What would you have done?"

The Zip said, "You mean the guy has your gun. The same as he took it from you." He nodded a few times before saying, "I get you another gun, *testa di cazzo*, you think you can hang on to it, not give it away?"

Was he smiling a little, thinking he was funny? Nicky wasn't sure. He was different, though, since being with the whore.

Then surprised Nicky again, saying, "We'll have something to eat."

He had told Benno he wasn't going in a room where the girls were sitting around waiting for him to choose one of them. So Benno spoke to the woman who kept the girls and for twelve thousand lire had the five of them put on their coats and walk past Vesuvio's one at a time. The Zip picked the one who seemed most like a girl from the country—though probably all of them were at one time—the one he judged to be the least professional, not putting on too much of an act, and arranged for her to come to the apartment. Her name was Rossana. She was twenty-one and did not speak a word of English; her breath smelled faintly of garlic. The Zip didn't care. He rode her hard, sweating, and it was over in less than a minute. That was okay: he didn't have to impress her and he'd ride her again before too long. He told her he was from Palermo and now lived in Miami Beach. He asked Rossana if she knew about Miami Beach, where it was. She nodded, lying in bed with her arms at her sides, waiting for him. He rested higher, against the headboard.

He said in Italian, "Do you see that suit?" It hung over the back of a chair in the bedroom. She raised her head to look and said yes. "I have twenty suits, each one costing at least . . . wait. One million two hundred thousand lire. Do you know why I came to Rapallo?" He waited for her to say no. "I came to kill someone. A man also from Miami Beach." He saw her eyes and how afraid she was, trying not to move. He said, "When I went to America they gave me a shotgun and five thousand dollars. That's . . . six million lire, to kill someone." He watched her eyes again as he told this girl who didn't know him that he had killed people and saw how it frightened her. He said, "I'm not going to hurt you. I was married to a woman like you, from the country, uh? Perhaps I'm still married to her, I don't know." He said, "I found out five thousand dollars wasn't enough for killing someone, so after that first one I got more. Once I got thirty million lire. Then, this is funny, I tried to give the same amount to a man so I won't have to kill him and he wouldn't take it. Can you understand that?" He waited, but could see she didn't know what he was talking about. He said, "I have all the money I want, but I work for a fool. So the time will come I'll pay someone to kill him. Maybe bring someone over from here and give him five thousand dollars. There is always someone who'll do it. Did you know that?" She stared at him with her frightened eyes, brown ones, without blinking. Now she blinked. It was hard to find someone who wasn't in his life to talk to. Almost always it was a woman. This time a whore, yes, but still not someone in his life. He told her again, "Don't be afraid of me. I'm not crazy. I won't even ask you to do something you don't like. All you have to do is listen to me. All right? Do you want some wine?" She shook her head no, barely moving it. He said, "Do you believe there are people who want to kill me because I kill other people?" She didn't move or nod or shake her head. "There is always someone who wants to kill me. I get new ones all the time. The fool I work for I think would like to have me killed and a punk who works for me would like to do it, but he doesn't have the nerve

that it takes. You know the word *punk*? A young
guy who acts tough, but has had no experience. I
used to ridicule him in front of others and then
they would start on him. You know. But I see
now it's a waste of time. If he's nothing to me,
why should I bother? Do you agree?'' She
seemed to nod. He looked at her pale comfortable body, a pillow to lie on, red marks on her
stomach from tight elastic bands. Her breasts lay
flattened, sagging to opposite sides. He moved
his head down and over her until their brown
centers were staring at him, unmoving, the
woman and her breasts waiting for this to be
over. She would come to life later, telling the
other girls about the man who killed people, rolling her eyes, saying how afraid she was and
maybe exaggerating, making him vicious, the
kind of guy who scared whores to death and en-
joyed doing it. When he was on her again, moving, and she was moving, he said, ''I was kidding you. I don't kill people.'' He said, ''Really. I
was joking.'' He watched her trying to smile.

While they were eating Nicky thought of asking
the Zip about the whore—How was it, any
good?—but decided to keep quiet and neither
one of them said much. When they were finished
and the Zip was having an espresso, Benno came

in and they talked to each other in Italian for a few minutes. Nicky watched the Zip looking at him as he said something to Benno, still in Italian. Right after that Benno left.

"This is the most I've spoken the language in ten years," the Zip said. "I think in it most of the time, but don't get a chance to use it. I told Benno to get you another gun."

Nicky gave him a nod and sat there wondering what the Zip was up to. If he was playing some kind of game with him. Setting him up. Otherwise it didn't make sense.

Like now, the Zip saying, "Maybe you'll have another chance at the cowboy."

Putting him on.

The Zip saying, "He left his hotel, checked out. We find out he's up in the hills again around Montallegro, or he was. He disappeared. Maybe he came back, sneaked down in the dark, but I don't think so. We wait till tomorrow, go up there and look around. One thing I know, we find the cowboy, we find Harry. And we find the other people, too, the colored guy and the woman, Harry's girlfriend. They must all be in the same place now, hiding. So we go from house to house up there from two directions. Where they going to go? I told Benno's guys, six hundred thousand lire to whoever finds the house."

Sitting there stirring his coffee and telling him all this shit like they were old buddies.

Nicky said, "When's he getting me my gun?"

EIGHTEEN

Wednesday morning, a few minutes before six, Harry moved along the upstairs hall, the heels of his leather slippers slapping the bare wood floor, boards creaking, from the master bedroom to Joyce's room. He pulled the covers back and crawled in with her and waited for her to open her eyes. After about a minute, when he couldn't wait anymore, Harry said, "You awake?"

Now they were looking into each other's eyes from the edge of one pillow to the next. She said, "What?" And then, "What is it?" with a note of alarm in her voice.

"Nothing."

She closed her eyes and after a few moments opened them again. They stared at each other.

"Everything's okay?"

"Fine, quiet."

"You're all right?"

"Reach down and see."

He felt her hand slip inside his pajama pants.

"Aw, you brought me a present."

"It's still there?"

"Sorta."

He waited.

She said, "It's coming back."

"Your magic touch."

She said, "I've been here three days, and this is the first time you've made any kind of move."

"We've had a lot on our minds."

"We don't anymore?"

"It's different now," Harry said. He'd awakened this morning with a hard-on, which hadn't happened yesterday or the day before. That was one difference.

She said, "Because Raylan's here?"

In the bedroom across the hall, or else downstairs. He and Robert Gee were taking care of security, dividing the watch between them, making up rules about going outside or turning lights on in certain rooms. Harry had to admit Raylan being here also made a difference, and said so.

"It's not that I like him personally; I can't see us becoming buddies. But I'll say this, you know he's one of the good guys."

"And the bad guys," Joyce said, "are still after you. So things aren't that different."

"No, but I feel like I've got more of a choice in the matter. I can go back if I want. Unless he's giving me a bunch of shit. If I had a phone I'd call Torres and find out for sure." Harry was quiet for several moments, feeling Joyce's magic hand on him. He said, "What do you think?" Meaning, did she think he was ready to perform.

She said, "I think Raylan's telling the truth. He's not here as a cop trying to extradite you. He has nothing to gain."

"Outside of some self-respect. He could be getting back at me. Twice, you know, I made him look pretty dumb."

"He was glad to see you," Joyce said. "I could tell."

"Of course he was."

"You know what I mean. He wasn't gloating. He likes you, he was glad he got here before those other guys."

Raylan had scared hell out of them last night

and almost got shot sneaking up on the house and around through the garden. Robert Gee had aimed a shotgun through the French doors of the library and blown half the leaves off an orange tree. He was about to fire again when Raylan yelled out who he was and Joyce recognized his voice. Someone Harry knew, all right, the same U.S. marshal last seen at Joe's Stone Crab telling stories, now arrives like Santa with Joyce's purse, her passport, her clothes, and full of good cheer about a dispensation, the wheels turning to get his murder charge dropped. Though according to Raylan, he'd still have to show up in court.

"The guy brought you your stuff," Harry said, "that's why you like him."

She said, "Harry, just the idea—you know what I mean? That he even thought of *doing* it. With those guys watching him. It's the most considerate thing anyone's ever done for me."

Oh? Was that right?

She didn't have to overdo it.

Harry said, "He's used to picking up suitcases, doing the heavy work. It's the kind of law enforcement he's in. Guarding, watching over people, taking them from here to there. He carried my bag that time in Atlanta. I bet I could talk him into working for me. Start in the garden, get it cleaned up. First, though, I'm going to talk to him about sneaking you out of here, put you on a plane."

"It wouldn't work, Harry. They've seen me."

"There might be a way."

She said, "You remember Cyd Charisse?"

"In the movies? Yeah, the dancer. But I don't recall what she looks like."

"Because she looks different every time you see her," Joyce said. "There was a story about her in *People* I read on the way over. Four pictures of her and she looked like a different person in each one."

"She was married to Tony Martin."

"She still is. The point is," Joyce said, "if I were Cyd Charisse I could walk past them in broad daylight, it wouldn't matter. I'd look different than I did before. But since I'm not Cyd Charisse, Harry, I think we'll all be going back together. You know you'll have to sooner or later."

"That's what he says, but I don't think the cops or the state attorney care one way or the other. Nobody's investigating Jimmy Cap anymore. Pretty soon no one'll even remember how this whole thing got started. Next year some reporter from *The Miami Herald* will come over here to interview me, do a story . . . 'Whatever

Happened to Harry?' You wait and see. In the meantime, how we coming down there?"

"I think we're losing it."

"You sure?"

He waited.

"It's not going to work, Harry."

He made a face.

"Nuts."

Robert Gee told Raylan, "That hat's *you*," saying Raylan knew how to wear it, just a touch over one eye. Raylan told Robert Gee he'd almost shot it off his head last night. "I felt the breeze."

They were in the kitchen now, 6:30 A.M., cleaning weapons: the two pistols Raylan had taken off Nicky and the Italian guy, his own revolvers, Robert Gee's Browning auto, his pump-action Remington, and the Beretta he'd gotten for Harry who kept leaving it, Robert Gee said, anyplace he sat down. They talked about serving in the military as they adapted to one another, Raylan learning you could use a made-up name in the French Foreign Legion, but they sent your prints to Interpol and if you were wanted anywhere they threw you out. This was at Aubagne near Marseilles before they sent you to Corsica for sixteen weeks of basic training. "Running your ass all over the countryside." Raylan asked

was it as tough as Marine boot camp, as seen in
the movie *Full Metal Jacket* and he had experi-
enced. Robert Gee said it was like that only
worse, 'cause they said all that bullshit to you in
French. The officers and most of the guys being
French, the rest East Germans, Portuguese, Span-
ish, Yugoslav, hardly any brothers. He said they
didn't wear those hats with the hankies to keep
the sun off your neck or shoot Arabs anymore.
"You see *Beau Geste*? You wonder now why they
were shooting those Arabs, huh? From the fort
waaay out in the middle of the desert, nobody
even living around there?" He said if you used
your real name and could prove it, they'd let you
become a French citizen when you got out. Robert Gee told them no thanks. He had been in the
U.S. Army and served a tour in Vietnam while
Raylan spent his Marine hitch at Parris Island on
the rifle range, instructing. Robert Gee did five
years in the Foreign Legion in Corsica and Djibouti while Raylan was in South Georgia at the
training academy. Robert Gee, Raylan decided,
knew how to soldier. But could he shoot?

Robert Gee said, "I'm better than fair."

Raylan said, "Then why didn't you kill me
last night?"

*   *   *

They talked about the house, how to defend it, walking through the ground-floor rooms studying views from the windows, fields of fire, and agreed it couldn't be done. Four marines or legionnaires with automatic weapons might hold out a few days if they never slept. The four here now would never make it, one to each side of the house, no communication between them. Knock one out, it was over. The Zip could bring a gang of people, put the place under siege. Feint coming in the back and drive a car through the front door. There were all kinds of ways in.

Robert Gee said, "So what do you think?"

Raylan said, "We got no choice, have to make a run. What's on the other side of Montallegro?"

"Nothing, goat trails. You go back down the way you came. Go to the police, if you get that far, what do you tell them? These guys are picking on us? These Italian guys with thirty million lire to give away? The police won't move till a crime's been committed. You know that."

"They might've already been contacted by Miami Beach PD," Raylan said.

And they might not have.

So think of something. Work out a way to make a run.

In the meantime try to make the place look

vacant. Keep the shutters closed. No smoke coming out of the chimneys. Try to keep Harry from going outside. Make a run or before you know it the Zip's people would be by to check. Knocking on the front door or poking around looking for the cars, a gray one and a blue one. It would happen within a few days at the latest; there weren't that many villas up here that a wealthy bookmaker might lease. Raylan had found the house asking around. The Zip could do the same, check real estate offices in town, find the one Harry used. That wouldn't be too hard.

"The first thing we'd have to do," Raylan said, "is get a different car. Trade the Fiat in on something bigger and faster."

Robert Gee said, "Get a Mercedes like they have, case they want to race." He said, "Why couldn't I do it? They don't know me."

Raylan said, "You sure?"

"Walk over to Montallegro and take the *funivia* down. Nothing to it. Get the car at Avis and drive it up here."

Raylan shook his head. "They've seen you before."

"When? The only time would be when I picked up Joyce at the café. You were there. They wouldn't have even noticed me till she got in the car and by the time they turn their heads we're gone."

"You met Joyce in Milan."

"That's right, but I didn't see anybody follow her. I checked to make sure."

"How'd they know to come here?"

That stopped him.

"They must've followed you. Or they saw her get in the car in Milan. . . ."

"Maybe. But it don't mean they got a good look at me. See," Robert Gee said, "I get to town I can put on my North African outfit, sell a few umbrellas and shit. You need a watch? I can do it today. Get a Mercedes, a Lancia, Alfa-Romeo, slip back up here tonight and I'll go with you as far as Milan or Rome or wherever you want to go. That'll terminate my employment as a bodyguard, and not any too soon. All the man does is fuss with me, keeps saying I'm gonna sell him out. Joyce says 'cause he's drinking again, it's the way he gets. Yeah, well, I don't need the aggravation. I don't even know what I'm doing here. Risk getting my ass shot off for what?"

"Didn't you make a deal with him?"

"I'm saying the man irritates me, that's all."

Raylan said, "If it turns out the Zip does know who you are and he puts his gun in your face, would you tell him where Harry is?"

Robert Gee frowned at him. He said, "Man, what kind of a question is that?"

Harry wished Joyce would leave the kitchen for a minute, go to the toilet or something so he could slip a shot of brandy into his coffee. No, she kept flitting around acting domestic, toasting bread in that medieval-looking oven and bringing it to them at the table that must have been as old as the house, a long oak table full of stains and knife scars. Joyce would put a plate of toast down in front of Raylan and he'd grin like he loved it burnt to a crisp. He had his hat off, for the first time in Harry's presence that he could recall, and was surprised to see the guy had hair, dark brown and cut fairly short, down on his forehead. They had coffee with boiled milk. Harry was the only one who passed on the toast and was dipping his bread in a saucer of olive oil. Mmmmm. He was in a good mood, in spite of not having gotten laid this morning; it was close.

"Coffee's not bad, is it?"

They both nodded.

"Where is he, anyway?"

They both looked at him again.

"Robert Gee. My cook."

"Watching the road," Raylan said. "We're going to have to take turns till we leave."

Something they hadn't discussed yet. Leaving. Harry hadn't made up his mind yet how to react to the idea. He said, "You're sure he hasn't sneaked off."

Neither of them said anything. They liked Robert and trusted him. Harry said, "Why wouldn't he tell where I am to save his own skin? Or for more money?"

Joyce said, "Why wouldn't any of us? You're so much fun to be with. This was not a good idea, Harry."

"What wasn't?"

"Coming to Italy. You know where you should go to retire? Las Vegas, it's more your style."

Harry turned to Raylan.

"Almost my entire life, all I think about is coming here someday. I save my money, plan for forty-seven years. . . . Did I tell you that?"

"In Atlanta," Raylan said. "At that time it was forty years you'd been thinking about it."

"But my friend here, after giving it some thought—how long, a couple of minutes?—says it's a bad idea, I should be in Vegas."

"Or stay home and retire," Joyce said. "You're Miami Beach, Harry. I think you miss it already." She said to Raylan, "You know what he does? He plays a tape of people calling in bets. You know what I mean? Phone calls he recorded."

Harry said, "I played it once," as Joyce got up from the table, "that's all, and you happened to hear it."

"Where is it, Harry?"

"In the bedroom. I don't even know why I had it in my bag. Robert happened to have a radio that plays tapes. . . ."

The moment Joyce was out of the kitchen Harry got up from the table, ducked into the pantry, and came out with a bottle of Galliano. He'd have one straight up, out in the open rather than slipping brandy or sambuca into his coffee, and if she said anything he'd tell her this was his house and if she didn't like it . . . But she wouldn't say anything. Not right away. Or never if he had just one drink. Two at the most. He raised the bottle to Raylan, who shook his head.

"I tried it last night. It taste like medicine."

"For what ails you," Harry said, getting a stem glass from the sink and bringing it to the table with the tall slender bottle of yellow liqueur. Busy busy. Talkative too.

"You say we can't defend this place. Why not?"

Pouring himself a generous one. Now taking a good sip.

"The house's too big."

Harry felt the sweet warmth of the alcohol seeping down to his stomach. He said, "You learn to do what you have to. I'd feel better if Joyce wasn't here. I invite her for a visit and look who she brings." Harry grinned.

Raylan didn't. Serious even with his official hat off.

Harry shrugged. "They have nothing against her, or you or Robert. I'm the only one they want."

"They come in here," Raylan said, "they aren't leaving anybody to tell what happened."

Harry sipped his Galliano. He said, "Twice before this, you might recall, guys have come to kill me and I shot them both. I throw that out for what it's worth. Or in case you feel I'm inexperienced. I might ask *you*, since you seem to be the expert in these matters, when the last time was you shot anybody."

"Yesterday," Raylan said.

Joyce came in with the portable radio, the tape already in place. She plugged it into an outlet on the counter and turned it on, looking at Raylan and then at the tall bottle of Galliano on the table. She didn't look at Harry.

"Hello, Mike? One of the missing. It's Jerry."

"Hey, how you doing, Jerry?"

"Not bad. What's the Saints today?"

"New Orleans? Seven."

"How about the Forty-niners?"

"Four."

"Okay, gimme the Saints and the Niners."

"Niners and New Orleans ten times reverse?"

"Right."

"Harry's idea of a good time," Joyce said. Raylan asked who Mike was and Joyce said one of Harry's sheet writers. Another one came on.

"Mike, Al, from South Miami."

"Yeah, go ahead, Al."

"The Bears ten times, the Giants fifteen times. Okay, then gimme the Eagles, Bears, and Steelers, nine-dollar round robin, twenty-seven-dollar bet. Okay, also the Oilers five times and the Cowboys five times."

"I got it."

"Tampa Bay four times."

"Yeah."

"The Falcons, the Eagles and the Broncos, nine-dollar round robin."

"Got it."

Silence.

"Mike, Billy. Too early?"

"No. Who do you want, kid?"

"Billy Marshall," Harry said, "works for the *Herald*."

"Niners minus four eight times. Detroit minus three forty times."

"Got it."

"And New Orleans minus seven ten times if Denver ten times. You have a figure for me?"

"Asking what he owes to date," Harry said.

"Just a second. Yeah, Billy? Five fifty."

"I'll see you during the week."

"Okay, you've got the Niners forty times, Detroit forty times and the Saints ten if Denver ten."

"Right. Have a nice day, Mike."

"Hello."

"Mike, Joe Deuce."

"Yeah, Joe."

"Gimme the Lions and the Forty-niners twenty times reverse, Bears a nickel, Chargers a nickel, Giants five times, New England ten times and the Browns twenty. Mike, I'll get back to you."

"Hello."

"Mike, it's Mitch."

"How you doing?"

"Mitchell."

"Yeah, I know who it is. Go ahead."

"He's a lawyer," Harry said, "in Broward."

"I want a thirty-dollar parlay."

"Yeah?"

"What're the Oilers?"

"Houston, fifteen."

"The Saints?"

"Seven."

"Seven?"

"Yeah, what do you want?"

"A thirty-dollar parlay. I told you."

"I mean who?"

"What?"

"Fucking lawyer," Harry said.

"Who do you want?"

"Both of them, the Oilers and the Saints."

"That's enough," Harry said, "turn it off. The same old shit over and over. And you think I want to go back to that?"

"In a minute," Joyce said.

Robert Gee said, "Okay, this is how it is. We got to leave here, right?"

Raylan nodded, since no one else was going to say anything.

"And the sooner we leave," Robert Gee said, "the better. Before they come looking."

They were in the front sitting room where Robert Gee had been keeping watch by the window and called them to come out there. It was going on eleven. He said, "Okay. I go get the car right now, no more talking about it. Or I quit, I walk out of here and you all can do what you like. I said before, I don't want to be here when they come, and nobody else should be either. So tell me right now."

Harry said, "You'll want your pay before you leave."

Raylan saw Joyce shake her head with a tired expression and then seem to grit her teeth. She said, "Harry—"

As Robert said, "Yeah, I want my pay. Why wouldn't I? I don't work for free."

"I know," Harry said, "you sell your services."

Joyce went after him again. "Harry, goddamn it—"

He stopped her with his innocent look. "What? I want to pay Robert what he has coming," Harry said, "and give him a credit card. I'm paying for the car, aren't I?"

Joyce seemed ready to jump on him again, but didn't say anything. Robert Gee didn't, either, till Harry handed him his money and said, "We square?"

"We square," Robert Gee said.

Handing him the credit card then, Harry said, "Don't forget to give this back to me."

After that Robert Gee didn't acknowledge him in any way, looking like he'd had enough of Harry to last him and anxious to get out of here. He touched Joyce's arm and said something to her Raylan didn't hear. Then looked toward Raylan and nodded.

Harry said, "Am I allowed to ask what time you'll be back?"

Raylan didn't think Robert Gee was going to answer him. He didn't until he was walking out. All he said was, "By dark."

Joyce got on him again, telling Harry he must be crazy and Harry put on his surprised look, innocent.

"What did I do?"

"Antagonizing him like that."

Raylan got into it saying, "It isn't how you treat a man that's going to help you out of a spot."

Joyce said, "If Robert takes off I wouldn't blame him."

Harry didn't seem to care what they were

saying. He walked over to a window in the south wall of the sitting room that offered a view, standing close to the panes of glass and looking west, of the green countryside sloping away from the villa.

His back to them he said, "I told you about Ezra Pound and his wife living with his mistress, Olga Rudge? In Sant' Ambrogio, over that way. The Germans kicked them out of their apartment and they had nowhere else to go, no money, he only got three hundred and fifty lire for his radio talks . . . the ones that got him in trouble. He claimed they were critical of Roosevelt and Truman, but not profascist. He did think Mussolini was a good guy though. When Mussolini and his girlfriend, Clara Petacci, were hung up by their heels in Milan, Ezra Pound called it 'the enormous tragedy of the dream in the peasant's bent shoulders,' in a poem he wrote. But can you imagine a man living in the same house with his wife and mistress? The three of them were together almost a year, until our army came through here on the way to Genoa. Ezra Pound went down to Rapallo looking for an officer, to give himself up or volunteer his services, I'm not sure which. He couldn't find anyone who knew who he was, or cared. A colored enlisted man tried to sell him a bicycle."

Harry turned from the window, Raylan and Joyce watching him. "The next day," Harry said, "Italian partisans picked him up and handed him over to the army. By the time I saw him he'd been arrested for treason, giving comfort to the enemy, and was being held in a cage."

"And that's why we're here," Joyce said. "You believe it?"

NINETEEN

A few days before Ezra Pound tried to give himself up or offer his services or whatever he was doing, Harry passed through Rapallo with a recon platoon from the 473rd Infantry Regiment. It was April 26, 1945.

He said they took some German prisoners in Santa Margherita and went on to Genoa, where about four thousand Germans surrendered the next day. Harry said he had been trained as a tank crewman at Camp Bowie, Texas, and went to Italy to join the Second Armored Group as a replacement. As soon as he got there the Group was disbanded and reformed as part of the 473rd. Harry was assigned to the Intelligence & Reconnaissance platoon as the lieutenant's driver. He was twenty years old.

"The war was almost over," Harry said, "so during the next couple months they had us rounding up deserters. There were some famous ones like the Lane Gang, a bunch of guys that stole all kinds of army supplies and sold them on the black market. Clothes, trucks, jeeps, everything. Others were soldiers who'd committed serious crimes and were wanted fugitives. Any deserters we caught we'd take to the Army Disciplinary Training Center, a military stockade they had not far from Pisa, between there and Viareggio. We were here in Rapallo looking for deserters working the black market when we picked up the guy from the 92nd, the one I shot, but didn't find out till later he was wanted for murder. He'd raped a woman and cut her throat. Temporarily we had him locked in a storeroom in the hotel we were using as headquarters, on the Piazza Garibaldi. This one time, because I happened to be standing there, in the lobby, the sergeant picks me to relieve the soldier guarding the storeroom, so he could go to chow. I'm going down the hall and who do I see coming toward me but the guy, the deserter, with the carbine he'd taken off the guy I was going to relieve. Coming fast, to club me with the gun rather than shoot me and let everybody know he'd escaped. Coming at me as I'm reaching for my sidearm, clearing it, a round already in the chamber. I know that 'cause it was the way I kept it. That guy in the parking lot last month . . . No, it was in October, wasn't it? He stopped when I pulled the gun. This one didn't, the deserter, he kept coming, raising the carbine to club me with it when I shot him and it stopped him. I shot him again and that one knocked him down. He'd killed the guard, so we never found out how he got the carbine away from him.

"A couple of weeks later, on May twenty-ninth, we delivered a deserter to the Disciplinary Training Center and that was the day I saw Ezra Pound for the first time, scruffy looking, like a skid-row bum inside one of the maximum security cells, where they kept the violent prisoners and the ones condemned to death. They had reinforced the cell Ezra Pound was in with steel wire mesh. He called it a gorilla cage and it did look like one. It sat on a concrete slab about six by ten, had a slanted roof, and was open on four sides, so the rain could come in from any direction. Other prisoners had pup tents inside their cages. All Ezra had the first few weeks were a couple of blankets. They kept a spotlight on him at night and no one was supposed to talk to him. You see," Harry said, "hardly anyone there knew he was a world-famous poet. The camp officials were told he was a traitor and to keep a close watch so he didn't try to escape or commit suicide. There was also talk the Fascists might try to rescue him. Finally, after a while, they eased up and moved him to the medical compound. They let him use a desk so he could continue writing his poetry."

"His *Cantos*," Joyce said. "He spent forty years writing a poem that hardly anyone in the world can understand."

" 'No man who has passed a month in the death cells,' " Harry said, " 'believes in cages for beasts.' You don't understand that?"

Joyce said, "Once in a while he made sense."

"He was a genius," Harry said.

"He was a racist," Joyce said, "and viciously anti-Semitic. He thought Hitler was right about the Jews; he said they started the war. He called Roosevelt President Rosenfeld."

Harry shrugged. "He said later that was a big mistake, those views, talking like that."

"He said later the *Cantos* were a mess, too, stupid all the way through," Joyce said. "I read

the books you gave me, Harry. Don't forget
that."

"He was old then," Harry said, but without
much conviction.

Raylan wondered how often they had this
discussion, Harry defending his hero, Joyce tear-
ing him down. There was a silence and Raylan
said, "You spoke to him, that time in the prison
camp?"

Harry nodded. "Once. I asked him how he
was doing. He said he was watching a wasp
build a house with four rooms. I saw him again a
month later, after he'd been transferred to the
medical compound. He was sitting at a desk typing. I'd heard that he wrote letters for prisoners
who were illiterate. They liked him, called him
Uncle Ez. Anyway, he was typing something, I
asked him how he was doing. This twenty-year-
old kid talking to Ezra Pound. He looked at me
and, while he was still typing, said, 'The ant's a
centaur in his dragon world. Pull down thy van-
ity. . . .' I said, 'What?' But now he was staring
at what he'd typed. 'The ant's a centaur . . .' I
remembered the line and found it three years
later in a book of his poetry, *The Pisan Cantos*, in
number Eighty-one."

Joyce said, "Does it make sense to you?"
Still after him.

Raylan thinking, It doesn't have to make sense. Not to Harry.

As Harry said again, "The man was a genius."

"You're taking someone else's word for that."

"Sure, why not?"

"A genius, and more than a little nuts."

"That too," Harry said. "But it got him off, didn't it? His friends said he had to be crazy to have made so big a fool of himself."

Joyce looked at Raylan. "You know what happened to him?"

Raylan shook his head. He knew the name, Ezra Pound, and that was about it. Following the trip to Atlanta he'd tried reading some of the man's poetry and had given up, telling himself he was too dumb. He was glad to hear hardly anyone else understood it either.

"He was declared insane," Joyce said. "Instead of doing time for treason he was sent to St. Elizabeths Hospital in Washington, D.C."

"Twelve years in St. Liz's bughouse," Harry said. "No way to treat the old darling of the U.S. expatriate intelligentsia. I think it was *Time* magazine called him that." He said to Raylan, "You know that hat you wear? There's a picture of Ezra wearing one just like it in one of my books.

I'll show it to you, taken in Rome in 1960." He looked at Joyce and said, "In the library by the big chair, the only good one in the house. You'll see two biographies there and a book of poetry, *Selected Cantos.*"

"Dinklage, where art thou,
         with, or without, your *von*?
You said the teeth of the black troops
         reminded you of the boar-hunt,
I think yr/first boar hunt, but
The black prisoners had such a nice way
with children,
Also what's his name who spent the night in
the air
caught in the mooring ropes.
                    Lone rock for sea-gull
who can, in any case, rest on water!
Do not Hindoos
                    lust after vacuity?"

Joyce closed the book with her finger marking the place. "You want me to go on?"

"You mean," Harry said, with his deadpan expression, "you don't understand that? A very nice reading, Joyce, we should have some wine and cheese with it."

She said, "It almost makes sense and then loses you. First I had to find a passage that's in English." She said to Raylan, "Some of it's in Italian, Greek, and he'll throw in Chinese characters every once in a while."

"He had a Chinese dictionary with him," Harry said, "and a book of Confucius, when they threw him in the cage. Show Raylan the photographs in the biographies. The gorilla cage, pictures of his wife Dorothy and Olga Rudge. The bigger book has the picture of Ezra Pound wearing the hat like Raylan's, taken in Rome in 1960. I remember that because after they let him out of St. Elizabeths he couldn't wait to come back here. Listen to this, with Dorothy and another girlfriend forty years younger than he was, Marcella, he thought he was in love with and ought to marry once he divorced Dorothy. What happened, Dorothy teamed up with Olga, who was still in Italy, and they sent Marcella packing. Then, it wasn't long after that he became depressed about his work, wouldn't eat or talk much. Dorothy gave up trying to take care of him and he came here to live with Olga, where I saw him again," Harry said, "in sixty-seven. Three days in a row, in fact, I saw them at the same café, Ezra Pound and his mistress, always with a group having lunch. Anytime I saw him there were people with him, friends, or writers getting interviews. Poets flocked around him. There always seemed to be a party at lunch, everybody laughing and talking. One time when I was at the next table, he had some kind of fish and complained about the bones the whole time he was eating it. That same day, I followed him to the men's room, got ahead of him, and held the door open. As he reached me I said, 'The ant's a centaur in his dragon world.' He looked at me and walked right past into the can, didn't say a word. So, that was okay. He had people bothering the shit out of him all the time. They'd come and ring the bell, tourists, and Olga Rudge would tell them, 'If you can recite one line of his poetry you can see him.' She'd turn a hose on them if they wouldn't leave." He said to Joyce, "We should be having lunch. Isn't it time?"

She said, "We have cheese and sausage. Some kind of cold pasta Robert put together."

Harry was going through one of the biographies. He said to Raylan, "Here, this is what he looked like when I last saw him. He was eighty-two then. Look at the hat. You ever see a brim like that? The coat and the walking stick; the coat's like a cape. The guy had style right up to the end, eighty-seven when he died in Venice the night of his birthday. Olga was there with him. Here's a picture of her. Good-looking woman, uh? They were together fifty years. Here, this is the one. At his wake, Olga touching him I guess for the last time. Born in Hailey, Idaho, died in Venice." He said to Joyce, "We going to have lunch or not?" He handed the book to Raylan and watched him turn to the photographs of the gorilla cages and the military stockade. "I went back there on one of my trips," Harry said. "You know what's there now? A nursery where they grow roses. Another time in Rapallo, you know who I saw? Groucho Marx."

They left Raylan to go out to the kitchen and fix lunch.

It was right after that, alone by the window, he saw a dark-colored Mercedes sedan drive past. Black or dark blue, he wasn't sure. The car slowed to a crawl, Raylan watching it until it was out of sight. He waited awhile before looking at the gorilla cages again.

Joyce came back with sandwiches. Harry had two glasses of wine on top of the Galliano and was taking a nap.

She said, "You'd think if he was going to recite poetry it would be someone more like . . .

I was going to say Edgar Guest and it reminded me of that Dorothy Parker line, 'I'd rather fail my Wasserman test than read a poem by . . .' Do you know what I'm talking about?"

Raylan nodded, eating the sausage-and-cheese sandwich. "So far."

"Harry picks a guy who wrote the most obscure poetry I've ever read. Nothing that makes sense, but Harry won't admit it."

"I don't think whether he understands it or not," Raylan said, "matters to him."

"I know, but he pretends he does. Now," Joyce said, "he even makes it sound as though he recognized the guy in the cage as Ezra Pound and was the only person in the camp that knew who he was. Harry might've known the name, but it was after the war he looked Ezra Pound up and found out, my God, this guy's famous. And started reading his work, if you can imagine, the Miami Beach bookie feeling some kind of rapport with the world-renowned poet who might be a little nuts. The next thing you know Harry returns to Rapallo. Comes back again, and again, and finally twenty years after seeing Ezra Pound in a cage, there he is again, an old dude now but still with that flair, the black hat and walking stick, a man who'd been dining with his mistress at sidewalk cafés all his life and Harry wanted to do it, too, see what it was like."

Raylan said, "And the bad guys came and ruined it for him."

"Even if they hadn't," Joyce said, "Harry would have changed his mind about sidewalk cafés. It's one thing to sip Galliano with an espresso on a nice day and watch the girls go by. But it can get cold and damp and the girls put on coats, the ones still around. On top of that he has trouble communicating and shouldn't drink, not even coffee. What Harry found out was, he's too late for sidewalk cafés. I don't think he'd last more than a few weeks, even with the sun out. Harry might be a romantic at heart, but he's a practical kind of guy, too, set in his ways. When he called and asked me to come? He tells me how much he misses me, he can't wait. And then he says, 'Oh, yeah, and bring me a couple bottles of after-shave. Caswell-Massey Number Six.' "

Raylan said, "That's after-shave?"

"His favorite."

"It sounds more like an East Kentucky coal mine."

He was alone again in the sitting room, looking around, wondering if he could live in a place like this, a museum with ceilings higher than he'd ever seen inside a house, and not a chair or table you dared put your feet on. Harry was right about the chairs, Harry dying to be left alone so he could get smashed. Put him in the car and go. Fly out of some other city besides Milan or Rome. Joyce had left to take the lunch dishes to the kitchen and check on Harry. She was easy to talk to. He'd asked if she and Harry were planning on getting married and she said, "Are you crazy?" Told him a couple of weeks in the same villa with Harry would be about all she could manage. She had been married to a real estate salesman less than a year when he divorced her. Raylan had said, "Well, we have something in common," and told about his wife, Winona, divorcing him for a real estate salesman. Joyce said maybe, like her marriage, it wouldn't last and he and Winona would get back together. He told her it would never happen; he missed his boys but not his ex, not for a minute. And was glad he'd made that clear. If it happened he and Joyce ever started keeping company, he didn't want complications in the way.

She should be back any minute.

Raylan looked from the doorway out into the front hall to the window again and saw the dark-colored Mercedes coming from the other direction, from Montallegro, creeping along. He thought it was going to stop, but it turned in the drive and was coming toward the house now. Dark blue, like the one those guys drove.

TWENTY

The time Robert Gee quit working for the Kuwaiti sheik they were in Cannes during the Film Festival, the sheik looking to meet movie stars. Robert Gee finally had enough of the man's shit and left him sitting in his stretch in the middle of traffic: said fuck it, got out and walked away, the sheik calling him nasty names as he joined the crowd that was causing the traffic jam, everybody wanting to see the starlet who'd taken her shirt off. It was the sheik telling him how to drive that got to him. To do what the man said Robert Gee would've had to kill people walking in the street. He looked at the rearview mirror thinking, You want to drive, raghead? But only said "Fuck it" out loud before he quit. The man was abusive: treated Asian girls working for him like slaves, liked to beat up on them. Robert Gee was afraid he might let go and deck the man sometime and end up in a Kuwaiti prison. So he'd walked away and felt good, even though it was dumb to leave without getting paid first.

This time he had money, he had Harry's Visa card, and if he walked away it would serve the man right for acting nasty to him. If it was just Harry up there in the villa he might even consider doing it, but not with Joyce and Raylan there, they never did anything to him. He didn't owe them his life, though, if it came to that. Like, tell us where they're at or we'll kill you. That kind of situation. He wasn't going to die for them. They wouldn't expect him to anyway. Raylan would know that if he wasn't back by dark, then something had happened to him and they had better move their asses out of that house quick.

Robert Gee settled all that in his mind riding down from Montallegro in the *funivia*, getting an aerial view of the town and then some close looks into apartment windows as the cable car neared the station. The room he rented was on this side of town. He thought of looking in to check on his umbrellas and jewelry and shit, stuff he'd bought off a Tunisian leaving the wannabuy business, going home. And then thought, Check on it for what? It was still there or it wasn't, all that junky stuff. Selling it was more something to do than a way to make a living. He sure couldn't live off the proceeds like the African dudes did, happy to have a chunk of hash to smoke and that sticky sweet tea they drank. Maybe give all the wannabuy shit away and go home, back to Houston, Texas, where all the northern people had left when the oil business went to hell and the ones that stayed were living under overpasses in cardboard boxes.

He thought of that riding across town in a taxicab, over to the Avis office on della Libertà.

Kiss his mama, hang around the house awhile and be gone before she got used to him, off across some ocean to offer his experience. He could drill to French with a German accent and field-strip Belgian FNs, Austrian Steyrs, versions of the AR15, both the Soviet and Chinese AK47s, the Valmet, the Sterling—name an automatic weapon—and was certain he could find a war somewhere that would accept him.

Two Avis men behind the counter, Robert Gee their only customer, and it took them close to a half hour to get a contract ready for him to sign. They said they weren't sure they had a Mercedes. Robert Gee said, what was that out front, the white one? They had to make a phone call in the office, they said to check on the credit card, Robert Gee hoping to God the man wasn't talking to who Robert Gee suspected he might be talking to. By the time he walked outside with the keys, ready to go, two guys were leaning against the car with their arms folded, trying to act cool. Robert Gee said, "Shit," as the one unfolded his arms to show the pistol he was holding and the other one said to the Avis guys, "*Grazie.*"

Raylan stood by the front door putting his hat on, getting it to sit lightly where it felt good, down some on his right eye. He put his hand on the doorknob, still not sure if he wanted to meet them outside or in the house, and heard Joyce in that same moment call to him.

"Raylan?" From the front stairs. She was about halfway up. "A car just pulled in the yard."

Raylan nodded. "I saw it."

"You're going *out*?"

"I was thinking about it." He wanted her to

stay calm. So far she sounded more surprised than excited. "Where's Harry?"

"He's asleep." She said, "Raylan, if we're quiet they won't know we're here."

"No, 'less they come in."

She said, "Stay with us," and it sounded like a better idea than going outside.

He watched her rear end go up the stairs ahead of him in blue jeans, a nice compact one, he had noticed before. Upstairs in the hall she said, "You were really going out there?" Still having trouble accepting it.

"Try to come up behind them," Raylan said. "I think since we're going to have words, it would be good to get a position on them. Some kind of advantage."

She stopped at an open doorway.

"Have *words*?"

"Show 'em they can't win."

"Or shoot them?"

"I don't know."

She said, "I have to get my gun," and went into her bedroom.

Raylan went on to Harry's room. He was stretched out on the bed with his mouth open, not exactly snoring, making a wheezing sound. Harry's pistol was on the night table next to the bed. Raylan moved to a window.

They were in the side yard, out of the Mercedes now, going toward the garage, the structure with the three heavy wooden doors, all padlocked. He watched the two guys pull on the locks and then look this way, toward the house.

Joyce came in saying, "There're fifteen shots in this?"

Making it sound like a simple question. He glanced over his shoulder at Joyce holding the Beretta he'd given her, Nicky's or Fabrizio's, inspecting it closely: a foreign object to someone who'd never fired a gun.

"Fifteen in the magazine and one in the throat, that's sixteen," Raylan said. "When it's empty the slide opens and that's it, you're done. But I doubt you'll have to shoot. Don't, okay? 'Less you have no other choice."

"How do I know when that is?"

"You see if you don't shoot you're gonna die. Then, squeeze the trigger. Don't yank on it."

"Take a breath first and let some of it out," Joyce said.

"Yeah, well, I wouldn't try to remember everything I told you. Just make sure the safety's off and hold the weapon in two hands."

Raylan turned to the window again.

"It looks like they're trying to find a rock, something they can bust those locks with and take a look in the garage. The one's the same guy that was driving the Mercedes the other day. Had on a white shirt? He's wearing a striped one today. No coat. The other one's wearing a suit coat that looks too small for him." Raylan didn't mention the guy's cut-down double-barreled shotgun. He said, "I guess you better wake Harry up," and heard her then as he looked out the window.

Her voice sounding calm as she said, "Harry? There's someone here."

Like friends come to pay a visit. Raylan half turned to look past his shoulder. He saw Harry pushing himself up, eyes wide open, Harry in a tan sweater and white socks, Joyce bent over helping him, aiming her good-looking rear end this way—not anywhere near the size of Winona's. It was funny, the things you thought of when you'd never think you would. He watched Joyce straighten and stand with one hand on her hip, the gun in the other, like she knew she had a good-looking behind. Harry reached for his gun on the night table and Joyce told him to put his shoes on first. Raylan liked the sound of that, her voice still calm. Harry looked bewildered, maybe from the Galliano and wine and just waking up. Twice, though, he'd shot a man dead coming at him. One more than you have, Raylan thought. Harry could do it again if he had to.

But then had to ask him, "Harry, you okay?"

"I'm fine."

Raylan looked out the window and turned back to them. "They're coming toward the house." He looked again and said, "Now they're out of sight. I imagine going around back. All the doors are locked. . . ."

He stopped as they heard the sound of glass breaking. A window, or one of the French doors.

"I was going to say, but if they want to come in, they will. Without bothering to knock."

"As soon as they look in the kitchen," Joyce said, "they'll know we're here."

"We could've left," Raylan said, "but you're right, they'll have to search the house."

Both Joyce and Harry were looking at him. Joyce said, "So what do we do?"

They came in through the library and strolled from room to room. The one with the shotgun was called Marco. Like Benno he was from Naples; he didn't think much of the north and had never been to Rapallo before. He thought the sea in the north looked different, a gray color without life in it; the food was bland and the houses were dark, the ones they had searched.

He said to Benno, "There's no one here."

But then had to change his mind when they strolled into the kitchen and saw the bottles on the table, plates in the sink. The stainless coffeemaker was unplugged. But when Benno touched it he jerked his hand away. So, if the people weren't here they had just left. Harry Arno and his people, Benno believed, because the woman in the real estate office said the villa Sr. Arno leased was on this road near Maurizio di Monti and showed them a photograph, an old one, of the place when it was a farm and this could be it. The reason they weren't entirely sure, they didn't have the photograph with them.

Benno had phoned from the car, after passing the villa twice, to say he believed he had found the right one, and was told the African had been taken, the one who drove for Harry Arno. They said to Benno wait and they would find out the location of the house and call him back. But Benno had a feeling this was the one, so they came inside.

Once they left the kitchen they no longer strolled but moved carefully now, thinking of the one in the cowboy hat and remembering Fabrizio sitting in the car with his head against the window, his eyes open, two bullet holes in him. It was Benno who said, "The one with the cowboy hat . . ."

Marco said, "If he's here I have something for him."

So when they came to the front hall Benno motioned to the stairway and Marco, with his double-barreled shotgun, went up ahead of him.

Joyce heard the floor creak and knew they were in the hall now approaching Harry's bedroom. The door was open so they'd look in there first. Look in and see Harry sitting in a chair waiting.

There. It was happening. One of them speaking Italian, surprised. Then silence.

"It has to be Harry sitting there," Raylan had said, "because these two have never seen him before and won't know it's Harry." They'd look in and it would stop them, hold their attention. See, Raylan said, then he'd come from across the hall—where he and Joyce were now—the room with the door closed, creep up behind the two guys talking to Harry, wanting to know who he was, and disarm them.

Getting their attention and holding it, Raylan had said, was the key. Otherwise, where were they going to hide?

Raylan opened the door and Joyce heard the

voice again speaking Italian. Now another one, in English with an accent: the two guys talking to Harry as Raylan crossed the hall, stepping over the board that creaked. Joyce stayed close behind him, entered the room with him, and stopped as Raylan said, "Put the gun on the floor. Right now." Joyce moved to the side, holding the Beretta extended in both hands, the way he had shown her.

The one with the shotgun, the short barrel across his forearm, didn't move. The one in the striped shirt turned enough to see them pointing guns at him from about ten feet away. Raylan approached him and took the automatic the man had stuck in his waist. Raylan said to the one with the shotgun, "You hear me? Put it on the floor. Now."

He still didn't move. The one in the striped shirt said, "Marco don't speak English."

Raylan reached over with his Combat Mag, held the revolver pointed at Marco's ear and cocked it.

"He understand that?"

Marco stooped and placed the shotgun on the floor as the one in the striped shirt said, "He knows a few words."

Harry picked up the shotgun, dug his pistol out of the chair cushions, and came around past the two guys. Joyce thought he looked a little sweaty. But he was still Harry: glancing out the window at the Mercedes and saying, "I see we've got a car."

Joyce said right away, "We have to wait for Robert," and looked at Raylan.

He didn't say anything.

The one in the striped shirt said to Joyce, "You mean his driver, the African? The one brought you here from Milano? You waiting for him, you going to wait a long time."

Joyce looked at Raylan again, expecting him to say something. All he did was stare at the one in the striped shirt, who stared back at him and seemed at ease, as though he had the advantage now.

He said, "I hear on the telephone in my car, they find the African. Looking for a Mercedes, uh? Like the one I drive. So I hear they take him someplace."

Telling it in a casual way, acting almost indifferent now. It got to Joyce. She said, "What do you mean *take* him someplace?"

"Someplace quiet, nobody bothers them."

She said, "For *what*—goddamn it!"

"Why do you think for what? You want to know something he knows, what do you do?"

She said to Raylan, "Jesus, you hear what

he's saying?" and waited. Raylan *still* refused to say one fucking word to the guy: staring at him but not even pointing his gun now. Joyce was pointing hers, holding the muzzle of the Beretta centered on the striped shirt.

"If they have him," Harry said, "then he's told them where I live and that's it, we better get out of here."

The one in the striped shirt was shaking his head, confident. "You too late. Take my word."

"Right now," Harry said, "it's time to leave."

"What we have to *do*," Joyce said, "is find out about Robert."

She saw Raylan look at her and then turn to Harry and take the shotgun from him, Raylan saying, "Whatever you want to bring along, get it ready," and looked at her again. "Can you pack in five minutes?"

She said, "I haven't *un*packed, but I'm not leaving without Robert."

"I'm going to talk to these fellas about that," Raylan said. "See if they can help us out." He said to the one in the striped shirt, "Is that okay with you?"

The man shrugged, indifferent. "I don't know what you talking about."

Raylan said, "What do they call you?"

This time the man hesitated.

"My name's Benno."

"And he's Marco, huh, I think you said? I'm Deputy Marshal Raylan Givens. You know what you two remind me of? Company gun thugs. People the coal operators hire during a strike to cause trouble. Benno, huh? I knew a gun thug in Harlan County, Kentucky, looked just like you, named Byron. Always had a speck of tobacco juice in the corner of his mouth." Raylan touched his lip. "Right here. Well, I'm going to ask you boys to step outside with me, if you will." He turned to Harry, saying, "I need a key to the garage. That door in the middle."

Harry found it in a little box on his dresser and handed it to Raylan no questions asked, Joyce watching, curious, as Raylan motioned to the two men now to come past him. Benno seemed to stroll toward the doorway, hands in his pockets. Marco didn't move until Raylan poked him with the shotgun.

Joyce said, "You're going out to the garage?"

"Someplace quiet," Raylan said, "where nobody'll bother us."

She saw Benno glance around to give Raylan a look, not as confident as before. When they were out of the room Joyce moved to the window. She said to Harry, already taking his clothes out of the armoire, "I think I know him, but I don't at all."

TWENTY-ONE

She heard Harry say, "I don't even know where we're going. I don't care either. I think you're right, I should've gone to Vegas, someplace like that, Tahoe, or stayed home. You hear what I'm saying? Don't tell me I never admit when I'm wrong." Harry busy, animated, saying, "I didn't think it ever got this cold here. You know it?" Saying, "Come on, we have to be ready."

Joyce didn't move from the window.

Finally, there he was in the side yard herding the two gun thugs past the Mercedes parked there, moving them toward the garage. She had never heard that expression before, company gun thugs, but knew what they were, strike-breakers in Kentucky, gangsters here or in South Florida. He'd waited until he had something to say before speaking to them.

Now he was handing something to Benno. The key? That's what it was. She watched Benno remove the lock from the middle garage door and with an effort swing it open a few feet. Raylan waved him out of the way then and motioned for Marco to go inside, into the empty middle area of the garage, between Harry's Lancia and Raylan's rented Fiat. He was in there now and Raylan was talking to Benno, Benno posing, standing in a slouch, one hand on his hip, gesturing with the other, and now Raylan was pointing the shotgun into the garage, holding it with one hand. He would have to be aiming at Marco; though she couldn't see him now. Benno gestured again. Raylan cocked the shotgun.

Joyce said, "Harry, come here, quick."

Benno was shaking his head. "I'm supposed to say, what? Oh, please, no, I do whatever you want. Like I believe you gonna shoot him? Or, I say, Okay, go ahead. But if you gonna do it, then

I want to *see* you do it. You don't shoot in there and I'm supposed to think you killed him." Benno gestured again. "So, go ahead."

"I can't fool you," Raylan said, "can I?"

"Anybody can look at you, know you won't shoot him like this. You don't have the *coglioni*."

"I don't?"

"You think I'm a fool, threaten me like that?"

"I felt it was worth a try."

"I told you I won't do what you want because why should I? Even though I could, because I wouldn't hurt nothing if I did."

"I didn't think it would."

"But you shouldn't have try to force me."

"You're right. So now that we have that cleared up, will you do it?"

Benno paused, as though giving it some thought.

"Okay, but not because you scared me."

"I understand."

"Or because I think you gonna shoot Marco."

"No, I understand that," Raylan said. "You're doing it out of the kindness of your heart."

"That's right. So come on."

They walked back to the Mercedes. Benno

reached in for his telephone and punched a number. He waited, began speaking Italian a mile a minute, and then waited again. Raylan heard a voice say in English, "Yeah, what?" and Benno handed him the phone.

"It's the punk."

Raylan nodded. He said, "Nicky? This is Deputy Marshal Raylan Givens. How you doing?"

He asked Joyce if she'd move the cars out of the garage so he could lock Benno up in there with his buddy. This was in case they knew how to hot-wire a car, start it without the key. Raylan said if they did they could bang Harry's car and his rented Fiat against those old doors till they gave way. After that he explained his plan: what he believed was the only way for them to slip out of the country without getting caught.

Joyce didn't care for the idea.

"Why can't you go with us?"

"If I do, how'm I going to check on Robert?"

"I mean we wait, all go together."

"We wait, none of us'd make it."

Harry said, "Let's get out of here."

By dark they were in the Mercedes headed down the hill, Raylan driving, Harry and Joyce in back, the two of them ducking down as they drove through Maurizio di Monti, past those pale buildings in the dark, light showing in some of the doorways, past a car where a figure stood with his radio, ready to report but not watching for a Mercedes. Raylan's hope, the guy would think it was Benno going by, fast.

Except for Harry it was quiet in the car. His problem, he still believed Robert had told where he lived.

"If he did," Raylan said to the rearview mirror, "they'd have been to the house before we left and we'd have taken our last breath."

Why couldn't he see that?

Harry said, "Which one did you talk to?"

"The young guy, Nicky."

"They try to make Robert tell?"

"He didn't say."

"Why didn't you ask?"

Raylan, steering through one of the hairpin curves, kept quiet.

"But why wouldn't he tell if they asked him?"

"I'll find that out," Raylan said, following his headlight beams. The narrow road and the darkness, no lights anywhere for long spells, reminded him of home.

"They must've at least beat him up," Harry said. "Done something to him out of meanness. I remember hearing one time how the Zip slammed a guy's wang in a car door. You ever hear of anything like that? They made the guy stand outside against the car and somebody inside the car held a string tied to the end of the guy's wang, you know, so it would stick out and they slammed the door on it. You imagine how the guy must've yelled? I get a pain in my stomach thinking about it."

Raylan would look at the mirror trying to catch a glimpse of Joyce, sitting back there in her wool coat not saying a word. She'd said as they were putting the luggage in the car, "I think I know you but I don't." Sounding like it was his fault, and he didn't know what to say to that. Did she want his life history? He could tell her that in about two minutes.

Looking at the mirror he said, "We just passed under the *autostrada* but there's no way to get on it here. I found that out driving around looking for your place."

Harry said, "They have ways of making people talk you wouldn't believe. They'll use an ax, chop off a guy's foot. Start there and work up."

Raylan said, "Maybe they didn't ask him," more to shut Harry up than give an opinion.

"I think Robert would've told them anyway," Harry said. "What I can't understand is why they didn't come."

Raylan let him think what he wanted.

Once they reached the outskirts of Rapallo, Raylan had to feel his way to Corso Mameli, one of the city's main streets. He followed it to Via Savagna, the road that hooked up with the *autostrada*, and started looking for one of the Zip's watchdogs, knowing he would have to be right around here. . . . Saw the car parked at the side of the road and pulled up behind it, a gray Fiat.

Raylan said, "Stay down, okay? Till I handle this," and got out of the car with Marco's sawed-off shotgun.

A figure was coming out of the Fiat speaking Italian, asking a question, it sounded like, a radio in his hand. He reached into the car and brought out a flashlight, still talking Italian in the dark at the side of the road, no cars going by, till Raylan asked him if he spoke English. The guy paused barely a moment and began talking again, putting the flashlight on Raylan. But now Raylan had the shotgun up in the light beam, pointing it at the guy's face, and he shut up.

He didn't speak English.

A couple of minutes later Raylan was standing by the Mercedes, opening the door and telling them it was okay, they could come out. They

acted surprised, looking around as they straightened up and he told them he'd locked the guy in
the truck of his car.

Neither of them said anything, Harry still
looking around in the dark. When they were in
the front seat of the Mercedes, Joyce behind the
wheel, Raylan said through the window, "This
gets you on A-12 north. It goes straight to Genoa.
What you have to do is find the airport and get
on the first plane out of there. I mean no matter
where it goes." When she didn't nod but kept
staring at him he said, "Will you do that?"

Harry came to life. He said, "We'll be okay."

Joyce looked away for a moment to start the
car. Now she was looking at Raylan again and it
gave him a funny feeling.

Harry said, "See you around."

Joyce said, "Take care of yourself."

He said, "Don't worry," and smiled.

She didn't, or even try to.

The Mercedes backed away from him to get
around the Fiat. As the car came forward again
he saw Joyce's face, her solemn expression, the
kind people have in church, and he wondered in
that moment if she was a religious person. Something he hadn't thought of before. Right then he
heard Harry raise his voice to him saying, "I
can't believe you'll find Robert in one piece."

TWENTY-TWO

The gun the Zip got for him was a .32 caliber Targa automatic, six bullets in the magazine. Nicky said, "*Six*, that's all?" And the Zip said, "You know what you're doing it's five more than you need." This was at the apartment where they were staying. Nicky looked the gun over, saw how it worked, and extended it in both hands, closing one eye and aiming at a picture of fruit on the wall nearest him. He turned to aim at something farther away and came to the Zip with his back to him, looking out the window. Nicky held the barrel on the middle of the Zip's back thinking, Man, it would be so easy, *pow*, and that was when the Zip turned around. He didn't act scared or excited seeing the gun pointing at him, so Nicky kept staring as he lowered it, showing the Zip he was cool, showing him it could be done. The Zip said, "There's only one way to shoot a man in the back. In front of a mirror, so he sees you doing it. The way Ed Grossi was shot. You know Ed Grossi, the one ran things before Jimmy Cap? They found him in the bathroom of an apartment he used sometime in Boca Raton. He's on the floor, but there's blood and parts of him all over the mirror, a big mirror, covered the wall. So you know he saw who it was and he saw himself get killed, shot in the back of the head."

That was yesterday.

Today, this afternoon, while they had the colored guy in the next room, Benno called asking for somebody who spoke English and Nicky had the phone handed to him. It was the cowboy saying he knew they had Robert and they had better not harm him. Nicky said, "That's what you called to tell me?" The cowboy said he wanted to talk to the Zip. So then Nicky had to go down the hall to the Zip's apartment and tell him.

The Zip said, "I thought he'd come looking after a while. How's he know we have the colored guy and where'd he get this phone number?"

Nicky said, "Why don't you talk to him?"

The Zip said, "I'm busy."

So Nicky had to go back and forth saying what one said and then what the other said. Should he tell the cowboy nobody had spoken to the colored guy yet or laid a hand on him? (Everybody wondering what the Zip was waiting for.)

The Zip said, "Don't tell him nothing."

Nicky went back to the phone and told him the Zip didn't want to talk to him.

The cowboy said, "Tell him I'll trade him Benno and Marco for Robert Gee. Two for one."

Nicky went back down the hall and told the Zip, who stood in the doorway of his apartment wearing a bathrobe and it looked like nothing under it.

The Zip said, "Tell him he can keep Benno and Marco. He wants to trade Harry he's got a deal. Tell him I been waiting for him to come around. He wants to talk to me, okay, be at that café he goes to and you meet him there. Tell him he can see the colored guy."

"Then what?" Nicky said.

"Bring him here."

The Zip closed the door. He had the whore with the white shoes in there with him.

Raylan had the windshield wipers on low speed, taking off the mist that would collect. The pavement looked dry. He came along Via Veneto to Nicky standing by the curb in the dark, café tables stacked up behind him, Nicky hunching his big shoulders in the leather jacket, stooping to see inside the car. Raylan imagined he'd be grouchy from waiting, standing out in the weather. Even on a good day he was the kind had an ugly disposition.

He opened the door, the first thing he said was, "Where you been? You know how long I've been standing here?" See? Like Raylan cared. Like his purpose in life was to make this asshole happy. Nicky wanted to know where he got this car and whose was it, but didn't wait for an answer. He said he was driving so come on, park it someplace and hurry up. All that bile coming out of him.

Raylan raised the sawed-off shotgun off the seat next to him and said, "Nicky, get in the car."

Nicky stood there, then eased himself in like there might be snakes inside. He closed the door and Raylan threw the shotgun over his shoulder, onto the backseat. Nicky didn't seem to know what to make of that. They were moving now. Raylan said, "All you have to do is tell me how to get where we're going. Can you do that?"

It turned out to be an apartment building up above town, newer than most, with balconies, but small, only three stories; across the street from red clay tennis courts. They got out of the Fiat and Raylan said, "Just a minute." Walked back to the trunk and opened it. The guy climbed out looking around, maybe not sure where he was. Raylan asked if he was okay, but didn't get anything from the guy except a bewildered look. About the same as Nicky's, watching him.

Two other guys came out. They took Raylan's guns and brought him down a hall through the ground floor to the back of the building, unlocked a door and shoved him into what looked like a utility room, bare except for storage lockers and a single light in the ceiling.

Robert Gee sat on the floor with his legs stretched out, his back against the concrete wall.

"They haven't touched you?"
"They haven't even looked mean at me."
"Or asked you anything?"
"Nothing."

"Where'd they get you, on the road?"

"I never got in the car."

"Brought you here. . . . They feed you?"

"Some pasta. It wasn't bad."

"Let you out to go to the bathroom?"

"Have my own. That door over there."

"Nobody else's around? Other people?"

"I haven't seen nobody else."

"What's his game?"

"Man, I'd like to know."

"I thought by now they asked and you told."

"I would've too."

"I know, and I wouldn't blame you."

"But they never gave me the chance. You understand? I even said to the man, 'Hey, ain't there something you want to ask me?' I don't know as maybe they gonna hurt me first, you understand? And then ask. I said, 'Listen, you don't have to rough me up any, pull my fingernails out, I'll tell you anything you want to know.' Trying to explain this ain't any of my business. The man walks out. This is when they had me upstairs. I only saw him a minute, he walks out. Dude type of man, had a sharp suit on, but kind of old-timey."

"That's the Zip. Tommy Bucks. The other

one has a leather coat on, Nicky, the one I spoke
to on the phone. He said either he knew I was
going to call or I was going to get in touch with
them. But I think it was the Zip knew it, or had a
hunch. See, Nicky's the kind I believe likes to
brag on himself. Or he'll tell you something another person said and make you think it was his
idea. I *know* he don't have a say in this deal. The
Zip's the one decides things."

"And he knew you were coming."

"Or thought I might."

"The man knew."

"Well, if you didn't get back . . ."

"You'd have come looking for me."

"I was going to say, I'd have thought of
some way, I suppose, to get in touch."

"And the man knew that, is what I'm saying. So what does that tell you?"

"If it's true? Then I think he wants to ask *me*
the question," Raylan said, "instead of you.
Wants me to be the one tell him where Harry is.
Like it's a personal thing between us."

Robert Gee said, "So, you going to do it?"

Raylan stood up when they came in, not out of
any kind of regard, but so the Zip and Nicky
wouldn't be towering over him. As soon as the
two were in the room, someone outside in the

hall closed the door. Robert Gee stayed where he was until the Zip looked at him and said, "Get up."

He did, taking his time, Raylan hearing him groan as he pushed himself up, stiff from sitting on the floor.

The Zip said to Nicky, "Watch him," before turning to Raylan. "I been waiting for you. I know, soon as you figure out I got this guy, you're gonna come try and make a deal, give me Benno and Marco. Where are they?"

"Locked up in a garage."

"Yeah? Where Harry is?"

"At his house."

"And Harry's there?"

"He left," Raylan said.

"Yeah? Where'd he go?"

"He went home."

The Zip kept staring at him.

Raylan heard Nicky say, "Lemme have him," and looked over to see Nicky holding a gun now, some kind of automatic. "Come on," Nicky said, "just me and him in here."

The Zip raised his hand as if to shut Nicky up without looking at him. He said to Raylan, "When was this Harry went home?"

Robert Gee answered. He said, "While

you're fooling around waiting for Raylan. You could've asked me where Harry lived. Man, I'd have told you in a second. But you rather wait and have him tell you. Well, that's what he's doing, he's telling you."

Robert Gee getting a kick out of this.

The Zip's face, listening to him, was made of stone. He didn't take his eyes off Raylan. When there was a silence he said, "Harry left when you did."

Raylan didn't say anything.

"That wasn't too long ago. You come here in the car belongs to the guy we put by the *autostrada*. But no one's seen Harry's car or the one you had. So you came down in Benno's car, uh? And that's the one Harry's driving. Okay, that gives them a jump on us, but not much of one. Where'd he go?"

Raylan didn't answer.

"He go to Genova with that woman?"

They stared at each other.

"Or to Milano. Or south, to Roma?"

"How about Turin," Raylan said. "Or maybe Bologna."

That stone face stared at him.

The Zip said, "Okay, tell me."

Raylan shook his head. "I don't know."

The Zip said to Nicky, "Put your gun on the jig."

Nicky glanced over. "I got it on him."

The Zip said to Raylan, "Where did he go? Tell me, or in three seconds this guy is dead."

Robert said, "Hey, come on. I'm not in this."

"He went to Genoa," Raylan said. "You're too late."

"I don't believe it. Where did he go?"

"To Genoa, whether you believe it or not."

The Zip said to Nicky, "Shoot him."

Nicky looked over, frowning. "What?"

Raylan said, "I'm telling you the truth!"

The Zip's hand slipped into his suit coat. "I said shoot him. Do it."

The hand came out holding a Beretta auto, the same one Raylan had at home. It came up in his face and stayed there. He heard Robert say, "I don't have no part in this, man. It ain't any of my business."

The Zip stared at Raylan as he said to Nicky, "You going to shoot him or not?"

Nicky said, "Jesus Christ, right here?"

The Zip said, "Right here, right now," swung the Beretta from Raylan to Robert Gee and shot him and shot him again, and swung it back in Raylan's face before he could move, the sound of the gunshots ringing in the concrete room.

The stone face stared from behind the muzzle.

The Zip said, "Where did he go?"

Raylan said, "He went to Genoa."

TWENTY-THREE

Buck Torres sat listening to Harry tell how overnight the Zip had more people working for him in Rapallo than he did here, real honest-to-God Mafia types. Harry said, "Like the Zip and these guys are the original cast and Jimmy Cap's bozos are the road company. I mean there's no comparison."

Harry trying to be himself again, the authority, in his rooms on the third floor of the Della Robbia, but moving to the window to look down at the street as he made his observations.

"I saw it was time to get out, so we left. You

want to know the truth? I was ready to go anyway."

Torres said, "What about Raylan Givens?"

"Yeah, he was there."

"I mean, didn't he help you?"

"Me personally? He had this idea he could help Robert. I said, 'You crazy? Robert don't need any help. Robert's told them by now everything he knows about me, what I had for breakfast, and they've let him go.' Raylan and Joyce want to know, well, where is he then? Like he's going to come back to the villa after finking on me."

"You expected him," Torres said, "to keep his mouth shut? Maybe die for you?"

"He knew the score, who those guys are. If I'm paying him I expect some loyalty."

Torres let that one go. He said, "So Raylan drove you down to the, what do you call it, the *autostrada*?"

"Yeah, the freeway, and we took off. I thought he'd be right behind us, at least by the next day."

"You didn't make any kind of arrangement for him to get in touch with you?"

"I figured he'd be okay," Harry said, "because he wouldn't have to lie. Where am I? Gone. Where'd I go? To Genoa. We're on a flight

to Rome that same evening and left there yesterday morning. We haven't even been home
twenty-four hours yet." Harry reached the window and turned. "Give him time, he'll be along."

"Joyce called me," Torres said. "She's worried about him."

"I'm the one they're after. She mention she's
worried at all about *me*?"

"Don't you want to know where he is?"

"I'm telling you, he'll show up."

"You know he went over there on his own."

"After I walked away from him not just
once but twice. This time he's thinking, I'm
gonna bring that son of a bitch home in chains if
I have to."

"Why do I get the feeling," Torres said,
"you wouldn't be here if it wasn't for Raylan?"

"I told you, I was ready to leave anyway."

"That isn't what I mean."

Harry wasn't listening. He said, "I'd be at a
sidewalk café watching the scene, trying to soak
up the atmosphere . . . I don't know why but it
was different this time. The weather was de-
pressing, that was part of it."

"You don't have an audience over there,"
Torres said, "anybody to bullshit with."

"I didn't before, the other times I went. But
those trips, I never stayed more than a few days,

a week at the most. This time I'm there close to a month and I'm thinking, Wait a minute. I'm going to *live* here? It was different." Harry stood at the window. He made his turn and started to grin. "These two guys come in the house, Benno and Marco. I'm telling you, real honest-to-God Mafioso, right out of *The Godfather, Part Two.* They come in the bedroom, they see me sitting there . . ."

Torres said, "By yourself?"

"It's a setup. They walk in the room, they see me—what is this? They look around. One of the guys, Marco's got a sawed-off shotgun. Not a pump, a regular double-barrel shotgun cut down. The other guy, Benno, sees me sitting there relaxed, he puts his gun back in his pants, in his waist. Marco says something in Italian; the other one, Benno, says, 'Who're you? What's your name?' I say to him, 'You walk in my house and you want to know who *I* am? Who the fuck're *you*? You understand, I'm the bait. I distract them. Raylan's across the hall with Joyce. He comes up behind them while I'm talking and I take the shotgun away from Marco."

Torres said, "They don't know who you are?"

Harry shook his head. "For all I know they still don't, they're back in Italy locked in the garage." Harry was smiling almost to himself. "Maybe I'll go back there sometime when the weather's nice. You know, like spend the winter here and the summer over there."

"I told you," Torres said, "the Zip came back. The surveillance guys have him talking on the phone to Jimmy Cap. He's saying, 'I chased him home. He might think he can hide, but there isn't anyplace he can go I won't find him.' That's you he's talking about."

"Of course it's me. So, you going to pick him up? That's a threat on my life."

"All he's saying is he can find you if you try to hide."

"So he can kill me, for Christ sake."

"We know that," Torres said. "The only reason we still have them under surveillance, I want to hear him say it. Otherwise we have to catch him doing it. You want, we can put you in jail till you're nolle prossed. That means the state attorney's office isn't proceeding at this time and most likely won't, but they can refile up to sixty days if they see a reason to."

"Like I shoot another guy they send?"

Torres said, "I'd like to know what you did to those guys. You must've actually been skimming big-time and they found out."

"You don't know how good it is to be

home," Harry said, "be able to talk to people again, communicate. Was I skimming on them? I've been skimming on those people all my life, but never once had any kind of trouble till this Bureau asshole set me up. Not even for anything I did. He makes up a story and they buy it. I get a contract put out on me and this Bureau prick McCormick drops his investigation. Decides he doesn't want Jimmy after all, makes up some excuse, right? But the real reason, there's no way he'd ever get a conviction. Meanwhile, I can't walk out the fucking door without very likely getting shot. That's why I told you, Christ, over a month ago, I didn't want any part of being a witness."

"All the years you and Jimmy are partners," Torres said, "why can't you explain to him you had nothing to do with it?"

"Do with what? It never *hap*pened. A guy says he lost a bet and paid me ten grand plus the vig. I say I never saw him before in my life and Jimmy believes the *guy*. Raylan even told the Zip that entire story was made up by the feds. I'll give him that. Christ, a United States marshal trying to help me."

"But it didn't make an impression on the Zip," Torres said. "Raylan told me about it that time he called."

"No, the Zip don't care if I skimmed on him or not, he still wants me."

"That's what Raylan said."

"But why? What'd I ever do to him? I mean that he knows about."

Torres said, "I'm starting to think it doesn't have anything to do with you personally. You know what I mean? They shoot you to prove a point, or to make an impression. Or because the Zip said he would and he's a man of his word. I don't know—they're your friends, Harry. If you can't figure out why they want to kill you, don't expect me to."

Harry said, "Shit, I'm stuck here, aren't I?" He turned to the window and back again, saying, "You want a drink?"

"The thing was," Nicky said, "they're talking Italian to each other the whole time and I'm suppose to know what's going on. Like they all get up from the table and walk away. I'm still sitting there. Tommy Bucks looks at me. 'What's wrong with you?' Tells me to come on. They meet, they hug and kiss each other? Man, I couldn't believe it. I got to know this one guy, the one I mentioned was killed? Fabrizio. I asked him what certain words meant. I find out Tommy's calling me an asshole all the time."

Gloria said, "How about *testa di cazzo*?"

Nicky was surprised to hear her say it. "Yeah, he calls me that. What's it mean?"

"Dickhead."

"Really? That's the only one I thought was okay, 'cause my name's in it, Testa. Like he was calling me Testa of the something or other."

"It means dickhead," Gloria said.

"What I want to know," Nicky said, "is if I have to take that kind of shit." He waited for a reaction from Jimmy Cap, but didn't get one.

They were in the Jacuzzi at the shallow end of the swimming pool, three faces in sunglasses above the foamy water: Nicky making his report; Jimmy Cap with his eyes closed, maybe asleep; and Gloria, Jimmy's girlfriend, running her toes up the inside of Nicky's thigh, beneath the foam. Nicky said, "Am I?" and waited.

Gloria nudged Jimmy Cap with her elbow. He said, "What?"

"Am I suppose to put up with that kind of shit, calling me *stronzo*?"

"Who you talking about?"

"Tommy Bucks, he's always calling me some name."

"*Stronzo*," Gloria said, affecting an Italian accent, getting a lilt in her voice. "Hey, *stronzo*."

"What've I got to do with it," Jimmy Cap said, "what he calls you?"

Gloria slipped her toes inside Nicky's athletic shorts and he jumped as he said, "I *wooork* for you."

"Yeah, so?"

"Okay, how about what he calls *you*?"

"What're you talking about?"

"With those guys over there, I hear him saying your name."

"So, what'd he say?"

"They were talking Italian. But I could tell by the way he said it, you know, the tone of voice, he was disrespecting you."

"Like what kind of tone?"

"You know, like he says your name and then laughs. One time he said something about you and right away he goes like this." Nicky raised his fists out of the water and punched the inside of his left elbow. "Or what about, I mean the whole idea of you sending us over there was to find Harry and whack him out. Okay, we get hold of this guy that worked for him I told you about, the colored guy? All Tommy has to do is ask him where Harry's at, where's he live. No, Tommy's too busy with this whuer. Spent all his time with her."

Gloria said, "This what?"

"This whuer."

Jimmy Cap said, "Yeah? What'd she look like, any good?"

"You kidding? She was a fucking dog. You put a cat in the room she'd go after it. He's with her when the cowboy called and I had to go back and forth delivering messages 'cause Tommy wouldn't speak to him."

Jimmy said, "What cowboy?"

Jesus, he didn't listen to any of it. "The U.S. marshal I told you about was there. With his star."

Jimmy Cap said, "Tommy's problem—don't tell him I said this—he's a Zip, pure Sicilian. That's why he's so fucking serious all the time. I tell him, 'Hey, try to kick back.' He don't know what I'm talking about."

"See, the thing is," Nicky said, "if it'd been up to me I'd've had the colored guy tell me where Harry lived and I'd've gone to his house and whacked him out. Like you asked me one time what would I do to that gas station guy owed you money? It's none of my business but I happened to hear you talking to the Zip a while ago about Harry, saying forget about him, Harry's more trouble than he's worth. And the Zip says you made a deal? He whacks out Harry he gets to run the sports book, so he's holding you to it. You don't mind my saying, I think you got a problem there. You give him the sports book, what's he gonna want next? A guy like him, he don't do what you tell him, what do you need him for?"

Gloria said to Nicky, "I can see you taking care of Tommy."

Jimmy Cap said to Gloria, "Who the fuck asked you?"

The Zip, wearing one of his beige double-breasted suits today, stood in the lanai, the open-air sitting room off the patio. He watched Nicky come up out of the Jacuzzi, turn and reach down to give Jimmy Cap a hand, popping his biceps to haul that 350 pounds of fat out of the water. Christ, naked, the guy all belly. Next came Gloria, topless; she picked up a towel and tied it around her like a sarong, covering her jugs. Now Jimmy was talking to her; he seemed upset, making a big deal out of something or other and now she was taking the towel off, handing it to him. He took it but didn't seem to want that towel. He threw it aside and it went in the pool. Now the asshole with muscle was saying something to him. Jimmy Cap shook his head, put his hand on the asshole's shoulder and said something to

Gloria. She picked up her bra and came this way putting it on.

The Zip waited, pretending to look out at the view, the Fontainebleau and Eden Roc over on the other side of Indian Creek. As she came past him hooking her bra, he said, "What's the problem?"

"He wants his own towel."

"I understand he hasn't seen his dick since he weighed two hundred pounds."

Gloria said, "He hasn't missed anything," and kept going.

The Zip said, "Hey, come here. Wait a minute."

She stopped and stood looking past her shoulder at him, giving him her profile.

"What were you having out there, a meeting?"

"Trying to decide," Gloria said, "if Nicky's a *stronzo* or a *testa di cazzo*," giving the Zip her idea of an accent.

He seemed to like it. He said, "You know any more words?"

Gloria said, "No, but I learn fast."

Joyce sat in the dark staring at the front windows. It was going on seven when Harry called.

She said, "You've been drinking."

"I have, as a matter of fact."

"All day?"

"More like fifty years. Why?"

She didn't hear resentment in his tone; that was a plus. But then had to give himself permission, a reason to drink, telling her:

"I'm a little edgy being stuck here. I needed something and that Xanax puts me to sleep. Torres came by. He said you called him."

"To see if he'd heard anything."

"He said you're worried about Raylan. I said, 'What about me? I'm the one they want.' "

"I'm worried about you too," Joyce said.

"Thanks. I asked Torres for a little protection, since it's not my fault somebody wants to kill me, for Christ sake. He says he'll have a squad car keep an eye on the hotel. Like these guys would come in with signs on them saying who they are. He says they'll be ready to respond, *in case.* That's supposed to be reassuring. And you ask me why I'm having a drink?"

"If you keep it up," Joyce said, "you'll end up doing something dumb. You know that."

"I'll tell you the worst," Harry said, "was one time when I blacked out. I wake up on a plane and have no idea in the world where we're going. I'm thinking, How do I ask the stew without sounding like an idiot? I'm sitting in first class, I have just a Perrier, I don't want to take a chance, maybe black out again. I get in a conversation with the woman next to me about something, I think the movie that was coming on. I know I have to ask her. So I say right out of the blue, 'This may sound like a stupid question, but would you mind telling me where we're going?' She gives me this look and says, 'Vegas,' like, where do you think we're going."

Joyce said, "Harry, I was with you."

It stopped him for a moment. He said, "You're right, you were the woman, huh?" He said, "You were wearing your hair different then."

She saw the headlights outside moving south on Meridian, creeping along looking for a number, making a U-turn now to pull up in front of the terrace apartments. It was about seven-thirty. Joyce watched from the dark living room. As soon as the figure was out of the car she jumped up and ran to open the front door and wait for the man coming up the walk in a dark suit and a hat like the one Harry Truman used to wear. Joyce put her arms out. He came into them not saying a word.

TWENTY-FOUR

Maybe he would tell her sometime how all the way back across the Atlantic Ocean he thought about her, couldn't wait to see her again, and how much he'd wanted to kiss her when she drove off with Harry and how much he still wanted to but didn't know if he should, thinking: What if he was wrong about the way she seemed to look at him? What if she thought he was dumb? What if, even though Harry was old enough to be her dad, she still liked him? All that. What if after flashing his star through Immigration and Customs and racing over here, she wasn't home?

She was though. And the way they started kissing each other on the front porch in the dark and some more inside the house, like they couldn't get enough of each other, he wondered how he could've had any doubts. He might tell her about them later, let her know how he felt. There were other things to tell her first.

Beginning with Robert Gee.

"The Zip said, 'Shoot him,' and the young guy, Nicky, said, 'Right here?' I think he wanted to, but he couldn't just, you know, *do it* like that; he wasn't ready. So the Zip shot him. The way he did it I guess there wasn't any need for him to get ready. He just looked over, shot Robert twice in the chest, and put the gun back on me and said, 'Where'd they go?' I told him the same thing I'd told him before. You were gone, so I had no reason to lie. I think he realized I was telling the truth and it stopped him. So right then the young guy, Nicky, says, 'This one's mine.' Meaning me. The Zip acted surprised then, putting it on. He said something about Nicky had told him before he was going to shoot me but didn't. The Zip says, 'Now you're ready to do it, is that right? Now that he doesn't have a gun?

What if I give him mine? You still think you can kill him?' See, what it was, the Zip had no respect for Nicky, so he wouldn't let him shoot me."

Joyce said, "If Nicky had shot Robert when he was told . . ."

"You're right, it would've been different."

"They just let you go?"

"I think it was like wanting to show he had power over me. He could kill a man in front of my eyes and let me go and there wasn't a thing I could do about it. They walked out of the room. . . . I still didn't know what was going to happen. I looked at Robert, didn't find a pulse. I went down the hall knocking on doors, but none of them opened. It wasn't till I was outside I knew for sure they were letting me go. I went to a police station, identified myself, and told them a man had been murdered. It took them an hour to decide I might be telling the truth, but then had to phone Washington, D.C., and check up on me. So by the time we got to the apartment house the Zip's guys were still around but Robert's body was gone, as I knew it would be. I told the police to forget it, we'd settle it when we got home."

Joyce said, "But you can't charge him with it here." Sounding surprised.

Raylan said, "No, we can't."

She looked at him for a time and said, "I don't know you, do I?"

What was there to tell? They got comfortable with drinks to sip, a lamp on now. Raylan said, "I grew up in coal camps, chewed tobacco when I was twelve. Went to Evarts High and played football, our archrival being the Harlan Green Dragons. What else you want to know? I've worked deep mines, wildcat mines—abandoned ones where you go back in and scratch for any coal left—and I've stripped."

"So have I," Joyce said.

"Pardon me?"

"Never mind."

"Stripping we'd cut the top off a hill and dig out the coal, mess up the countryside. . . . My mom put her foot down, wouldn't let me work for those people. Let's see, I walked a picket line over a year when we struck Duke Power. Learned about company gun thugs. During that same time my dad died of black lung and high blood pressure. My mom said, 'That's enough.' Her brother was shot and killed during the strike. We picked up and moved to Detroit, Michigan. I went to Wayne State University, graduated, and joined the Marshals Service. What else you want to know?"

"Two boys, I wanted to call the first one Hank and the next one George, after Hank Williams and George Jones, old Possum, the greatest country singers that ever were. See, we'd agreed each time that if it was a boy, I'd name him, and if it was a girl, then Winona'd pick the name. But when the babies were born, Winona got her way as usual and named them Ricky and Randy. I attended the same church back home as the one where George Jones learned to sing, Assembly of God? I mean the same denomination. His church was in eastern Texas, the Big Thicket country, and mine was over in eastern Kentucky. Winona, if she had a girl, was going to call her Piper, Tammy, or Loretta. Her favorite song was Loretta Lynn's 'Don't Come Home A-Drinkin' with Lovin' on Your Mind.' I don't know why, 'cause it wasn't something I ever did."

Joyce said, "You know what happens when you play a country tune backwards? You get your girl and your truck back, you're not drunk anymore and your hound dog comes back to life." She said, "I was born in Nashville."

* * *

He wanted to know why she hadn't told him and asked if she'd ever been to the Ryman Auditorium and Tootsie's Orchid Lounge. It seemed important to him. Joyce was sorry to have to tell him they'd moved when she was two: first to Dallas, then Oklahoma City, then Little Rock and then here. She said her dad sold cars, any kind, and drank; her mom smoked and played cards and neither one was still living. Raylan asked if she was a religious person. Joyce said she seemed to be doing okay and hadn't yet felt the need. She said, "Are we going to tell everything there is to know about each other the first time we've sat down without looking out the window, waiting for something awful to happen? I guess we're still waiting, but taking time out and getting things said, is that it? Making up for lost time? You want to know what my favorite color is? What vegetables I hate? I won't eat stewed tomatoes. I like rock and roll, short of heavy-metal head banging. The highlight of my life happened almost twenty-five years ago: I went to Woodstock, I was there with all those people in the rain, the mud, nothing to eat, and at the time didn't think it was much fun. I was married once, I told you that. Patton is my maiden name, I never gave it up. I went to the University of Miami three years, majored in psychology, and I worked as a stripper for three years in topless bars in Miami, but not the grungy joints. I never took off my G-string or did private parties or got hooked on dope or got pregnant or had an abortion. What else do you want to know?"

There was a silence till Raylan said, "What're you mad at?" He touched her face, laying the palm of his hand very gently on her cheek.

Harry said, "You hear that?"

"I sure did," Joyce said. "Right in my ear."

"I dropped the goddamn phone."

"Are you okay?"

"Am I *okay*?"

"That's not a hard question, Harry."

"You mean outside of being stuck here, not knowing what's going to happen to me or when? Yeah, I'm just great. How're you doing?"

"I'm worried about you."

"Is that right? Torres said you were worried about Raylan, but didn't know if you were worried about me or not."

"We covered that the last time you called."

"We did? Come over and keep me company, allay my apprehensions."

"Harry, you're drinking again. That's what

I'm worried about. You're right back where you left off."

"Come over and I'll quit."

"You're acting like a child."

"Come over and I'll grow up right before your eyes. I'm starting to feel horny."

"I'm not coming, Harry."

"Why not?"

"I'm in bed."

"It's only—it's not even ten o'clock."

"I'm tired. Why don't we talk tomorrow?"

"Raylan's home," Harry said. When he paused, Joyce kept quiet. "I thought you'd want to know. Torres called, he's been checking with Immigration at the airport. That's how he found out the Zip was home. They said Raylan Givens arrived on a British Air flight around six. So he made it. I knew he would; they're after me, not him." Harry paused. "I tried calling him just now but there was no answer." Harry paused again. "He gave me his number that time he was watching over me. He said if I had the least suspicion anything was wrong I was to call him. Even if there was another marshal downstairs in the lobby. I thought that was kind of odd."

"Harry, let's talk tomorrow, okay?"

"You haven't heard from him, have you?"

She said, "Who, Raylan?" lying on her back staring at the ceiling.

Harry said, "I listened to him and came home and where am I? Worse off than before. I shouldn't have let him talk me into it."

"He didn't. You had no other choice."

"I could've gone somewhere else. I could've gone to Africa. I could've gone to the French Riviera. Paris."

"Harry, I'll call you tomorrow."

"You promise? What time?"

"I don't know, in the morning sometime." She said, "Good night, Harry," reached over to replace the phone, and rolled back to Raylan's face on the pillow, watching her.

"Why didn't I tell him you're here?"

"You feel sorry for him. He's alone, he's scared."

"He's doing it to himself."

"Not all of it."

"He's using it as an excuse to drink. Being stuck there, not knowing what's going to happen. The police won't help."

"I could hear what he was saying. You want to go see him?"

"Tomorrow."

"He's blaming me, huh?"

"He's drunk."

"Yeah, but he has a point. Bringing him home didn't help any."

"What will?"

"Maybe if I have a talk with those boys."

TWENTY-FIVE

Gloria heard him grunt and then gasp, you'd think in agony, the air going out of him, and felt his belly collapse on her hips, Christ, her kidneys, Gloria on her hands and knees in the king-size bed—the only way they could make contact —Gloria terrified that if her arms gave out with Jimmy on top of her she would suffocate beneath his mass of flesh and he wouldn't find out she was dead until he rolled off, if then. She said, "Oh, God, don't, please." She said, "Honey? Don't go to sleep on me, okay? Please?" Her arms shaking, losing strength. She said,

"Honey?" And screamed at the pillow, "God, will you get off me!"

It worked. He slipped off and rolled and she scrambled against the sagging mattress to get out of there and make it to the bathroom arching her back, moving her head from shoulder to shoulder, having lived through another life-threatening experience, nap time with Jimmy Cap. Maybe there wouldn't be too many more. She wanted to take a shower and wash her hair, but was meeting the Zip in a half hour and had to hurry.

Gloria returned to the bed with a glass of water for Jimmy, part of the ritual. After that he might snort a few lines off the bedside table and want to go again. She hurried to get into her panties.

"What're you doing?"

"I'm getting dressed." And picked up her white shorts from the chair.

"I want to talk to you. Get your advice on something."

"The last time I told you what I thought you go, 'Who the fuck asked you?' "

" 'Cause I didn't ask you that time. Okay, now I am. You see the difference?"

She had the shorts on. "What do you want to know?"

"Where you going?"

"I promised my mom I'd stop by."

"Tell me what you think of Joe Macho."

"Nicky? What do you mean, what I think of him?"

"Is he all mouth or what?"

"How would I know?"

"What's he say about Tommy?"

"Not much. He doesn't like him. Even less than before, since they got back."

"You know what Nicky calls him, the Zip. Yesterday we're in the Jacuze talking?"

"I was there."

"I know you were. Nicky says Tommy says things about me? You ever hear him?"

"Who, Tommy? I don't think so."

"You never talk to him?"

"Hardly ever."

"You hear Nicky? He says I should watch him. Says if Tommy gets the sports book, what's he gonna want next?"

Gloria said, "Yeah?" pulling a black T-shirt over her head.

"He says what do I need him for?"

"You mean like fire him?"

Jimmy Cap smiled at her. He very seldom did that and it surprised her.

"No, he don't mean like fire him, he means

like whack him, take him out, get rid of him. For my own good."

"Yeah?"

"Nicky wants to do it, whack him out. You know, you didn't hear that word so much till I read John Gotti uses it all the time. Or he used to. 'Whack him,' and it became popular again."

Gloria stood looking at the soles of Jimmy Cap's feet, his belly rising from the white spread covering the bed and behind the belly, peeking over it, his head propped against pillows.

"Nicky's serious?"

"Every once in a while."

"I can't see him doing it."

"Me neither. Nicky's more for having around, pick up a pizza, carry your suitcases. The trouble is," Jimmy said, "I don't have a guy right now, outside of Tommy, who I know is any good at it. I don't know why, but you just don't find the kind of guys today you used to. I mean white guys who want to do that kind of work. Latins and colored guys, shit, you can get all of them you want. It's like in pro sports today, you know it? The same thing."

He was smiling at her again.

"You ever consider that line of work?"

"What?"

"Whacking guys. There's good money in it."

* * *

Raylan drove to Jimmy Cap's house in a confiscated Jaguar sedan he happened to have the keys to; stopped at the gate on Pine Tree Drive and reached out to press the button below the speaker in the stone pillar. A voice that sounded like a recording said, "State your name and the nature of your business."

Raylan said to the speaker grille, "This is Deputy United States Marshal Raylan Givens. I have business of a confidential nature with Mr. Capotorto. I'd appreciate your opening the gate so I don't have to drive this car through it." He had to wait about five minutes before the gate opened and he went up the drive lined with coconut palms and shrubs to his favorite type of house, a tan-colored hacienda with dark-wood trim and a red tile roof. Some guy let him in. Raylan looked around, heard steps clicking on the terrazza floor, and there was Nicky and a blond-haired girl in a black T-shirt. Nicky said something to her. Raylan watched her look this way, a cute girl, right out front about studying him. She walked off. Nicky said to the guy who'd opened the door, "It's okay, Jack," and motioned for Raylan to follow him. They went down a hall and came to an open-air kind of room with white furniture, the pool and patio right outside. Jimmy Cap was sitting on the sofa, taking up half of it in a white robe.

Nicky said, "You want me to pat him down?"

Raylan had to smile. He waited while Jimmy Cap looked him over and said, finally, "So you're the cowboy."

Raylan touched his hat brim. "With the Marshals Service, but at the moment acting on my own."

"And you have something you want to tell me. All right, have a seat."

"It's of a private nature," Raylan said, easing into a fat white chair. "You don't mind my speaking in front of this boy?"

"What's it about?"

"Harry Arno."

"Go ahead, I don't care."

Raylan was aware of Nicky standing off to his right, but kept his attention on Jimmy. He said, "I want you to leave Harry alone. Call off your dogs. Anybody touches him I'll hold you responsible and cause you more trouble than you can believe."

Jimmy kept staring at him, no doubt thinking it over. Raylan wanted to look at Nicky, see what kind of face he was putting on, but knew he'd better stay with Jimmy. Finally Jimmy said, "You're on your own time?"

"Right now I am. Touch Harry and you become my life's work."

Jimmy seemed easy enough to talk to; he didn't put on any kind of act. He said, "I don't know why you're looking out for Harry; I don't care either. What I'll do is make you a deal. Take somebody off my hands I don't need and Harry won't have to worry anymore. He can go back to work if he wants, run his book."

Raylan said, "Are we talking about the Zip? The one you don't need?"

"Tommy Bucks, the same."

"Take him off your hands, how?"

"I don't care, long as I don't see him again. When he's gone, Harry's got nothing to worry about. I give you my word on it. What do you say? You have to think it over or what?"

Raylan said, "Where's he live?"

Jimmy looked at Nicky.

"What's wrong with you?"

"Nothing."

Raylan thought he looked mad, or like he was pouting.

"Tommy still live at the Esther?"

"Far as I know."

Jimmy said, "You're not sure, find out."

"I'm sure." He looked right at Jimmy as he said, "I know Gloria's meeting him there, so that's prob'ly where he lives."

Jimmy's tone changed. "Meeting him for what?"

"That's all she said, she's meeting him. Have a drink—I don't know."

Raylan stood up. He didn't need to listen to these two pick at each other. Now Jimmy was looking at him again.

"You don't take your cowboy hat off in the house?"

Upset about Gloria going out on him, it sounded like, and looking for something to fuss at. Raylan said, "Being in your house has nothing to do with it. My hat stays on 'cause I won't take it off to you or anybody like you." He looked at Nicky again as he turned to go. "What was that, the Hotel Esther? Ocean Drive about Fourteenth?"

Nicky moved his big shoulders. "Around there."

Raylan said, "Thank you."

He knew where it was: one block up the street from where Harry lived.

* * *

The Zip said to Gloria, "I got another word for you. See that guy? The one in the shorts, thinks he's hot stuff?"

Walking by in a tank top and tight athletic shorts.

"Nice buns," Gloria said.

"The word for him is *frocio,* a fag."

"*Frocio,*" Gloria said, putting on her accent. "There's one I want to ask you. How do you say fuck off?"

"You say *va fa in culo.*"

Gloria tried it. "I used to hear guys, I thought they were saying fangool."

"Yeah, that's close."

The waitress came with their iced tea and Gloria said, *"Va fa'n culo,"* as though she was thanking her. She said to the Zip, "You want to see a lot of *frocios,* you ever been to the Warsaw Ballroom on Collins? The straights go to Egoiste, but the Warsaw's more fun." She sipped her iced tea and said, "We're a little north of the action, Tommy," looking around at the tables on the porch and the sidewalk in front of the Esther: all tourists, but none of the trendies from New York City. "This is kind of the edge of nowhere." When she arrived Gloria had walked up to Tommy the Zip sitting at the table in his white silk sports jacket and black silk shirt open at the neck, the Zip casual this Saturday afternoon, and said, "Hey, we're twins." Both of them in black and white.

He said now, "Okay, tell me what's going on."

Gloria gave him a look over the rim of her iced-tea glass. "What do I get?"

"You mean if you don't tell me? What do I do to you? Let's see . . ."

"Nicky wants to whack you out."

"You're kidding me. He told you that?"

"He told Jimmy and Jimmy told me."

"He's a joke, Nicky. I could stand with my back to him all night, off someplace nobody sees us, he could never do it. I believe he's *frocio*. He jumps you so you won't get it in your head he's queer and tell Jimmy."

"Who says he jumps me?"

"I just said it."

"He'd like to." Gloria shook her head. "I got a three-hundred-and-fifty-pounder likes to lay on top of me as it is. Can you picture that?"

"How do you do it?"

"Like the bow-wows, doggie fashion. Man, it's a full-time job. I'm sure as hell not going to entertain this muscle-bound geek on the side. Those guys, those bodybuilders, they're always picking you up, flexing, looking at themselves.

. . . They won't fuck unless it's in front of a mirror. What I need is a normal guy for a change," looking the Zip in the eye.

He said, "We get some time I'll give you what you need. What I like is for you to help me kill a guy. I don't mean I want you to do it, that's my job. But you can help me."

Gloria wasn't sure she wanted to. She frowned at the Zip as she said, "How?"

"See, what I do is call this guy and tell him I want to talk to him, settle a dispute we have between us, a misunderstanding. He's going to think I'm setting him up and he's right, that's what I'm doing. So I have to get him to trust me."

She was interested and liked the Zip's accent; it was soothing.

"How do you do that?"

"I tell him he can choose where we meet, a public place like a restaurant, lot of people around, so he'll think, Sure, he can't do nothing to me there. And that's where I do it. Pop him, get up, and walk away."

Gloria hunched over the table. "But people will see you."

"Yeah, what? Ask them, they all see something different. One or two witnesses, they can identify you. A lot of people there, you got no problem."

"Jimmy's going to freak. He's already scared to death of you."

The Zip raised his eyebrows. "Oh, is that right?"

"You know that," Gloria said, still looking right at him and getting some sparkle in her blue eyes. "Can I watch you do it?"

"Sure, you'll be there."

"What do I do?"

Raylan saw them as he approached the Hotel Esther from across Ocean Drive: three stories of rounded Art Deco corners, cream and aqua: all the tables occupied and the two of them at a table for four on the porch, out of the sun: the little girl pressed against the table to get closer to the Zip, hear what he was telling her. Raylan walked up the two steps to the porch they called "Dining on the Terrace" and over to the table. The Zip had stopped talking and was looking at him. Raylan stood at one of the empty chairs and touched the brim of his hat to the girl looking at him now.

He said, "Miss, your name's Gloria Ayres?"

She seemed surprised. "Yeah?"

"I'd like you to be a witness to what I'm going to tell this fella. Will you do that?"

She looked at the Zip. "Is he for real?"

The Zip said, "Listen to what he has to say," still looking at Raylan. "Is this official business? You have a warrant or something?"

Raylan shook his head. "I've come on my own, like the last time."

The Zip was quiet, maybe trying to guess what was in Raylan's mind. He seemed curious. Finally he said, "Okay, what do you want to tell me?"

"Here's the deal," Raylan said. "I'm giving you twenty-four hours to get out of this county and never come back." Raylan looked at his watch. "That means you have until . . . two-fifteen tomorrow afternoon to clear out. If I see you're still around after that, I won't hesitate to shoot you on sight. You have any questions?"

The Zip hadn't moved as Raylan spoke. He said, "The fuck you talking about?"

"That's your question?"

"You think you can make me leave?"

"It's your choice," Raylan said. "You go of your own free will. If you choose to stay, then I'm coming after you with a gun. I won't give you much of a warning, if any, though I doubt I'd shoot you in the back. If for some reason I was to find you unarmed? I'll keep in mind Robert Gee wasn't armed either."

Gloria said, "Wait a minute," looking at the Zip and then turning to Raylan again. "Aren't you a cop?"

"United States deputy marshal."

"Well, you can't shoot somebody just 'cause you happen to feel like it."

"He does," Raylan said.

Gloria kept staring at him.

"Doesn't he?"

She didn't answer.

"So I thought, okay, we'll play by his rules." Raylan looked at the Zip now in his sporty black-and-white outfit. "You have till tomorrow afternoon," Raylan said. "Two-fifteen."

TWENTY-SIX

Gloria told Nicky it wasn't like he was actually threatening the Zip, because he didn't say it that way. It was like leave town or I'll kill you. Okay? No, it was leave the *county*, that was what he said, or I'll come after you with a gun. "With his cowboy hat on," Gloria said, "cocked down on one eye. I couldn't believe it. Get out of the county by—listen to this. Get out of the county by two-fifteen tomorrow. Exactly twenty-four hours from when he was saying it."

Gloria had just come in the door and was in the kitchen telling Nicky about it while he got the bucket of ice water and hand towels ready, the ones Gloria used to wipe Jimmy down. It was almost time for his 3:00 to 4:00 P.M. sunbath.

"So after, I asked him what he was going to do."

Nicky said, "Yeah?" wanting to hear about it without seeming too interested.

"He goes, 'I'm not going to do nutting about this,'" Gloria giving her version of the Zip's accent. "'You know why? 'Cause he ain't going to do nutting. All he was trying to do was scare me.'"

"I don't know," Nicky said, seeing the cowboy up on that ridge, telling Fabrizio if he took another step he'd shoot him.

"Tommy goes, 'You ever hear of a fed walk up and shoot somebody? Sure, they might do it, but they don't tell you about it first, ask you to be a witness to what he's saying,' like he did me. He even knew my name. Tommy goes, 'I'll take care of this cowboy after.'"

"He was here," Nicky said.

"I know, I saw him."

"That's right, I forgot."

"No, you didn't. Nicky? What do you want to tell me?"

"Nothing."

"Come on, I know you, Nicky. What?" Like

talking to a muscle-bound baby. "You told Jimmy something while the cowboy was here, didn't you?" She was getting close. She said, "You told the cowboy where the Zip lives. That's how he knew—" Gloria stopped. "What else? Come on, Nicky."

"I told them that's where you went."

"Oh, shit."

"It slipped out."

"Thanks a lot, you creep. Now I have to think of something to tell Jimmy."

"I couldn't help it."

"Nicky, do you hear yourself? The guy who wants to whack out the Zip—you sound like a little kid. You know how you're going to do it?"

"I'm working on an idea."

"Well, if you want to see how it's done—" Gloria paused. "Don't tell anybody, but Tommy's going to take out Harry Arno tomorrow."

Nicky said, "Come on, how do you know?"

"That's what I went to talk to him about."

"He *told* you he's going to do it?"

"He wants me to help him."

"You kidding?" It didn't make sense. "Does Jimmy know about it?"

"It's going to be a surprise."

"He'll freak."

"That's what I told Tommy, my exact words."

"He'll go hide in the closet. You going to tell him?"

"No, and don't you either. I want to see his face when he hears."

"You're helping him? What do you do?"

"I give Tommy the gun."

It was funny, Joyce asking him where he lived after they'd spent the night together. He explained he'd bought a house expecting his family to come once they sold the place in Brunswick, Georgia. It was a ranch in North Miami off 125th Street, not too far from the Broad Causeway, the one he took to get to Miami Beach. Joyce said she'd like to see the house sometime. When he told her all it had in it was a bed, two plastic lawn chairs, a card table, and a twelve-inch TV, she said, "Are you going to show me the house or not?" It was way too early to discuss marriage or even the possibility, but Raylan had the feeling Joyce would like to set up housekeeping and try it again.

He didn't know what would happen tonight, Saturday, if they were going to Joyce's or what. Six P.M. they arrived at Harry's with Chinese takeout. He had told Joyce last night he couldn't think of anything he didn't like to eat, though in the Chinese food line he'd only had chop suey and the other one. He had never heard of any of the dishes they had in the sack, standing at the door to Harry's apartment still talking, grinning at each other. After a minute or so they knocked again and waited some more. Finally the door opened.

Raylan said, "Harry—"

As Harry said, "Guess who I just got done talking to." Sounding pleased with himself.

He said those guys would never admit they made a mistake. What must've happened, they put some bozo in to run the sports book who didn't know the system, who owed and who didn't, and got it all fucked up. So they have the Zip call to suggest a sit-down, like there was a disagreement to discuss. That was the way those guys had to do it. The Zip referred to it as, listen to this, "the dispute between us."

Joyce said to him, "You haven't seen Raylan since Rapallo."

"I nodded, I acknowledged him. Excuse me, but I got something on my mind here." Harry turned to Raylan to say, "How you doing?" and that was that.

Joyce gave him kind of a worried look and

Raylan shrugged. They got ready to eat then, serving themselves out of the cartons on the table. Raylan liked the looks of the Mongolian Beef. Harry said, "Sit where you want," taking his plate over to the sofa where a drink was waiting on the coffee table. Joyce sat down next to him, looking at the drink. Raylan stayed at the table with the takeout cartons. He tried the chopsticks and picked up a fork. He could watch Joyce using hers and not have to pay close attention yet to what Harry was saying. It sounded like he was taking credit for the phone call and bragging on himself. It was hard to tell how much he'd had to drink. Joyce was with him earlier in the afternoon and she said he was fine then.

"You have the urge," Harry said, "you want to tell him, 'You moron, this isn't a dispute. Somebody set me up and you guys bought it. You took the word of a colored guy you don't even know over mine. Why, because you won't accept even the possibility somebody skimmed you and got away with it. So I sit down with the Zip, this Sicilian hard-on, and act grateful to be there. Kiss his ass in front of a hundred people, the contract's forgotten. And if I want to run the book again, like it's an afterthought, fine. In other words if I want, I can start skimming on them again Monday. Back in the saddle again. You know that one, Tex?"

"Out where a friend is a friend," Raylan said.

"Where's your hat?"

"I didn't wear it this evening."

"That was it, I didn't recognize you. You come in, I'm thinking, Who's this guy with my girlfriend?"

Joyce, sitting over there next to Harry, gave Raylan that worried look again.

He let it go.

"Harry, where you meeting him?"

"The Terrace, the café at the Esther."

"That's where he lives."

"So? It's only a block up the street."

"What time?"

"One. Have a bite while we settle our dispute, as he calls it."

"Phone him a few minutes after one," Raylan said, "and tell him you'll meet him someplace else. Like across the street, the Cardozo."

"You think he's setting me up?"

"Why take a chance?"

"He let me name where we're meeting."

"And you picked his hotel?"

"We talked about different places, he mentioned that one, and I said okay. I didn't *pick* his hotel."

"Harry trusts him," Joyce said, "because he thinks they need him."

"I'll bet money on it," Harry said. "I pick the place, I can pat him down if I want. These are his inducements."

"So you do trust him."

"Not ordinarily, no."

"He wants to," Joyce said, "more than anything."

Raylan said, "What about guys that work for him? Or some gun thug he's hired to come by while you're talking? You're outside there, they could drive by and do it."

Harry started eating again. He didn't seem worried.

"If you phone him at his hotel and he goes in to take the call," Raylan said, picturing it from across the street, "he could call whoever's doing the job while he's in there, tell his guy or this gun thug where to go. So you don't want to call. There has to be another way to do it."

"Send somebody," Joyce said.

"Yeah, with a message for the Zip." Raylan thought about it, Joyce watching him and Harry eating, unconcerned.

"Use one of the bellhops from the Cardozo.

Give him five bucks to run up the street. Wouldn't take him but a couple of minutes. Once he delivers the message," Raylan said, picturing it again, "if the Zip goes in the hotel, where he could be making a phone call, then the meeting's off. You go home right away."

"I'm at the Cardozo?" Harry said.

"That's right."

"Well, if he's up the street at the Esther, how do I know if he goes in his hotel?"

"I'll let you know."

"Yeah? Who invited you? I know I didn't."

"I told the Zip I might see him," Raylan said, "around two-fifteen."

Harry left them to visit the bathroom. Raylan said, "He hasn't gotten any sweeter, has he?"

"It's you," Joyce said. "Or me talking about you this afternoon, saying nice things. I could feel him closing up."

"You tell him about Robert?"

"He said it was too bad."

"What's wrong with him?"

"He doesn't like to be wrong. Listen, why don't you leave pretty soon. He'll expect me to stay the night, so I'm going to have to explain what's going on. You and I are what, seeing each other?"

"I guess you could call it that. It's going to tear him up, though, isn't it?"

"At first he won't believe it. Then he'll act hurt, he'll use it as an excuse to get drunk. He'll use it whatever way he can. He might even start smoking again. Wait for me downstairs, okay? In the park?"

That's what he did: sat on the low stone wall separating Lummus Park from the beach and watched the two-lane bumper-to-bumper Saturday-night traffic on Ocean Drive. He'd read that movie stars had bought condos here, but had never seen any of them. There were quite a few homosexuals, though, all neat-appearing young fellas with haircuts. Raylan had nothing against homosexuals; he wasn't sure if he had ever met one. Not just some of them but others down here wore clothes Raylan had never seen in any stores. Where did they buy their outfits? A guy in a regular suit of clothes, like the one in the seersucker suit coming along the walk, was from another planet . . . Jesus, or the Miami Bureau office. The guy coming this way in the suit, sport shirt open at the neck, hands in his pockets and looking kind of aimless, was Special Agent McCormick. He looked this way. Raylan didn't move. McCormick looked again, no recognition on his face. He seemed about to walk past when he stopped.

"I thought that was you. I don't believe I've seen you around lately."

"I took leave."

"What was your name again?"

Raylan stood up as he told him.

"Right, you're the one wears the cowboy hat."

"It's western, yeah."

"You probably haven't heard, we shelved the Capotorto investigation. Turns out Jimmy's small potatoes, the kind you can take to a grand jury, but is it worth the effort?" He said, "Well," starting to edge away, "I'm meeting one of my favorite snitches for a drink. Nice talking to you, Raymond."

Joyce walked up as McCormick left.

"Who was that?"

"Just some guy."

"He looked lonely."

"I wouldn't be surprised."

"You have to watch yourself around here," Joyce said, "you never know who you're talking to." She slipped her arm through his and squeezed it, telling Raylan, "Don't worry, I'll take care of you."

TWENTY-SEVEN

Nicky said after, if Jimmy wasn't in the middle of his breakfast he would've gotten up from the table and slapped her around, her talking to him like that.

Eleven-thirty, he was having his usual Sunday morning breakfast of runny fried eggs on waffles with bacon and a few English muffins after with apple butter. Gloria was having a Coke with her toast. Nicky was serving, because the Cuban guy who usually did it was off Sundays. The cook fixed the stuff and then he left too. What happened:

Jimmy said, "We're going to Butterfly World today."

Gloria said, "Gee, I'd love to but I can't."

Jimmy said, "Oh? You going to see your mom again?"

Gloria could tell by his tone what he was getting at. She said, "I *did* go see my mom yesterday," beating him to it. "On the way back I drove through South Beach, see if there was anything new. You know how it changes all the time? And Tommy saw me. I was stuck in traffic and he asked would I have an iced tea with him. That's all."

Jimmy said to Nicky, "Take that hot coffee and pour it on her fucking head for lying to me."

"I'm *not* lying."

"You told Nicky before you left you were going to see Tommy."

"I was putting him on. Why would I see Tommy?"

"That's what I'm asking you."

"It *hap*pened that I did see him. Or he saw me. I can't help that, can I?"

"You say you stopped on the way back from your mom's?"

"That's right."

"Only it isn't on the way. Is it, Nicky?"

Gloria said, "It is if you take the MacArthur,

South Beach is right there, you go through it. Jimmy, you don't drive, so you have kind of a weird sense of direction."

"What I have," he said with his mouth full, "is a sense of when somebody's bullshittin' me. We're going to Butterfly World."

Gloria said, "You're going to make me look at butterflies when my mom's dying of terminal cancer and it may be the last time I see her?"

Jimmy Cap said, "You're in the car when we leave or hit the fucking road. I'll get a replacement for you."

Gloria shined her eyes at him. "You don't mean that, do you?"

Jimmy said, "Try me." Maple syrup on his chin.

He finished and left the dining room. Gloria sat at the table looking at *Tropic,* the *Herald*'s Sunday magazine, while Nicky cleared. He asked what she was going to do and she said without looking up, "Where were you? You didn't hear what I told him?"

"Yeah, but he'll throw you out."

"You think I'm going to turn the Zip down to go see some fucking butterflies?"

"You could've told Jimmy that."

"The Zip doesn't want Jimmy to know till

after; so don't tell him. Look at the butterflies and keep your mouth shut."

"I've never been out there."

"You walk through like screened-in jungles, natural settings, full of all kinds of butterflies. Jimmy's favorite, they have a giant moth that's about six inches wide and doesn't have a mouth. Jimmy kept staring at it. He goes, 'How'd the fucker get so big if it can't eat?' You could see Jimmy thinking, Jesus, not have a mouth."

Nicky said, "Well, how's it stay alive?"

"It doesn't. It only lives a few days."

"Shit," Nicky said, "I don't want to go look at butterflies. I want to see what the Zip does."

"So tell Jimmy you can't go," Gloria said. "Make up a story." She shrugged in her tank top. "Tell him you made plans, you're going to whack out the Zip."

He'd wear his hat today for sure, so he put on his navy-blue suit—he liked the way the light-tan Stetson went with it—drew his Beretta nine out of its holster and slipped the pistol into his waist, tight against his belly, and buttoned his suit coat. It would work.

At 8:45 A.M., early enough to find a place on Ocean Drive, he parked the Jaguar across from the Esther and walked to Joyce's on Meridian.

He had left there two hours earlier to go home and get dressed for today. Joyce fixed grits and hot biscuits for breakfast, to please him, and they grinned at each other. He had worked out a part for Joyce in this business, but didn't plan on telling her about the deadline, 2:15 P.M., until last night they were in bed holding each other in the dark and he changed his mind.

He told her and she said, "But you can't do that," was silent a few moments, and said, "Can you?" He said it made sense to him, telling a gun thug to leave town.

She said, "But if he's meeting Harry at one—"

"If he shows up he doesn't think much of the deadline, that I was only trying to scare him."

She said, "When he finds out you're serious—"

"I doubt he'll run," Raylan said. "A person like him, they back down they're out of business."

"But he'll be unarmed. He told Harry he can search him."

"Don't worry, he'll have a gun," Raylan said, "or somebody'll bring him one." He said, "Get a table inside against a wall and sit down across from Harry."

In the dark she said, "Maybe I still don't understand you."

He said, "You didn't see him shoot Robert."

By 12:45 Raylan had returned to the Jaguar and was sitting behind the wheel. All the tables on the hotel porch, the Terrace, and along the sidewalk appeared to be occupied. He didn't see the Zip.

At 1:10 Joyce came up the street in a pair of white slacks, a navy top; she walked up on the porch looking around, was out of sight for a minute or so, and reappeared, the Zip with her, coming from the Fourteenth Street side of the porch. The Zip said something to Joyce and she waited on the sidewalk in front while he went over to the dark-haired maître d', peeled a bill from a roll, and handed it to him. After that the Zip and Joyce started down Ocean Drive toward the Cardozo.

Raylan waited.

Not long. At 1:25 Gloria Ayres came around the corner from Fourteenth. She carried a straw beach bag with a big blue flower on it, went up the steps, and stood looking around the Terrace. Raylan watched the dark-haired maître d' approach her. He said something. She said something. He said something else, touched her bare shoulder in the tank top, and she walked off with her beach bag.

Raylan got out of the car. He followed Gloria down Ocean Drive to the Cardozo as people crossed the street going to the beach. It was a beautiful day.

Nicky stood in the bedroom doorway holding up the gun they'd gotten for him in Italy, the .32 caliber Targa, showing it to Jimmy Cap.

Jimmy said, "Yeah, what about it?" still in his robe, getting ready to take a shower.

"It's the one I'm gonna use. Perfect kind of piece. I leave it at the scene, there's no way they can trace it back. Holds six."

"You think that's enough?"

"I put every one of 'em into him."

"How you know where he is?"

"Gloria told me."

"Gloria's a bullshitter. Where is she?"

"She left already."

"Where'd she go?"

It was unbelievable. You tell him something —the man refused to fucking listen.

"I thought I mentioned it. Didn't I? About her helping him take out Harry Arno?"

"You believe that?" Jimmy chose a pair of Bill Blass designer briefs from the bureau, green ones, and closed the drawer. "He don't tell me, he tells Gloria?"

"He don't tell you, Gloria says, 'cause he's showing everybody what a hard-on he is on account of pretty soon, if I don't stop him, he's gonna take over. Gloria says while you're out looking at butterflies."

Jimmy was taking off his robe. "I got to have a talk with Gloria before I kick her ass out. Maybe you should squirt some gasoline on her, what do you think?"

"If I could get you to picture it," Nicky said, wanting to hit him, drive his fist into that huge gut. "The Zip's sitting there with Harry. He don't even see me. I time it. He pops Harry, I walk up and pop the Zip. Let him see me so he knows it's from you."

Jesus, he had the robe off now. All that fat, no muscle, it barely looked like a human body.

"I know you want me to whack him out, you said so. I was just thinking that right now—"

"I told you where we're going," Jimmy Cap said, walking into the bathroom.

The lobby in half light, only a few tables occupied, reminded Joyce of Italy, Harry's villa. Their table was across from the entrance, the doors standing open. The Zip walked up taking off his suit coat, held his arms outstretched, and turned around in front of Harry. "Okay?" Harry said to sit down and have a drink; Harry on his third beer, sunglasses covering his watery eyes. The Zip looked at Joyce's white wine and ordered iced tea. He slipped his coat back on saying, "How you doing? I haven't seen you in a while."

Joyce said, "Not since you were lying on my living room floor."

When the girl walked up with her straw beach bag she said, "Well, hi," to the Zip. "I just happened to come in to use the john." The Zip asked her to sit down and the girl said, "Okay, for a minute," took the empty chair across from him, and shoved her beach bag under the table. The Zip said, "This is Gloria," and Gloria said, "Boy, what a day," laying her sunglasses in her hair. "Everybody's outside, on the porch." Joyce watched the Zip. He said, "We like it in here. Harry, you picked a good table." Harry said, "What?" Joyce watched the Zip's gaze raise. She looked over to see Raylan standing in the entrance. Harry didn't see him until he was approaching the table.

The Zip glanced at his watch and said to Raylan, "I got forty minutes yet. Right?"

Harry wasn't listening. He said to Raylan,

"You're late. I already checked him out and he's clean."

Raylan said, "You look in his socks? He took an ankle gun off me in Italy. I doubt, though, he's wearing it."

"Not my style," the Zip said. He seemed relaxed in his light-gray double-breasted suit, white shirt, and dark tie; in charge. "So what do you want? Is that all you have to say? I'm not going to talk to Harry about personal business in front of you. Can you understand that?"

Now Raylan looked at his watch, studying it for a moment. He said, "I don't see you're going to have time to talk much at all. You have less'n forty minutes to the deadline. Figure it'll take you a good half hour to get out of Dade County from here, that means you actually have only about eight minutes."

Joyce kept quiet. Not Harry. He said, "You know what you're talking about? If you do, let me in on it."

"What it means," Raylan said, "he can't hurt you."

Harry seemed confused now. "Why not?"

"He won't be around."

"What're you talking about?"

"He's going out of business," Raylan said,

and laid his hand on Gloria's bare shoulder.
"Honey, you're through here, aren't you?"

She didn't move right away, not until Raylan helped, pulling her chair back. Gloria got up
and said, "Well . . ." She didn't seem to want to
leave. Or she was waiting for the Zip to tell her it
was okay.

He said, "Good to see you."

Joyce watched her walk off across the lobby:
in a tank top, shorts, and high heels; only in
South Beach.

Raylan was seated now across from the Zip.
They seemed to be watching each other without
staring directly, eye to eye. Harry said he had to
take a leak and left for the men's room. Raylan
said to Joyce, "Would you excuse us for about
seven minutes? Wait for Harry and take him into
the bar? I need to get something cleared up
here."

She wanted to stay with him, not walk away
now to put up with Harry, argue with him.
There were so many things she wanted to say to
Raylan. Joyce hesitated a moment and picked
one from the front of her mind.

"I think Gloria forgot her beach bag."

Raylan said, "You bet she did."

* * *

The Zip had it upright between his legs. All he had to do was lean forward on the table, slip his hand into the straw bag, and bring out the piece with the towel still covering it. Use it below the table. Gloria did okay: pushed it over as she sat down and he got it in position right away. It would've been nothing to do Harry. It would be done by now.

This cowboy was something else. Lays it out for you, this is how it is. He remembered Nicky telling how the guy had shot Fabrizio up on the mountain and remembered Fabrizio's face against the car window with his eyes open.

This time, though, it sounded like the guy was trying to fake him out, telling the broad excuse us for seven minutes. That was bullshit. The guy was a cop, wasn't he? A fed? They had to have warrants and court papers before they made you do something. All that legal shit. Tell him, I got news for you, I ain't going nowhere. Or don't tell him nothing. Wait him out.

"You got five minutes."

"The fuck you talking about?"

"Five minutes," Raylan said.

It was weird seeing Jimmy Cap naked from behind, as big and fat as he was his ass was a normal size. Jimmy was in there brushing his teeth, in the pink glow of the bathroom. Nicky was still in the doorway, across the bedroom from him.

"I don't see where you need me, if all you're going to is this butterfly place."

"They got a moth there, great big fucker, that don't have a mouth."

"I heard about it."

"Can't eat."

"I mean if Jack's driving he'll be with you."

"You're driving. I gave Jack the day off."

Nicky moved across the bedroom toward the pink glow repeating what Jimmy said, that he'd given Jack the day off, but sounding amazed.

"He asked me last week."

"You could've changed your mind." Nicky was in the doorway to the bathroom now. "What I want to do isn't way more important? Christ, whack a guy for you? I got the piece"—the Targa, still in his hand—"the perfect time to do it, and you give him the day off instead of *me*?"

Jimmy was shaving now.

"They got an insectarium there with bugs in it you wouldn't fucking believe. Grasshopper as big as a fucking bird. You know stick bugs, they look like sticks? They got one must be a foot

long. They got these big fucking beetles with
horns—"

Nicky shot him in the back of the head. He
didn't say to himself, I'm going to shoot this son
of a bitch. He didn't have to think. He aimed the
Targa at the back of Jimmy's head, saw Jimmy in
the mirror holding the razor to his face looking
at him and then with the noise didn't see him as
the mirror turned red and shattered, both at the
same time.

They had eye contact now, not more than five
feet between them. A waiter came over and
asked the Zip if he'd like another iced tea. The
Zip shook his head. The waiter asked Raylan if
he'd like something. Raylan said, "Give me
about three minutes and come back."

They still had eye contact.

"You don't look at your watch," the Zip
said. "How do you know it's three minutes?"

"I'm estimating. Now it's two minutes."

"You don't know that!"

"Why's it upset you?"

"You don't have the permission, what
you're doing, the authority."

"An officer of the law tells an undesirable
like yourself to get out of town. It's done all the

time. If you don't choose to leave, then we have to play by your rules."

"I don't *have* rules."

"That's what I mean. You have one minute."

"You just got done saying *two* minutes."

"Time flies, huh? Make up your mind."

"You're crazy, you know it?"

"Get up and leave, that's the end of it. I'll tell Jimmy Cap you quit the business."

"I'm not going anyplace."

"You still have thirty seconds."

"You're trying to fake me out or else you're crazy. No cop I ever heard of does this."

"Twenty seconds," Raylan said.

"Harry told you, I don't have a gun."

"Look in the bag."

"Come on, cut the shit. You want me to leave Harry alone? I don't care, he's nothing to me."

"He ain't much to me either," Raylan said. "Ten seconds."

The Zip didn't say anything. He nodded, taking his time. When he spoke again his tone was different, quieter. He said, "Okay," face-to-face with Raylan across the table. He said, "You're going to get what you want."

* * *

Joyce saw it.

She was a few steps behind Harry coming out of the bar into the lobby, leaving because the bartender was taking all day to mix a row of pastel-colored ladies' drinks. Didn't have time to open a *beer*? For a regular customer? Harry said fuck it, in his hung-over state, he had a beer on the table over there where nobody had asked Raylan to sit down. Harry said, "I don't need him. What do I need that redneck for?" and walked out of the bar. Joyce hoped to catch up and grab him by the arm, keep him away from the table.

She saw the Zip from the front, Raylan more in profile, his left side.

Just as she caught up with Harry she saw the Zip pulling something red from under the table. A towel? That was what it looked like. Now his other hand came up and Harry stopped short. He yelled out, "He's got a gun!" Loud, but sounding more surprised than to mean it as a warning. Joyce saw it, dark metal, an automatic. And saw the same kind of gun already in Raylan's hand aimed point-blank at the Zip, butt resting on the table. She had time to wonder which one Harry meant. *He's got a gun!* What she saw then might have taken three seconds, no more, from the time:

Raylan shot him.

Bits of glass and china flew and the Zip hunched over with the sound of it, punched against his chair. Raylan had to bring his gun up again to lay the barrel on the edge of the table.

Raylan shot him again.

Jolting him, causing the Zip to fire into the table, and more glass and china flew.

Raylan shot him again and this time sat waiting, the butt of his gun still resting on the table.

The Zip looked at him, stared before letting his shoulders go slack, and appeared then to lower his head to the table.

Joyce was aware of the sound fading and a silence before she heard voices coming from outside, the hotel porch. Raylan had turned his head and was looking at her with a solemn expression in his eyes, beneath the cocked brim of his hat. She watched him lay his gun on the table before he rose and came over to her.

TWENTY-EIGHT

Harry said to Torres, "I don't get it. This is a pretty sharp young lady we're talking about here, knows the score. Right? I wouldn't have been going with her all these years."

"She's intelligent," Torres said, "she's aware," and bit into his pastrami sandwich.

They were at Wolfie's, a bowl of cherry Jell-O in front of Harry. "Then why does she ride off with the Lone Ranger, somebody she's got nothing in common with?"

"They're around the same age," Torres said.

"So? They're not going to raise a family. She

used to talk about her biological clock? Well, that stopped ticking some time ago. Raylan's got two kids they're going to stop off and see in Brunswick, Georgia, Ricky and Randy, named after a couple of country music hotshots. I said to her, 'What's all this you-all shit? You don't go for that, you like Frank Sinatra, Count Basie.' She says, 'Yeah, but I was born in Nashville, don't forget.' She says she thinks that side of her is starting to come out, like she's a latent redneck. She tells me he's taking her home for Christmas. I'm thinking, Harlan County, Kentucky, Christ, they're going to have Christmas in a coal mine. No, it's Detroit, where they all move to from Kentucky. I save the guy's life and he takes my girlfriend of long standing to Detroit to meet his mother."

Torres said, "You believe what you read in the paper, huh? 'Warns U.S. Marshal . . .'?"

" 'Warning Alerts Federal Marshal,' with one of those lines over it, *He's got a gun!* The last time in the paper I was 'South Beach Resident Charged in Fatal Shooting,' page three. I've moved up to the front page, but I'm still South Beach Resident in the story."

"That was a weird investigation," Torres said. "There still some questions haven't been answered. We going to bring up this Gloria Ayres, accessory to attempted murder of a federal officer? Or was the Zip after you? You're not saying. What about this kid Nicky Testa? Is there some kind of connection? Says he's lifting weights when two guys come in wearing ski masks, pop Jimmy, and run out. McCormick wants to talk to him, somebody he thinks he can take. He says he might reopen the racketeering investigation. I told him Nicky Testa won't last three weeks running that show. Crimes Persons talked to him, they said he's in a daze, Gloria's leading him around by his dick."

"I don't know him or want to," Harry said. "McCormick mentions my name, tell him I'm leaving town any minute."

"I hear you're back running the sports book."

"Just till after the Super Bowl."

"Then what?"

"I don't know. I may give Italy another chance. Find someplace a little farther south. See what Joyce's doing, if she's still with the Lone Ranger. She wants to come along to Italy, fine. She doesn't, that's okay too."

"Just a sweet old guy," Torres said, "aren't you?"

Harry shrugged, eating his Jell-O.

A SNEAK PREVIEW OF

RAYLAN

BY

ELMORE
LEONARD

Featuring U.S. Marshal Raylan Givens

Available in hardcover from

WM

WILLIAM MORROW
An Imprint of HarperCollins*Publishers*

BUZZ HICKS, the senior detective in the room, said, "Now we're getting to it, aren't we? You're lookin for Reno's little girl, aren't you? Jackie Nevada."

Raylan said, "Isn't Reno her stepdad?"

"That's right," Hicks said. "The name on her birth certificate's Rachel Nevada, but Reno started callin her Jackie when she was a kid."

One of the detectives down the table said, "Her mom was called Jackie. She got knocked up by some loser passin through and took up with Reno. She has the child and acts like a mother till she got tired of home life and hit the road. Was Reno named her Rachel, after his own mother, but started callin her Jackie before too long. Had a soft spot for the broad walked out on him."

Hicks said, "Lloyd, how'd you come up with all that?"

"Talkin to her," Lloyd said, "while we had her in custody."

"So now," Hicks said, "she's raised by Reno, this suspected colored guy passin as Latino and runnin a sports book."

"They musta got along," Raylan said.

"Well, they lived in the same house," Hicks said, "till she went to Butler. Listen to this, and paid her way through college playin poker at night. The only girl livin in a house with seven guys, all students. You know what they called her? 'Mother.' She had a poker table, cards and racks of chips. You wanted to play you had to bring your own chair or borrow one. We went over there and talked to 'em. They said you oughta see her shuffle cards."

"I understand," Raylan said, "she won twenty grand betting Duke over her school."

"That's right, but Reno says he covered her for ten, in case Butler managed to pull off a win. We asked Jackie—" Hicks turning to look down the table. "Lloyd, what'd she tell us?"

"That game," Lloyd said, "Reno put up *nada*. He was too busy losin on the spread. Jackie said the students laid down twenty and that's what she picked up."

"You look into it?" Raylan said.

Hicks said, "What are we, the gaming commission? It was Duke minus seven, the spread *BetUS Sportsbook* was offerin online, and Reno took a bath."

"How'd Jackie take gettin busted?"

"Didn't make a fuss. I guess thinkin about the hole she was in, broke. This A student who plays poker you might say for a living. I asked the woman runs poker games we busted. Elaine? I said, 'You musta known those guys'd eat her alive.' Elaine said, 'She lost her cool. But you could tell the girl's a player.' We set Jackie aside while we're arm-wrestlin these high-priced lawyers and she walks out."

"Didn't show up in court," Raylan said.

"Took off on us," Hicks said. "Reno swears he hasn't heard from her. What do you think this girl's doin now?"

Raylan said, "Well, I hear she's sticking up banks to get back on her feet. You got tape on her?"

"Jackie and two other girls," Hicks said. "We have 'em in different banks in Lexington. Now take a look at what she's doing." Hicks glanced down the table. One of the detectives—it was Lloyd—slid the stack of surveillance prints to him and Hicks passed them on to

Raylan, telling him, "We showed Reno. He said his little girl don't rob banks. These are some girls lost their way. He said, 'But they're mellow, riding some kind of high.' He said, 'My little girl don't do drugs either. She keeps her mind on poker.' "

Raylan went through the tapes, seeing the girls with shopping bags at separate tellers.

Hicks said, "Watch 'em come away, the two looking back at the one still at a window. They're stoned. Had to get fixed to rob the bank."

"I've heard of ones have to get ripped before they go in," Raylan said. "These girls look like they just cashed their paychecks."

"What do they get paid in," Hicks said, "yen? Have to bring store bags to carry it?"

"I guess what I mean," Raylan said, "we don't see that many women stickin up banks. I think it's maybe five or six out of a hundred. Here you've got three at once. Which one you think's Jackie?"

"The one wearing the baseball cap," Hicks said, "down on her eyes. Some of the other tapes you'll come to, you see her lookin up." He stood to watch Raylan go through the prints.

Lloyd said, "Buzz, you recall we had two girls doin banks at the same time?"

"Not around here," Hicks said.

"Was down toward the state line," Lloyd said, "seven, eight years ago. They'd hit a bank in some dinky town off sixty-four and cross over to Louisville. A guy with the girls was teachin 'em how to rob banks."

Hicks said, "How you remember that?"

"It stuck in my mind," Lloyd said. "I remember a confidential informant fingered them, but were released for lack of evidence."

Raylan said, "You remember what happened to the snitch?"

Lloyd was squinting, trying to recall before nodding his head. "A guy blew off his right arm with a shotgun."

Raylan said, "Delroy Lewis?"

"*That's* the guy was questioned," Lloyd said, "about the bank jobs."

"You mind," Hicks said, "if we settle on this job here?" and said to Raylan, "That one, where she's lookin up. All of us but Lloyd said that's Jackie Nevada or her twin."

"It could be," Raylan said. "I stopped by Butler and got a look at her picture. I can't see the girl in the year-book playing to a surveillance camera."

"We like her motive," Hicks said. "She needs dough."

Raylan was shaking his head. "These two comin out, mugging right at the camera."

"Doped up and think it's a hoot. It's your people in Lexington," Hicks said, "sent us all the bank photos. They picked out Jackie and asked for our confirmation."

"The three almost look alike," Raylan said. "Young, the same size. Three girls having fun."

Hicks said, "Robbin banks."

"Your fugitive," Raylan said, "I can see why you want her to be Jackie. I hope you're right and I'm dead wrong. But I can't see three girls wanting to rob banks. I *can* see some guy putting 'em up to it. Gives the girl's some toot and drops 'em off. I don't know for sure, but we'll find out, won't we?"

"We respect your opinion," Buzz Hicks said, "but hope you're wrong this time. We been followin you since you called out that Zip in Miami, Tommy Bucks? You gave him twenty-four hours to get out of town. He drew on you and you put him down."

"And got demoted to Harlan County, Kentucky."

"But then shot it out with that transplant nurse."

"You're havin fun with me, aren't you?"

"Well," Hicks said, "you're doin a job the way we like to see it done."

LIZ BURGOYNE CAME in the sun parlor from the patio to see Jackie Nevada waiting, getting up from the sofa, and it made Liz think of Raylan, the time she walked in and he asked her about Cuba stealing kidneys. Liz crossed the room in jeans and cowboy boots offering her hand, saying:

"Jackie Nevada. Harry's told me about his poker-playing buddy. He makes you sound like a little girl, but you're quite something else, aren't you?" Liz smiling now. "Harry mentioned you're wanted by the police?"

"It's a misdemeanor thing," Jackie said. "I didn't show up for a hearing."

"Picked up in a raid," Liz said. "Harry told me about it. He said you like manhattans, is that right?"

Jackie said, "If that's what we're having."

They were both on the sofa now, the nearly empty pitcher on the cocktail table, both smoking cigarettes.

"You ever cheat?" Liz said.

"Why do only women ask that? You mean at poker."

"Or on a guy."

"Poker, I've never had to."

"You're that good?"

"You have to work with another player. Didn't you see *Rounders*? They cheat playing with a bunch of cops. I've never cheated on a boyfriend either. Right now I don't have one, but I live with seven guys. You know what they think is funny? Farting."

"Why do guys love to fart?"

"They're expressing themselves."

"You hop in the sack with any of them?"

"Nope. There's some fooling around, girls come for a party and we get high, but I don't recall anything really inappropriate. You might hear a girl tell some guy to quit grabbin her ass. We have great parties."

Liz said, "You like to go down on guys?"

"Not *guys*, no. But I have polished the occasional knob."

"Wow," Liz said. "You're not bashful, are you?"

"You know what I'm talking about or wouldn't've asked."

"You have to meet some of my friends from olden times, they'd love you."

"I'm not a lay," Jackie said. "I've only gone to bed with three guys in four years, ones I thought I was serious about."

"What happened to them?"

"They graduated."

Liz poured the rest of the manhattans.

"You like to do it standing up?"

"I never have," Jackie said. "In movies they look like they're ringing the bell, but I think it would be uncomfortable."

Liz said, "I bet I know the movie you're thinking of. The girl walks in the bar—"

"That's the one."

"She can't get any attention and yells out, 'Who's a girl gotta suck around here to get a drink?' "

"She gets into the cute guy's pants, in the booth."

"Then you see them in back doing it standing up."

"You ever do it with a black guy?"

"No, and I'm not racist," Jackie said. "Or maybe I

am and didn't know it. I've never had any chills and
thrills yet when I meet black guys at parties. I know
you have."

"Our driver at the time," Liz said, "Harry thought
was from West Africa, so Cuba always had to put on an
accent, one he picked up from cabdrivers." She said, "I
can't imagine Harry trying anything with you."

"Why?" Jackie said.

"He's too old. He might ask you to strip, promise
he'll just look."

"Would that upset you?"

"Not in the least, if he can pull it off."

"He sure goes to the bathroom a lot."

"His tired kidneys," Liz said. "And here's your boyfriend now."

Harry came in from the hallway telling Jackie, "I got
three guys so far want to play you: my friends the breed-
ers, Ike and Mike, and a World Series of Poker pro they
dug up called Dude Moody."

Jackie was nodding.

"He's been at the final table. I think he won a couple
of bracelets. They call him Moody Blues or just Blues."

"I said to Ike and Mike, 'For Christ sake, what do
you guys need help for?' And there's a guy in town I
asked to stop by. You met him, Liz, Raylan Givens? The
marshal lookin for that driver we had. He called, I asked
him to come by for a drink and say hello."

Jackie said, "Harry, don't tell him I play poker, okay?"

Jackie watched Raylan take off his hat shaking hands
with Harry and they stood talking for a few minutes.
Now they were coming over to the sofa, Raylan saying,
"Don't get up, ladies, you look comfortable."

"We *have* had a couple," Liz said. "Raylan, it's so

good to see you. It seems to me that you and I sat here having martinis one time. Harry, where were you?"

"Tendin business. I believe I was helpin a foal come into the world. She's still lookin like a possible."

Jackie saw Raylan stare at her for a moment and turn to Liz again, Liz saying, "This time my guest said she might try a manhattan. They seemed to've worked just fine." Jackie wondering how she'd be introduced. These people got in conversations and forgot she was there.

Not Raylan.

Harry said, "Liz makes it sound like she's never had a manhattan."

Jackie watched Raylan smile, being polite, watched his eyes come back to her. She said through her buzz, "Hi, I'm Jackie."

Raylan came over to shake hands telling her not to get up, but she did and stood with her feet planted.

"Harry's latest partner," Liz said.

Raylan gave her hand a nice squeeze and said, "Is that right?"

Jackie told herself she'd get out of this or she wouldn't, and said, "Harry's my banker, he stakes me to poker games, but doesn't pay too much attention." Smiling then to show she was being funny. "He has no idea how we're doing."

No one laughed. Liz said, "If you've been playing no limit for the past week you're winning, or Harry would've left you off somewhere."

Harry said, "You make me sound heartless."

"I'll bet," Liz said, "she's up at least a hundred grand."

Raylan said, "You play poker as an occupation?"

She said, "I'm not sure. I'm looking at it."

"You were in a game," Raylan said, "in Indianapolis recently that was raided, weren't you?"

Jackie said, "You know how much I lost?"

Harry said, "You never want to be in a game when the cops bust in. They take all the cash and chips as evidence. What happens to the dough after that?" Harry said to Raylan. "Maybe you can tell me."

"Isn't part of my job," Raylan said.

"I'm always careful," Harry said, "pickin games for Jackie. What I do is call the chief of police, tell him who I am, and say I want to play some poker without gettin in the way of a raid. I ask him if there's a police fundraiser I could help out."

Liz asked Raylan if he had time for a drink. He said, glancing at his watch, he'd better get back. "We're tryin to locate a guy wants to shoot me on sight."

Liz said, "I'd think you'd have them lining up."

"Well, some are dead," Raylan said, and looked at Jackie. "I'd like to hear more about what you're doin. I haven't played a lot of poker but've always had a good time. Are you stayin here by any chance?"

"Till we hit the poker trail again," Harry said. "Jackie's takin on some guys tomorrow in a big cash game."

Raylan touched his coat pocket and said, "Excuse me," taking out his cell phone and turning away.

Jackie watched him, telling herself it was a case they were putting him on and he had to leave right now, forget about her walking out of jail, and heard him say, "Come on, you're kiddin." He turned his back to them now and stepped away to listen. *Come on, you're kiddin,* his voice raised but not much, was all she heard. She watched him fold his cell and come back to stand with her as he told Liz and Harry, "I'm sorry, but that was my job callin."

"About the guy who wants to shoot you?" Liz said.

"Something else," Raylan said. Then paused, like he

was getting around to what he wanted to say. "You don't mind, I'd like to have a word with Ms. Nevada."

Liz said, "I hope you're not going to cuff our guest. Are you?"

"I'm not arrestin her," Raylan said. "There's something I'd like to talk to her about."

Jackie gave Liz a shrug and walked out to the hallway with Raylan.

"Where we going if you're not turning me in?"

"I want to talk to you," Raylan said. "The first time I came here I said, 'This's a sun parlor? I'd like to see what they call the living room.' Liz told me it's been a sun parlor for eighty-five years."

Jackie stopped. "If you're not arresting me, where we going?"

"Forget about Indy," Raylan said. "I'll appear at your hearing and tell the court you owed a shylock and was hopin to pay him out of the twenty grand you blew." Raylan, turned enough to see the Burgoynes watching, said, "Come on," and they continued walking down the hall, Raylan telling Jackie, "I stopped at Butler and saw your picture in the yearbook. I said to myself, Whatever it was, you didn't do it."

"I have no idea," Jackie said, "what's going on."

"I want to take you out," Raylan said, "if you're not playin tonight. You are, I'll come and watch."

She said, "Like a date?" Thought for a moment and said, "You know those two girls who were murdered? I'd love to see where it happened."

"There's nothin there now but police tape. He paused a moment and said. "Hey, you want to come with me? I'll show you a scene hard to believe."

THE UNDISPUTED MASTER
OF THE CRIME NOVEL

DJIBOUTI
A Novel

978-0-06-173521-9 (trade paperback)

Elmore Leonard brings his trademark wit and inimitable
style to this twisting, gripping—and sometimes playful—
tale of modern-day piracy.

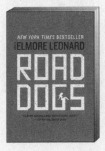

ROAD DOGS
A Novel

978-0-06-198570-6 (trade paperback)

The further adventures of Jack Foley, out of prison
but right back into trouble.

PRONTO

978-0-06-212033-5 (trade paperback)

A brilliant combination of suspense and black
humor featuring Raylan Givens, the inspiration
behind the FX series *Justified*.

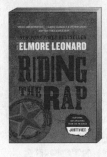

RIDING THE RAP

978-0-06-212247-6 (trade paperback)

Raylan Givens returns to bust open a kidnapping ring
in the sequel to *Pronto*.

FIRE IN THE HOLE
Stories

978-0-06-212034-2 (trade paperback)

This short fiction collection features a few beloved
Elmore Leonard characters, including Raylan Givens in
the title story that was the basis for the pilot of the hit
FX series *Justified*.

MAXIMUM BOB

978-0-06-200940-1 (trade paperback)

Florida Judge "Maximum" Bob Gibbs has thrown the
book at so many felons, it's beginning to look
as if one of them is throwing it back at him.

TISHOMINGO BLUES

978-0-06-200939-5 (trade paperback)

The Dixie Mafia is aiming to shoot high-diver Dennis
Lenahan from the top of his 80-foot ladder.

RUM PUNCH
A Novel

978-0-06-211982-7 (trade paperback)

Cops try to use Jackie Burke to get at the gunrunner she's
been bringing cash into the country for, but she hatches a
plan to keep the money for herself.

FREAKY DEAKY
A Novel

978-0-06-212035-9 (trade paperback)

It's only after he transfers out of the bomb squad that
Chris Mankowski begins playing with dynamite.

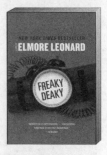

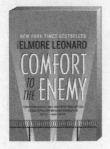

COMFORT TO THE ENEMY AND OTHER CARL WEBSTER STORIES

978-0-06-173515-8 (trade paperback)

First time in print in the U.S.
A collection of 3 stories about the legendary lawman
Carl Webster.

GET SHORTY
A Novel

978-0-06-212025-0 (trade paperback)

A Miami shylock, Chili Palmer, goes to Hollywood
and becomes a movie producer. Why not?

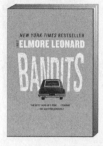

BANDITS

978-0-06-212032-8 (trade paperback)

An unlikely trio targeting millions of dollars is
sure to make out like bandits—if they survive.

KILLSHOT
A Novel

978-0-06-212159-2 (trade paperback)

After witnessing a scam, Carmen and her husband
must outrun the thugs bent on eliminating any
living evidence.

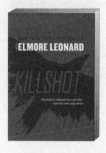

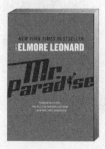

MR. PARADISE
A Novel

978-0-06-211905-6 (trade paperback)

Elmore Leonard presents a whole new cast of
characters—the kind that only he can create—in
this Detroit homicide book.

GLITZ
A Novel

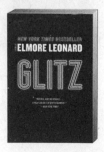

978-0-06-212158-5 (trade paperback)

A classic Elmore Leonard novel, spinning from the lazy
beaches of Puerto Rico to the mean streets of Miami to
the non-stop jangle of Atlantic City's one-armed bandits.

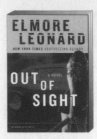

OUT OF SIGHT
A Novel

978-0-06-174031-2 (trade paperback)

Minutes after pulling into a prison parking lot, Deputy U.S. Marshal Karen Sisco meets legendary bank robber Jack Foley and the fun begins.

THE COMPLETE WESTERN STORIES OF ELMORE LEONARD

978-0-06-124292-2 (trade paperback)

This collection is a must-have for every fan of Elmore Leonard.

SWAG
A Novel

978-0-06-174136-4 (trade paperback)

Used car salesman Frank Ryan sells Ernest Stickley, Jr. on his "10 Rules for Success and Happiness in Armed Robbery".

LABRAVA
A Novel

978-0-06-176769-2 (trade paperback)

Ex-Secret Service agent Joe LaBrava gets mixed up in a scam involving a former movie actress and bad guys.

BE COOL
A Novel

978-0-06-077706-7 (trade paperback)

Chili Palmer searches for his next big hit as murder blurs the line between reality and the big screen.

SPLIT IMAGES
A Novel

978-0-06-212251-3 (trade paperback)

When homicide cop Bryan Hurd takes a vacation, he lands in Palm Beach and finds murder in the Sunshine State.